CW01664425

MIAMI IN VIRGO

A NOVEL BY

SALLY MANSFIELD ABBOTT

Woodbine Odyssey
San Francisco

Miami in Virgo, a novel
Copyright 2019 by Sally Mansfield Abbott

ISBN: 978-1-7333771-0-2

Library of Congress Control Number:2019913468

Cover and book design by Damonza
Back cover photo by Cappy Coates

Woodbine Odyssey

San Francisco, California

For you

CHAPTER 1

Gorten Brothers was a carnival circuit that worked its way down the Central Valley, stopping at all the little two-bit towns between Sacramento and Bakersfield, hooking up with the local county fairs. My mother, Lilah, always went to the County Fair so she could enter her begonias, amaryllis, sweet alyssum and whatever was having a particularly good year in the horticulture competitions. She'd gone every year since we moved to La Grange and always used to take me with her. I stopped going years ago when I lost interest in stuffed animals and Ferris wheel rides and The Spinner, but then I got my Nikon and it was like I was seeing it all with new eyes. Suddenly I was into it again, and the County Fair was the high point of my summer just like when I was a kid. It was an oasis in the desert of blandness of the Valley, and the only place I could get the kind of shots I wanted for miles around. I was trying to get a portfolio together for the California Arts Council's Young Photographers Contest, and I was thinking of doing a photo essay on the County Fair. I had a show at our school library last year of some portraits of my girlfriends K.D., Glenda, and Jane, and I wanted to develop some new material.

I carried my mother's fuchsia tub to the main tent, and we made a second trip for the potted plants. Then I took my three entries to the photography booth. The one I liked best was a picture of lightning streaking across the sky in a freak storm. I set the camera on a tripod and did a time exposure to get it. Another was a bowl of persimmons on our dining room table by moonlight, also a time exposure, and the last one was a portrait of Ms. Richmond, my English teacher from last year who was my mentor. She had an interesting face with short black hair and thick bushy eyebrows that met over her nose like Frida Kahlo's. I looked at the other pictures on display but only one caught my eye—a wide angled shot of a New England-style clapboard church up on a hill. A lot of energy was compressed into the frame, and the church was so distorted, it looked as if it was about to burst its seams and split the sky.

I got out my camera and picked my way through the crowd while I focused the lens. Everything looked like it had a halo around it or a glow, and the colors were brighter than usual. Looking through the lens of the camera, I picked up on things I would have missed otherwise, like the quality of the light. The noonday sun flattened everything and leeched the color out of it. The late afternoon was best, its long shadows turning everything into the camera's friend. Even landscapes became intense, and previously stolid, opaque faces took on a ruptured look that revealed their souls. Their secrets spilled out of them and I was there waiting to capture them in my shots. My friend K.D. said the camera was my third eye that looked into a hidden dimension and revealed it to others.

A pretty Mexican woman with a head of frizzy hair and an older man, stiletto thin, strolled ahead of me, their arms braided together. A man selling slices of melon from a cart had a leathery

CHAPTER 1

Gorten Brothers was a carnival circuit that worked its way down the Central Valley, stopping at all the little two-bit towns between Sacramento and Bakersfield, hooking up with the local county fairs. My mother, Lilah, always went to the County Fair so she could enter her begonias, amaryllis, sweet alyssum and whatever was having a particularly good year in the horticulture competitions. She'd gone every year since we moved to La Grange and always used to take me with her. I stopped going years ago when I lost interest in stuffed animals and Ferris wheel rides and The Spinner, but then I got my Nikon and it was like I was seeing it all with new eyes. Suddenly I was into it again, and the County Fair was the high point of my summer just like when I was a kid. It was an oasis in the desert of blandness of the Valley, and the only place I could get the kind of shots I wanted for miles around. I was trying to get a portfolio together for the California Arts Council's Young Photographers Contest, and I was thinking of doing a photo essay on the County Fair. I had a show at our school library last year of some portraits of my girlfriends K.D., Glenda, and Jane, and I wanted to develop some new material.

I carried my mother's fuchsia tub to the main tent, and we made a second trip for the potted plants. Then I took my three entries to the photography booth. The one I liked best was a picture of lightning streaking across the sky in a freak storm. I set the camera on a tripod and did a time exposure to get it. Another was a bowl of persimmons on our dining room table by moonlight, also a time exposure, and the last one was a portrait of Ms. Richmond, my English teacher from last year who was my mentor. She had an interesting face with short black hair and thick bushy eyebrows that met over her nose like Frida Kahlo's. I looked at the other pictures on display but only one caught my eye—a wide angled shot of a New England-style clapboard church up on a hill. A lot of energy was compressed into the frame, and the church was so distorted, it looked as if it was about to burst its seams and split the sky.

I got out my camera and picked my way through the crowd while I focused the lens. Everything looked like it had a halo around it or a glow, and the colors were brighter than usual. Looking through the lens of the camera, I picked up on things I would have missed otherwise, like the quality of the light. The noonday sun flattened everything and leeched the color out of it. The late afternoon was best, its long shadows turning everything into the camera's friend. Even landscapes became intense, and previously stolid, opaque faces took on a ruptured look that revealed their souls. Their secrets spilled out of them and I was there waiting to capture them in my shots. My friend K.D. said the camera was my third eye that looked into a hidden dimension and revealed it to others.

A pretty Mexican woman with a head of frizzy hair and an older man, stiletto thin, strolled ahead of me, their arms braided together. A man selling slices of melon from a cart had a leathery she was a man with a penis and balls and everything, just like any other man. But it was weird because she had breasts too.

It made my skin crawl to look at her. Him. Whatever. But I stood there riveted, and I couldn't move and kept blinking my eyes because it was like I was seeing double. She held her skirt up in this delicate way and smiled a little slur of a smile. All the while, the sides of the tent flapped like sails, like the evangelists' tents off Route 3 when you went by at night and saw the shadows moving around inside. I fumbled with my camera and finally got the lens cap off and started snapping pictures, because I didn't know what else to do, and besides, I told myself, that's what I was there for.

Then she stopped smiling and dropped her skirt and in a hard, nasty voice that was neither male nor female but somewhere in between said, "Now, get out, before someone comes in and the whole thing gets busted. You got what you came for. Maybe a little more." She said this with a smirk that made my hair stand on end.

I thought she was going to be mad at me for taking her picture, but she didn't seem to notice. She just looked me up and down and said, "Take a good look. You may be headed the same way yourself."

My eyes ricocheted around and I tried to exit as quickly as I could, but I was enveloped in the nylon folds and had trouble extricating myself. I could barely breathe and had worked up a sweat by the time I got out of the tent. The barker had a friend with him now, which was lucky for me because they were so engaged in their beer and conversation, I don't think he saw me come out of the tent. He noticed me soon enough, though.

"What, are you still hanging around?" he asked. "Now, git.

Scoot. Skidaddle. Buy yourself a ticket if you're so interested. You're old enough."

He guffawed and looked at his friend and the other guy chuckled. The friend had a red face and wore a purple and blue plaid cowboy shirt with mother of pearl buttons.

"She's a man, and she's a woman both," the friend said in a quiet voice. He had sort of a Southern accent. "Both at the same time. She's a hermaphrodite."

I stared at them and then back at the sign. My eyes were stinging and I wanted to cry, but I couldn't because I was mixed up and divided within myself. I shouldn't have gone in there, and I don't know why I did unless there was something wrong with me to begin with. At the same time, I felt violated even though no one had laid a hand on me. I felt like I did when Eddie Harris and Charlie Gompers chased me down the stairwell in the second grade. They ganged up on me and pulled my pants down and I couldn't even get back at them, because I was too ashamed to tell the teacher or anyone about it. I felt humiliated and helpless like that now until I remembered the pictures. I must have gotten two or three good ones, so that was like telling someone, and I decided to get away before they figured that out.

"Hey, wait a minute," the barker called after me. "Come back here."

I didn't stop or turn around. I dodged through the crowd and the show pigs, the oversized watermelons, the chickens with their scaly claws and clipped wings, the cocks and carrier pigeons, and the red-faced women from the 4-H clubs with their hefty arms and skinny children. Meanwhile the heat was overpowering. It was dusty and people were sweating and there was a cast over everything like I was seeing through a red filter.

I went to the main tent to look for my mother. I walked

down the aisle between the rows of pickle jars, jams, canned tomatoes, on the one side and on the other, the homemade quilts, Afghans, embroidery, and knitting. Pens of prize-winning pigs, heifers, and rabbits lined the sides of the tent. I finally saw her standing in front of a booth advertising a giant mushroom and stopped in my tracks. "World's Largest Puffball," the sign read in dripping red letters. "23 pounds, 11 ounces, raised by Jonathan Graham of Chehaw, CA." I didn't know whether to believe that or not and I looked at the big chalky mushroom and back at my mother. I was just about to rush up to her when I realized she wasn't alone.

My mother had aquamarine eyes and curly chestnut hair, and she wore a white seersucker dress that accentuated her tan. Her hair was damp from perspiration but her frown lines were gone, and she had some kind of new, pretty smile on her face.

She was talking to a man in a bright blue suit and a white straw hat. He looked a little older than her, and he had a thin, lined face, with curly brown hair, and startling blue eyes. His hand rested on the small of her back and there was a glow on her face and a haze over her eyes. It looked like they had quite a conversation going, although they were too far away to hear what they were saying. Then he leaned over and whispered something in her ear and she giggled and he kissed her. He seemed to be looking for excuses to touch her, and then I got it—they were in love and it was like the movies almost.

The sight of him triggered an interior alarm, possibly one that registered all the boyfriends my mother had had in the last eleven years, which was none. When I was a little girl she'd had a lot of boyfriends, but that was a long time ago and she'd changed a lot when she sobered up. The man looked familiar to me, and I wondered if I could be remembering him from all the way back then.

I was only a few yards away, but they were so wrapped up in each other they didn't notice me. Then they both saw me at the same time and he dropped his hand from her waist.

"Miami," Lilah said and took a deep breath as if she was steeling herself for something. "There's someone I'd like you to meet—Ben Beasley. Ben, this is my daughter, Miami."

Beasley, I thought, but the name didn't ring any bells, and he didn't look so familiar anymore either.

"I'm happy to meet you," he said, stretching out his hand. "I've heard a lot about you, Miami."

I nodded and smiled but thought, Why haven't I heard anything about you? His eyebrows were raised in a question that gave his face an open look, and he had a friendly smile, but his eyes were sad as if he had responsibilities weighing on him, and I wondered if he was a minister.

"Where do you two know each other from?" I asked.

There was a silence and I could tell that whatever they came up with would be a total fabrication, and I was wondering what the reason was for all the secrecy.

"We met at work," she said simply.

"You work at Yarborough's?" I asked Ben and he shook his head no.

Yarborough's was the department store in Modesto where my mother worked in the notions department. It was hard to feature the two of them meeting over the sale of some snaps or thread.

"I'm a football coach at Alvarado Middle School in Merced County," he said.

"The school had an auction to raise money for the team," my

mother chimed in. "And Yarborough's donated a few things—a couple of lounge chairs and a China tea service—and I was there on the part of the store to give them away."

"I ran the raffle," Ben said. "And to me your mother was the brightest part of the evening."

The main tent was next to the Holy Roller arcade and gospel music was playing with Eddie and the Apostles singing "Blessings Shall Rain down from Heaven." With all that going on, I could barely hear them. The whole time I looked at them, I kept seeing the Hermaphrodite in the bridal dress and remembered what she looked like when she raised her skirt. That was the last thing I wanted to be seeing right now, but the more I tried to stop thinking about it, the more it came to mind.

Ben shifted back and forth with his hat in his hand. The three of us looked from one to the other and no one knew what to say. All I could think was, I should be getting a picture of this, so I picked up my camera again. It wasn't going to be any good. There was too much going on in the background and the composition would be off, but I didn't know what else to do so I took it anyway.

"When was this raffle?" I asked quietly.

"Last spring," she said. "Around Easter."

I couldn't believe they'd been seeing each other for almost six months without me knowing anything about it. I hadn't noticed any mysterious absences on her part, and I was pretty sure he'd never called the house, at least not when I'd answered the phone. It seemed like they'd gone to a lot of trouble to keep it secret, and they'd covered their tracks pretty well. She must have met him away from the house, telling me she was going out with friends.

"Enjoying your summer?" Ben asked. "I love teaching but I couldn't do it without summer vacations. Lounging around the house, drinking iced tea, mowing the lawn—it recharges the batteries. Finally, the house and kids get some of my time. Are you about ready to go back?"

I nodded halfheartedly. I'd spent the summer loafing around the house reading *Anna Karenina*, getting together with my girlfriends occasionally. Resisting my mother's efforts to get me a job in the stockroom at Yarborough's was my sole achievement.

"Your mother tells me you go to Alamo," Ben said and I nodded. "I know some of the faculty there. Jim Tompkins and Leslie Forester. How do you like it?"

I shrugged and he and my mother exchanged glances.

"I guess that was a stupid question," Ben said. "I've got three boys in high school myself. They all go to Mission and of course I can never get them to say a positive word about the place."

Mission was our rival high school on the other side of the county.

"You have three sons," I repeated and he nodded.

"Marvin. He's my oldest. And Cal and Jason. They're a handful. Actually, they *were* a handful. The truth is I barely see them anymore. Now that they're practically grown up they don't want to have much to do with the old man anymore."

He smiled a reassuring little smile; meanwhile, my socks were wilting around my ankles and I knelt down to pull them up.

"I think they like Mission well enough. Of course I can't get them to admit it. I guess they like it as much as they like anything at their age. Other than cars and rock 'n' roll, not to mention girls, of course."

He winked at me and looked at his watch.

"Speaking of the boys, I'd better get going," he said. "I told Jason I'd pick him up at the rifle range almost twenty minutes ago. Nice meeting you, Miami. We'll get together soon so you can meet the boys. We'll have a barbecue in the backyard."

He kissed Lilah goodbye and turned and I watched him disappearing through the crowd. I thought, Rifle range, and shivered. Meanwhile my mother picked her way back to the horticulture booth and started gathering up her plants—the tuberous begonia, glads, freesia, and the fuchsia bush. Most of the other plants were gone but a smell of damp earth lingered in the tent.

"So who *is* this guy?" I asked.

"We just told you," she said. "Ben Beasley. He's a P.E. teacher over in Merced County."

"Yes, but you know what I mean," I said. "Who is he? What is he to you? How long have you known him?"

"Not long," she said. "Maybe five or six months. Look at this. My giant amaryllis won the blue ribbon."

She started plumping the dark glossy leaves, but I didn't let her change the subject.

"So what's going on between you?" I asked. "Is he your boyfriend or something?"

She brushed a damp lock of hair off her forehead.

"You might say that," she said smiling sweetly. "I guess so. Your mother has a boyfriend. Imagine that!"

"Five months you've been seeing him and you didn't tell me anything about it?" I asked. "Why the big secret?"

"No secret," she said trying to be matter of fact. "I just thought it made more sense to wait until I was sure how I felt about him. I didn't want to alarm you unnecessarily, but now of course you feel like I'm springing it on you."

"I don't just feel that way," I said. "You *are* springing it on me."

"I'm sorry," she said looking at me helplessly.

"And if I hadn't surprised you like that, who knows when you would have gotten around to telling me about it? You weren't even planning on telling me today, were you?"

I glared at her so hard she lowered her eyes.

"Where did you meet him?" I asked.

"At the raffle," she said. "Like we said. His wife had just died, and he was lonely so he struck up a conversation and we clicked and started seeing each other shortly after that. It wasn't necessarily a big romance. It was more that I felt like I'd known him my whole life."

She tried to make it sound like the most natural thing in the world, and it might have been for anyone else.

"So how serious is this?" I asked.

"Pretty serious, I guess," she said.

It was almost five o'clock, and she'd gotten me up at six to get there and I was drained and exhausted. We put her plants in the back of the car and went by the photography booth to pick up my prints. Of course none of them won anything and I felt even more depressed. They weren't that great maybe, but the one of the lightning I thought had a chance, and I looked around at the photos with the ribbons next to them. A dog with a hat on won honorable mention and a picture of an oak tree second prize. The blue ribbon was hanging on the picture of the clapboard church I had noticed earlier. The Warped Church, I called it. There was no title on the print but the photographer's name leapt out at me. Marvin Beasley.

"Hey, look," I said, pulling on Lilah's arm. "Beasley."

She looked at it and smiled.

"Marvin," she said. "That's Ben's oldest son. Well, good for him, he won first prize. That's funny, I wonder if he's here. Ben didn't even mention it. We could have introduced you. It would have been fun."

We looked around but there was no sign of Ben anymore either. My mother didn't say anything about my prints being any good or about them not winning any prizes and I felt vaguely cheated out of something. I looked at the blue ribbon on Marvin's photo again and remembered how humiliated I felt back at the Hermaphrodite's tent and realized I hadn't gotten back at anybody by taking the pictures. I could never submit them to the CAC and I probably wouldn't even be able to get them developed anywhere. I was on the verge of crying either from exhaustion, disappointment, shock, or all three.

CHAPTER 2

Since I stumbled onto them at the County Fair, Ben began stopping by the house on a regular basis, up to two or three times a week. I expected it, but it was still strange the first time he showed up. I wasn't used to my mother singing and daydreaming around the house either. She was off in her own little world, oblivious to my presence. I wondered if she'd been acting that way all along and I hadn't noticed. More likely, she saw no point in hiding her feelings anymore now that she'd come out in the open about the relationship.

From my room, I watched her get ready for a date with Ben—putting on pearl clip-on earrings and makeup, trying on an orange sheath and a green floral sundress before she finally settled on a navy blue dress with a flared skirt. Then I heard the click of her high-heeled sandals against the hardwood floor going down the stairs.

When Ben arrived, I had to be dragged into it. I guess he was just trying to get to know me, but I thought he was smarmy and ingratiating. He chatted with me for a while, and then I went back upstairs and watched them drive off in his two-tone Chrysler, my mother snuggled up next to him like a teenager.

When they were out of sight, I pulled the phone cord into my room and plotzed on my rumpled white chenille bedspread and got on the phone to Glenda.

"My mother has a boyfriend now," I said.

"Great!" Glenda said. "But you don't sound happy about it. Isn't it about time? When did that happen?"

"I don't know," I said. "It sounds like they've been sneaking around behind my back for a while. Five months she says. I stumbled onto them together by accident at the County Fair about a week ago. That was the first she ever said anything. Otherwise I'd still be in the dark about it."

"What's he like?" Glenda asked.

"He's OK, I guess," I said. "He seems like a nice enough guy, a middle school teacher. A football coach, actually, over at Alvarado Middle School. He's trying hard to get to know me and seems genuinely crazy about my mother."

"Well, great. Good for Lilah," Glenda said. "She deserves it after all this time. Kind of a late bloomer."

"You could say that."

"Her little girl is all grown up now," Glenda said. "Sounds to me like she's getting herself ready for when you go away to college so she won't be left all alone."

"Yeah," I said. "I thought that, too."

"It'll make it easier on you to leave if you know she has someone. It'll be better for both of you, so it's a good thing."

"I guess so," I said. "It's kind of hard to see what she'd see in him after my father, though."

"Maybe the fact that he's alive for starters," Glenda said. "Someone that loves her, is stable, likes kids, is nice—what's not to like?"

"Nothing, I guess," I said. "It's just that he seems so ordinary and my father was something special—a professor and a prominent man."

"Why does that have to be so important?" Glenda asked.

"You tell me," I said. "You're the one who wants to be a movie star."

"That's different," she said. "Not so highbrow."

"It turns out he has three teenage sons at Mission High," I added.

"Ah," Glenda said. "See, I told you it would be a good thing for both of you. Now you'll get to meet some cool guys from Mission High. God forbid you should wind up going out on a date!"

"God forbid," I said.

Glenda was my oldest and best friend. Probably my first real friend. I don't remember exactly when we met but it was either in the second or third grade, shortly after we moved to La Grange. I felt like I'd known her all my life, and she was closer to a sister. Along with that went a sibling rivalry, which was for the most part genial and good-natured but could take on an edge, and we'd had plenty of spats and the occasional feud that resulted in our not speaking to each other for months at a time.

Glenda was a towhead with a bright, sunny personality—sort of a Shirley Temple type—Heidi, or Pollyanna, giggly and buoyant. She wanted to be an actress, preferably a movie star, which was a little on the grandiose side, but I could see it. She had certainly entertained me plenty over the years. Even as a kid, she wanted to go on stage and took tap and ballet, and I must have gone to countless of her recitals. As we got older, she taught me how to dance and dress and turned me on to Nina Simone and Joni Mitchell. She had blossomed into a bit of a beauty, although her chief asset continued to be her personality.

I'd half grown up in the Richters' sprawling, ramshackle

house, her family welcoming me into it for whole weekends at a time, in spite of the house being full to overflowing already. There were six kids, the family dog, and several cats had the run of the place. There were terrariums full of plants, and an old aquarium for Glenda's hamsters. It was totally different from our lonely little bungalow, just my mother and me, each lost in a book. Perhaps that was where Glenda got her friendly disposition.

After I got off the phone I settled back into *Anna Karenina*. It was unusual for me to have anything interesting enough to compete with Anna, Dolly, Kitty, Vronsky, and Levin, but my mother's boyfriend almost qualified. I liked having a good, long book to lose myself in, and I must have fallen asleep reading because I don't remember my mother coming home.

Ben invited us for a barbecue like he said he would, so Lilah and I drove over there in her old olive-green Mercury one Thursday afternoon. The temperature was up to a hundred and fire warnings were posted along the road. It was so still nothing moved and the cows stood like statues. It was just the way it felt before the 6.1 came along that wiped out the Tracy tower a couple of years ago, and I was thinking, that's all we need now—an earthquake.

I wore orange pedal pushers and an aqua blouse and my hair was pulled back out of my face with little barrettes and I looked OK, I guess. The main thing I had going for me lookswise were my eyes. They were big and gray like amorite crystals. I looked a little like Patty Hearst except I wasn't skinny and didn't wear bangs. I'd seen cops looking at me sometimes and wondered if they were thinking the same thing, and for all I knew they might actually haul off and take me in one day. But my friend Jane said I was paranoid and they weren't looking at me at all, and besides I didn't look anything like her.

I had a picture of Patty, Tanya actually, her nom de guerre, on the wall in my room wearing a black beret and holding a machine gun, looking like she was ready to blow somebody away. Patty Hearst was a newspaper heiress who had been kidnapped from her Berkeley apartment six months earlier and was being held by the Symbionese Liberation Army in exchange for food and education programs for the poor. In the meantime, she'd joined forces with her captors, and they were all on the lam after the rest of their cadre had been firebombed in a house in Los Angeles. My mother thought she was an idiot, but I thought she was cool because she used to be this little rich girl, but she'd had a change of consciousness and now she was trying to help poor people. I'd like to do something myself one day, only I didn't know if I'd do what she did or not, but I wouldn't exactly rule it out.

It took us about an hour to get there. I'd been to Coombs maybe fifteen times before but this time I sat up and took notice. I thought the streets were a little wider than they were in La Grange and the houses set further back. There was a used auto dealer on one corner, a Federal Home Savings Bank next to an A&W root beer stand, and the Rosarita Tamale Parlor across the street. A sign on my side of the road said the elevation was 304 feet and the population was 7,854, which made it even smaller than La Grange. She drove down a couple of side streets and finally pulled up in front of a two-story stucco house that was water stained a dull charcoal gray. The screen door opened, and Ben came out holding a can of beer. He was wearing khaki pants and a red madras shirt and looked flushed from the heat. Two Dobermans came tearing out of the house after him and jumped up on me with their big paws, practically knocking me down.

"Down, Donner, Blitzen!" Ben yelled at them and they finally left off.

"Quick," Ben said, after he kissed Lilah hello. "Nixon's giving his resignation speech. It's on TV right now. You're just in time."

My mother squealed with excitement, and they went off to the living room to watch the denouement of Watergate. I never got why everyone made such a big fuss about the whole thing. I could have cared less, because I always knew the government was full of crooks, although I would have to agree Nixon was a worse slime than most. But it seemed small time compared to the secret bombings in Laos and Cambodia, Black Panthers gunned down on the streets of Oakland and Chicago, children napalmed and villages strafed in Vietnam, not to mention elected governments sabotaged and overthrown on covert orders from the CIA throughout Central America. I guess their cherished illusions of democracy were threatened, but the veil had fallen from my eyes a long time ago.

I stood in the doorway for a few minutes surveying the living room. There were no curtains on the windows and no carpets, just a bunch of hockey sticks and kneepads lying around on the bare hardwood floor. The place had a drafty, grungy feel to it and looked like it hadn't been cleaned in a long time. The walls were a grimy beige and the only ornament to speak of was a tacky print of the Grand Canyon on a calendar a couple of months out of date.

The dogs' nails clicked against the floorboards as they ran the length of the hall, and I went off to prowl around the rest of the house. There was a big funky kitchen at the far end with a worn blue-and-white-checked linoleum floor. A bottle of barbecue sauce and a platter of raw chicken gathered flies on the Formica tabletop.

I went out the back door and saw two guys throwing a baseball back and forth in the backyard. One of them was tall and lanky wearing blue jeans and a white shirt, and the other one was short with a thin, wiry build. He wore wide blue and green plaid Bermudas and a green polo shirt.

I stood there for a while, then slowly walked down the steps and over to where they were playing. I didn't know how they could stand it in the heat, but they hadn't even broken a sweat. The ball whizzed by hard and fast and made a loud thwack as it hit their gloves. I didn't see them miss once—they made it look totally effortless. I sat down at the picnic table and watched for five or ten minutes. I know they saw me, but they didn't let on or hazard a look in my direction. It wasn't until I got up and headed back to the house that they finally stopped throwing and came over.

"So," the shorter one said to me. "I'm Jason and this is Cal, and you must be..."

He squinted at me under a black Yankees cap. He had a gaunt face and curly, almost kinky brown hair, and his eyes were an intense blue like Ben's. He seemed a little friendlier than the other one.

"Miami," I said.

"Miami," Jason repeated, screwing up his nose. "What kind of a name is that?"

"It's a city," Cal said. "What do you think?"

Cal's hair was cut in a long shag and he had dark eyes and a big horsey mouth. They were both good looking, which somehow unnerved me.

"Miami Bitch," he said grinning at me. "Aren't they having race riots there or something?"

"I think so," I said. "But I wasn't named after the city, I was named after the Indians. You know, the Miami of Ohio?"

They both gave me a blank look, so I went on.

"They're an Indian tribe that lived all through the Midwest a long time ago. Chicago was originally a Miami settlement. They're supposed to be related to an ancient tribe who built the Mound Culture of the Mississippi—big burial mounds full of artifacts, like the Great Serpent Mound along the Allegheny Plateau. They were forced to relocate to Oklahoma and practically wiped out.

"My father was an anthropologist," I explained. "He wrote a book about them and died right before I was born, so my mother named me that to commemorate his work. Miami. It means something like 'crane calling to her young.'"

There was a changing line about crane calling to her young in the *I Ching* that went something like, "The superior man's thoughts originate in the quiet of his room and yet have consequences throughout the land. Must one not then pay great heed to one's thoughts?" It was my namesake, but the changing line I usually got when I tossed the coins was, "Big ambition coupled with lack of skill and unbridled appetite seldom escapes disaster."

"No one ever told me your father was an anthropologist," Jason said.

"No?" I said. "Nobody's ever told me anything about your family either. He wrote a book called *Indian Tribes of the Miami Confederacy*. I'll show it to you sometime if you come over."

"What was his name?" Cal asked me.

"Derek Montague," I said.

"Miami Montague," Jason said with a laugh. "It sounds like a sportscaster or something."

"What happened to him?" Cal asked.

"He died in a car crash," I said. "Back before I was born. I never even met him."

"Rough luck," Cal said.

I followed Cal to the grill by the back fence. He squirted lighter fluid on the briquettes and flames flared up and a sooty, black smoke filled the air.

"So have you been seeing much of our dad?" he asked.

I shook my head.

"No," I said. "I've only met him a couple of times."

"It's kind of sweet, isn't it?" Cal asked. "Love among the older set. Your mom's been over a few times. She made dinner once—corned beef and cabbage, I think—and we watched TV together and played Scrabble. Nice lady."

Cal had a space between his front teeth and there was a shadow on his jaw. He reminded me of someone, and I realized it was the barker outside the Hermaphrodite booth. There was a silence for a minute and we could hear the sound of the TV coming from the house.

"That your camera there?" Cal asked pointing to the table and I nodded.

"Her and Marvin," he said to Jason. "The two camera freaks."

"Yeah," Jason said. "The fuckin' paparazzi."

I looked around because I'd been wondering where Marvin was, but neither of them said anything more about him.

"So you guys are really into baseball, I guess?" I asked.

They looked at each other and shrugged like they could take it or leave it. Of course they were playing like a couple of fanatics a few minutes ago, so they were just trying to be cool. Guys were such idiots sometimes.

After a while Ben came down the back stairs carrying the platter of chicken, and my mother followed with bowls of potato salad and coleslaw. She wore blue espadrilles and a crepe dress covered with blue and yellow flowers and looked somehow cool and refreshed even in the heat. While we waited for the chicken to cook, I set the table and we were finally ready to eat when Ben suddenly stood up.

"Wait, a minute," he said. "Where's Marvin?"

His face was sweating and greasy from bending over the grill.

"He's not here, Dad," Cal said. "I think he went out to the Strip with Jimmy La Tour."

"You've got to be kidding," Ben said shaking his head, his voice rising. "I must have told him about this barbecue a week ago. I guess you can't tell that kid anything anymore. The first time the family all tries to get together and he doesn't even show! How do you like that? He's got to be off doing his own thing."

"I'm sorry about this," he said to my mother and me and threw his hat down on the bench.

I was kind of disappointed, but it didn't seem like that big a deal, and no one knew what to say to calm him down. Cal started talking about Oakland's chances of making it into the Series that year. Then Jason asked Ben about Nixon's speech, and that finally turned his energy around, because once he got started he wouldn't shut up about it.

"Here's to the fall of King Richard," he toasted with his beer can. "His immense ambition and grab for power fueled by a misguided attempt to compensate for his boundless insecurity. That's his flaw, but he's no tragic character, because that would imply some dignity or nobility to begin with, which is precisely what he lacks. A more graceless slob, it's hard to imagine. Socially inept, ill at ease, the type no one would have played with as a kid. Old tricky Dickie—with the cutthroat, killer instinct. Terrified of losing because he knows he's such a loser, that he doesn't dare play fair."

"Amen," Cal said and we all toasted too and finally sat down to eat.

I had a Coke and large portions of the coleslaw and potato salad to compensate for not having any chicken. I'd been a vegetarian for a couple of years, ever since the first time I saw the big stockyard off I-5 near Hanover. Shoulder to shoulder, cows in all directions as far as the eye could see, like a Cecil B. DeMille film, and the stench hit you long before they came into view. It was an overwhelming vista and you knew there was something terribly wrong with the whole setup. I didn't want to have anything to do with it and was eating low on the food chain.

"Did you get a look at the house?" Ben asked. "Go in and feel free to take a look around, if you like."

"OK," I said, wondering why he was so eager for me to look the place over. I thought someone would show me around, but neither of the boys got up to go with me, so I walked back to the house by myself.

Upstairs the beds were unmade and jeans, books, papers, and album jackets were scattered over the floor of the boys' bedrooms. I flipped over a jacket for *Catch a Fire* and a paperback of *Naked Lunch* lay on the floor. A big print of a beautiful Chicana girl with long black hair hung over the bed in one room. It had the same grainy quality as the photo at the County Fair, and I figured Marvin must have taken it and she was probably his girlfriend. I don't know what I was expecting but I got the same cheated feeling I had when he got the prize at the County Fair, and I kicked one of the album jackets and it skidded across the room. The floorboard creaked behind me and I turned, thinking he might have come home unexpectedly, but it was just one of the dogs, Blitzen, I think, snuffling up behind me.

The basement was a storage area, full of boxes and orange crates and a rusty swing set and an old treadle sewing machine. I was on my way back upstairs when I heard the refrigerator door slam and Jason's and Cal's voices in the kitchen.

"He said he couldn't handle it on account of Mom, so he was going to split," Jason said. "He always was too close to her, if you ask me, or too sensitive or something."

"Like Dad says, you can never tell him anything," Cal said. "He's always got to be right and he can never see anyone else's point of view. He's never been able to see Dad's, that's for sure, especially not on the subject of Mom."

"He hasn't gotten over it yet," Jason said. "The way it happened and all. I don't think he's been quite the same since. Do you?"

"Everything's always harder on him than anyone else and he never lets you forget it, either. I get pretty sick of hearing about it all the time, that's all."

They spoke in a half whisper, and I peeked through a crack in the door and strained to hear them, but they didn't say anything more. They picked up a watermelon and a half-gallon of ice cream and headed back out to the yard, and the screen door slammed behind them. I waited a few minutes before following them out.

I picked up my camera and took some pictures of the house before the light completely faded, and then I sat down and recorded my exposures in a notebook. Ben cleaned off the grill and Lilah looked at the flower beds by the back fence. Jason and Cal tossed a Frisbee around and after a while I got up and joined them. It was day-glow chartreuse green and it sailed over the yard in a neon curve, and the dogs tore after it and jumped up and tried to snag it with their teeth. After a while my mother came over and said it was time for us to head back.

"Well?" she asked me when we were out on the highway. "How did you like the boys?"

"I liked them," I said. "They're a little heavily into sports for my taste, but that's what boys are all about. Other than that they were OK."

"It's too bad Marvin wasn't there," she said. "He's the one you'd probably have the most in common with.

"That garden could certainly use some tending, couldn't it? It's crying out for it. Nobody's ever cared for it, you can see that. It's just flat and dark with no grass or ground cover, nothing but hard, bare earth. It's been nicely terraced, though. If they pruned the trees and the sun could get through, I'm sure things would grow nicely. That house doesn't look like it's been cleaned in a century, does it? Big old, drafty place. I'm sure everything he said about that woman is true."

She prattled on but I snapped to attention at the mention of Ben's wife. It was completely dark and lights from the oncoming cars flashed on and off her face like a strobe.

"What did he say about her?" I asked. It came out suddenly in a staccato rhythm and she looked at me surprised.

"Just that she was a little bit crazy," my mother said. "I don't think it was a happy marriage."

"Crazy," I repeated. "Crazy, in what way?"

She'd lost the dreamy look she had earlier and her mouth was set and tense.

"Not exactly the ideal wife and mother. You know, just a little nutty."

"Wasn't there supposed to be some mystery about the way she died?" I asked.

"What makes you say that?" she asked sharply. "What did the boys say about her?"

"Nothing, really," I said. "What was she like, anyway?"

"Like I said, she was kind of out of it," she said quietly. "I never met her. I didn't meet Ben until after she died. I think she died of cancer of the pancreas."

All I could see were the distant outlines of trees against the landscape and the taillights on the big semi ahead of us. I thought about Marvin not being there because he felt bad about his mother, and I had some of the same feelings about Ben and my father, and it made me feel even closer to him than the photography connection.

We drove in silence and she started singing, "Cry Me a River." Her voice was deep, throaty, and sexual, and for a minute I got a sense of a whole dimension to her that was totally unknown to me. The tule fog was beginning to move in and everything looked fuzzy and ethereal like a fairy tale or the pageants in elementary school where the Holy Family and the clay oxen emerge shimmering through the mist from the dry ice. The fog lifted for a minute and I saw what was left of an old barn with its back wall fallen away. Then the fog closed in again and it was gone.

CHAPTER 3

Sunday afternoon a few days after the barbeque, my mother was ironing an apple-green work dress when I sauntered into the kitchen. I pulled a Fanta out of the refrigerator and sat on the stepladder and watched her. We had two fans going but all they did was blow the hot air around. The yellow paint was faded and beginning to flake off the ceiling. I'd finished my book and had nothing better to do, and it was a bit on the early side, but it felt like a countdown of the remaining days of summer before school started. I was actually looking forward to it at this point.

She shook and sprayed an aerosol can of starch and the iron hissed and a big cloud of steam filled the air. I thought briefly of the billowing steam that filled the railroad station when Anna killed herself.

My mother pushed a lock of damp hair off her forehead with the heel of her hand, and stood the iron on end.

"I know," Lilah said. "Let's us get out of the house and go for a drive. It's much too hot to be stuck here in the kitchen ironing on a day like this."

The car was hotter still but cooled off some after we got out on the highway. We'd been driving for a while when a giant image from *Alice in Wonderland* loomed up ahead of us on a billboard for Down the Rabbit Hole with Alice Miniature Golf. The billboard was painted in streaky brush strokes that fell short of the Disney ideal. It depicted the episode where Alice grew ten times her size and her head went through the roof and a foreshortened red-and-white-striped stockinged leg stuck out the front door.

I used to badger my mother to take me there when I was a kid, but it looked stale and faded now and wasn't a place I had much interest in anymore, so I was dumbstruck when she veered out of lane and pulled into the narrow parking lot off the shoulder of the highway.

"Shall we stop and play a round?" my mother asked. "It might cool us off."

I don't know why we didn't just go to an air-conditioned movie theater and sip Cokes, but I shrugged and went along with it. She was already dressed for it in plaid madras culottes and a pink shell, and I was wearing baggy yellow Bermudas and a chartreuse halter-top.

Each of the holes was designed around an episode in the story. My mother picked up an orange ball and I took a yellow one. The rabbit hole in the tree was a straight shot down the Astroturf and we both scored a hole in one. Hole number two was the tiny door in the wall that Alice had had to experiment with drugs to get through, and the pathway was blocked with barriers for the ball to ricochet off. The concrete had been painted forest green and was chipped and cracked, adding another challenge. Grace Slick's voice belted out over the loud speaker: "Go ask Alice/ I think she'll know,/ When logic and proportion have fallen sloppy dead...".

The concrete figures of the Mad Hatter and the March Hare

looked like garden gnomes and the Cheshire Cat grinned cheerlessly. We were at the ninth hole, where the Queen of Hearts played croquet with the flamingos and the hedgehog, and the score was 36 to 25. I was winning, of course. My mother seemed to have defeat programmed into her when it came to me, perhaps it went with the territory of motherhood, a totally foreclosed property. She transitioned smoothly from throwing me the game early on as encouragement—be it tennis, Ping-Pong, canasta, Monopoly, or Scrabble—to my eventually being able to beat her fair and square.

"You liked Cal and Jason well enough the other day, didn't you?" she asked as she aimed her swing.

"Mmm hmmm," I said. "They were cool."

"That's good. How about the house? Did you get a chance to look around?"

"I did. I went upstairs and snooped around. I can't say I was really crazy about the house. Why? Why the third degree about Ben and his family all of a sudden?"

She gave me a sideways glance and bit her lower lip.

"Because we'll be seeing a lot more of them from now on."

"How so?" I asked.

"Because I've got some news for you," she said haltingly. "Which I hope you will see as good news. Ben and I have decided to get married, so we'll be moving over there pretty soon."

I had to steady myself on the metal railing by the side of the tee.

"When is this going to happen?" I asked.

"We haven't set the date yet, but we're thinking of November first. I thought I'd see how you felt about it."

The sun beat down steadily and beads of sweat poured off of

me. How I felt about it? How did she think I would feel about it? She might as well have delivered a swift punch to the gut.

"Whoa," I said. "Don't you think you're rushing things? After all, you barely know the man."

"We've been seeing each other for five or six months now, and besides, it's not like he just came along and swept me off my feet or anything. It's much more solid than that. I'm so comfortable with Ben, he feels like an old family friend. I think it was meant to be. It feels like my whole life has been leading up to this."

"So we'll be moving over there?" I asked.

She nodded and her eyes sparkled.

"I'm afraid we'll have to," she said. "There certainly isn't room for them to move in here with all those boys."

"How am I going to get to school from all the way over there?"

"I'll drive you to school if you want. Or better yet, you could change schools and go to Mission along with Ben's kids. That would probably be the simplest arrangement."

"Which is it?" I asked. "You're going to drive me or I'm going to have to switch schools? I don't want to change schools. This is my last year of high school. I don't feel like leaving Alamo in the middle of the year."

My eyes welled with tears. Her hair was clustered in damp ringlets and the late afternoon light accented the blond highlights, but the veins in her neck stood out and I thought she looked haggard and harsh. I had been so wrong about her sacrificing and letting me win. She gave in on the little things and claimed the big ones for herself.

"Why can't you wait until after I graduate?" I asked. "And then there won't be a problem."

It wasn't just that I didn't want a big rupture right in my last year, I was also shocked at her recklessness.

"I'm afraid we're not prepared to wait *that* long. We want it to happen sometime this fall or winter, before the first of the year. I'm getting to be an old lady. I'll be forty on my birthday. And how long has it been since I've had a man in my life?"

"I can't believe you're doing this to me," I said.

She stood there staring at me, her mouth crumpled into a whorl.

"Look, I'm sorry you feel this way," she said. "I really thought you'd be happy about it—not for my benefit but your own. You're the one who's always talking about how bored you are by this Podunk town, and how you can't wait to get out of here. Well, now you can. You're always bemoaning the fact that you never had any brothers and sisters, and now you're going to have three brothers."

I was so frustrated by her obtuseness that I purposely hit my ball into the drainage ditch by the hurricane fence, officially putting an end to the game. We stood glaring at each other. The Alice in Wonderland figures looked almost demonic now. Even the White Rabbit seemed to have a wicked grin.

"I never said anything about wanting stepbrothers," I said. "I wanted regular brothers and sisters that you grow up with your whole life. It's too late for that now. I'm not sure how I feel about moving in with a bunch of stepbrothers that I barely know. It sounds vaguely creepy. And I don't want a father. I already have one, remember? Or have you completely forgotten about him, too?"

I paused and she looked sort of sad for a minute, and then her eyes brightened and she winked at me.

"Those boys are bound to have some friends, you know. I

can pretty much guarantee that things are going to get a lot more interesting pretty soon. Think about it. You're going to have a whole new family now—with boys your age. Doesn't that sound exciting? Don't you want to change schools and have some new experiences?"

"No, I don't," I said. "I can barely handle the ones I have now. Don't pretend you're doing this for my benefit. You're thinking of yourself, pure and simple. You're in love with the man. I don't know exactly what you see in him, but that's your business, I suppose. And now I'm going to have to leave all my friends."

"It's not that far away," she said. "And you can see them any time. I'll personally chauffeur you over here whenever you want and you'll probably be learning to drive yourself before long.

"Look, Honey, I'm sorry to inconvenience you like this and I understand that you're upset about it. I wish we could wait until after you graduate, I really do. I know it would make things a lot easier for you. But there'll be some bright spots for you, I promise. There'll be more money for college for one thing because I'll be selling the house."

We were interrupted by a chubby guy in plaid Bermudas.

"You two have been arguing here for a good twenty minutes," he said to Lilah. "There are six people waiting for your tee, and you're holding everyone up. Can you please just get on with it?"

A cadre of the irritated stood behind him. Normally, I would have been mortified, but I was beyond being fazed by it.

"Let's just go home," I said.

I ripped up the scorecard and threw it away. As if on cue, a tinny recording of the Queen of Hearts said, "Girl, *keep* your temper."

I sulked in silence in the car and my mother gave me my space. We were both tired and wanted to retreat into our corners, but when we got back to the house, Ben was seated on the glider on the front porch, fanning himself with his hat. From the looks of him, he completely belonged there, and was staking out his territory.

Lilah looked palpably relieved at the sight of him.

"What inspiration led you to drop by, Ben?" she asked. "Have you been here long?"

"No," he said. "I was hoping you'd be back soon. I was going to wait another twenty minutes."

I took the measure of him sitting there with his skinny legs and his khaki shorts and his wrinkled face. He was a harder sell now that I knew he was going to be my stepfather. I visualized the big drafty house with his reindeer dogs running through it. No wonder he was so anxious for me to look around. He seemed to be appraising me too. I thought he was assessing how much I knew and I decided not to give anything away.

"It's too darn hot," he said. "How about we go skinny-dipping down at the old swimming hole where the river deepens?"

"Now that sounds like a good idea," Lilah said. "We just went out to play miniature golf but it was too hot even for that. I'll go upstairs and get my suit."

"He said skinny-dipping, Mom," I said. "I don't think you'll need a suit."

"Well, I'm going to take one just in case," she said. "You never know who you're going to run into. I might be struck with a sudden burst of modesty. He might not have meant it literally. Ben can be a bit of a joker sometimes."

"How are Jason and Cal?" I asked him.

"Oh, they're out and about, making the most of the dog

days before the grind starts up again. I'm not entirely sure what they've been up to. I've been spending half days over at school going through the equipment, getting rid of the broken stuff, and cleaning out the supplies closet."

"Sounds like fun," I said.

"I don't mind," he said. "I wouldn't be there if I did. I always look forward to the start of a new year—the anticipation, the strategizing, seeing what kind of team we're going to have."

Lilah came down wearing a green muumuu over her suit and the two of them drove off.

I sat on the couch in the living room dazed from the news. I looked across the room at the bronze Buddha head on the coffee table and tried to tune into its calming essence. Lilah had a tendency to accumulate furniture and tchotchkes, and the house had the look and feel of a secondhand shop. A framed Toulouse Lautrec poster hung on the purple wall ahead of me with a gilt statue of Isis below it, next to a straggly Wandering Jew growing out of a Chinese porcelain pot. A fake oriental rug covered the floor, and old *National Geographics* were stacked on the sideboard with the inlaid facing.

It was still stiflingly hot, and it felt claustrophobic and confining. Suddenly I wasn't sure why I was making such a fuss about leaving. Perhaps I was being bratty and immature or else it was just a knee-jerk reaction of defiance, but I'd had the rug pulled out from under me and I thought she owed me more of an explanation. I could still see the sign in front of the hermaphrodite's tent with the painting of the bride and groom merged into one person like a split personality. "He's a wedding all in himself," the barker had said. It was directly after that that I met Ben, and now there *was* going to be a wedding and my world would be turned upside down. It had been hard enough to imagine them having sex, and now they were actually getting married.

It was clear she wasn't going to change her mind about the wedding, and I would have to adapt to the move. She had briefly offered to drive me to Alamo but abandoned the idea in favor of my transferring to Mission. That was what she was pushing for, and I hadn't really fought against it. Perhaps part of me was more open to this than I realized, although being prematurely wrested away from K.D., Jane, and Glenda in my last year of high school came as an unimaginable blow. High school was a challenge as it was, and it was hard to imagine surviving it without my friends.

I had some tuna fish salad, corn on the cob, and iced tea for dinner and went for a walk. I followed Baedekker Place out of town past the 7-Eleven and the Scoffield's house and walked out on the levee, scanning the flat horizon. The heat had lifted and a breeze ruffled the water pouring into the sluice, and it reflected back a shimmering, golden light. The evening sky turned violet and a flock of crows flew overhead cawing noisily, their wings beating the sky.

I sat down and dangled my legs over the embankment. The water shimmered back at me like a mirror, and the sunset glinted a shiny copper on the horizon. The sky dwarfed everything on the landscape and the horizon looked expanded and limitless. I'd purged some of my anger in the argument with my mother, but something still bothered me, and I finally figured out what it was. When I tried to bring my father into the discussion, she neatly sidestepped it. I guess she didn't want to be reminded of him anymore. I planned on remaining loyal to my father's memory no matter what, and it looked like it was solely up to me now. Her marriage would never make me Ben Beasley's daughter, although it might be more of a struggle to preserve my essential identity. She had been so devastated by my father's death, I took it for granted that he was irreplaceable and a second marriage was out of the question. I hadn't realized she would heal with time.

Having pinpointed what was bothering me gave me some relief, and I inched a little further in my openness to the thing. My mother was right, I *had* always wanted to move and now we were, and who knows what it would be like? It might be OK. It wasn't exactly the exodus from the Valley I was waiting for, because it was just a neighboring town, but it was still a change, and an expansion of my horizons. The fact that as much harm as good could come of it didn't fill me with dread anymore, but posed a challenge, and I felt momentarily invigorated by it.

It had grown dark while I was sitting there and the lights from Fresno blinked on the horizon. Further up, stars radiated their haloes so that the entire night sky seemed to be pulsing with visions and swirling like a Van Gogh painting. I thought I heard the "Hallelujah Chorus" coming from somewhere but I must have imagined it. There wasn't a house anywhere around and it was August, not Christmas.

I lay down on the ground and the strawlike grass prickled my back as I tried to make out a few of the constellations. I had never been good at picking them out, but if there was ever a night for it, this was it. It was around the time for the Perseid meteor showers and Orion's belt and Cassiopeia were up there somewhere. There was a constellation I'd heard of, of three brothers who went out boar hunting and been impaled against the sky, but I didn't remember what it was called and didn't know where to look for it. The only one I could see for sure was the Big Dipper, but perhaps that was all you needed. Draw a straight line from the bowl to the handle of the Little Dipper, follow the Drinking Gourd, and you were home free.

Jane would know the planetary alignments and whether they were auspicious or not for journeys and new beginnings. A giant golden orb hung low on the horizon in the north sky, and

Jane would probably know what that was too, maybe Venus, the first star of evening. Directly overhead I saw a falling star, which meant a soul had entered heaven. My mother echoed what Glenda said about the boys having friends, and a shiver of excitement went through me. Glenda would probably see the move as an exciting adventure. It might be good for me to have this built-in exposure to boys, although I couldn't help having cold feet about it. Built-in also meant there would be no getting away from it if it didn't work out.

My mother might not be so off base after all and the move might be all right. I wasn't going to tell her that, though. The same way I didn't tell her about the secret supply of Twinkies, Hostess cupcakes, and M&M's in my underwear drawer that I binged on when I had a bad day. It was to my advantage for her to continue thinking that she was seriously inconveniencing me with this move. That way she owed me one. If I held my cards close to my chest and didn't reveal my feelings, there was a chance I could finesse better treatment out of her, although there was nothing special I was angling for. She'd already promised me more money for college from the sale of the house.

The light reflected off the water in the irrigation ditch, and I picked up a flat stone and skipped it one-two-three-four times before it finally sank out of sight.

CHAPTER 4

I woke up sweating in the middle of the night, my head aching from grinding gears and screeching brakes, and the smell of burned rubber singed the air. I must have had the dream about the car crash at least fifty times. The car went into a prolonged skid followed by the collision of steel and shattering glass. A siren sounded and the revolving red light of the ambulance flashed, and my father was carried away on a stretcher with a coarse wool blanket over his face.

My father was killed in a car crash three months before I was born, at a four-way stop by a drunk driver. He was on his way home from teaching a class at Cal State Stanislaus in Turlock. It was as if I was there and felt the impact myself. It became a recurring nightmare of mine, the closest I've gotten to what hell must be like. Sometimes the car was yellow and sometimes blue. Sometimes it was a station wagon and other times a sedan, but other than that, the particulars of the dream remained the same. Not to be morbid, but it would have been fine with me if my mother was in the car with him and I had never been born. It might have been for the best.

Glenda said that the loss of life of a 90-year-old man wasn't valued as highly in insurance payments as 50-year-old man, and so forth. Her father was an insurance claims adjuster, so she knew about such things. I'd have to get the actuarial tables from her on what that accident cost, and what a lifetime with no father was worth in dollars and cents. I know it wasn't worth much to me, not to mention what it did to my mother. Another wasted life.

I considered the fact that I'd never gotten to know my father to be the greatest single deprivation of my existence, although he probably occupied a bigger place in my life in absentia than he ever could have if he'd been around. He loomed over me like a big myth and I had long talks with him at night the way other people prayed to God. If I had a bad day, I didn't talk to my mother, I went to him, and he helped me reason out my conflicts and gave me wisdom or advice. He was always interested in what I had to say, so in a sense he was the ideal father, even though it was all in my mind.

I had a framed picture of my father hanging on the wall over my bed. He was standing in a field of pampas grass with a mountain range in the background. It had been taken out on a dig somewhere. He was a field anthropologist before he became a professor at Cal State Stanislaus, and my mother was one of his students. He was wearing a khaki shirt in the picture and was smiling and handsome with thick, bushy hair like the Kennedys. He had a light in his eyes that looked more like a dreamer than a scholar and radiated their same sense of optimism and curiosity about the world.

My mother was pretty close-mouthed on the subject of my father, because his death had wracked her up so bad, and I had to cadge whatever bits of information I could get out of her. I wondered why there weren't royalties from his book or some kind of pension from the university, but she said lawyers and academics had screwed us out of all that a long time ago.

My father was pronounced Dead On Arrival at Mercy Medical from internal hemorrhaging. The other driver, the one who had been drinking, walked away from the crash, although he wound up doing a few years in Soledad for criminal negligence and vehicular manslaughter.

My mother did some time behind bars too, the kind you get seriously drunk in, although the one led to the other and she was arrested a few times for being drunk and disorderly herself. Then Child Protective Services had to be called in. You'd think she'd have known better since that's what killed my father, but I knew how she felt and couldn't really blame her. Still, for me it was like losing them both, because my mother was little more than a thirsty ghost.

When I was little, she used to take me to the bars with her. I sat on the floor close to her ankles where the bartender wouldn't see me, sort of like a ball and chain, I guess, with a set of paper dolls to keep me occupied, listening to the drunken palaver going on over my head. Drinking seemed to make instant friends of strangers, before the fights started anyway. In no time, they carried on like they'd known each other all their lives. Drinking buddies were the closest things to friends my mother had in those days, before she met her union pals Agnes and Mabel at Yarborough's. I was frequently used as an excuse for not going home with someone who'd been buying her drinks all night. They'd say "Come on, Lilah, she can come too," or "She's old enough to be left alone. She's practically a toddler."

When she was sober, I dragged her to the library to read to me whenever I could. She enjoyed reading and it seemed like the most fun we ever had together. We schlepped a stack of books around with us whenever we moved, half of them overdue library books. When they wouldn't give her a library card anymore, I got one and when they took that away, she read to me at one of the nicked wooden tables in the library and reshelved the books when we'd finished.

My mother landed a few jobs that got us off welfare for a while, though our lifestyle didn't change much as a result. We were still living in firetraps, but she was away more and I was left on my own. She worked as a Licensed Vocational Nurse, a seamstress in a sweatshop, and an aide in a greenhouse. The greenhouse job was by far her favorite and gave her a passion for plants and gardening that stayed with her. She brought home six-packs of seedlings, along with her other six-packs. They thrived on the fire escape or windowsill of our hotel room for a while, until we had to move, and then were left to wither and die.

Me, I was taken along to wither and die. One hotel was as good as another to her. She drank up the welfare money so we stayed until we got bounced for nonpayment of the rent. I thought if we stayed in one place long enough, I could have finally made some friends. Other welfare families took up permanent residence, and their rooms looked homey and lived-in with crystals and curtains in the windows and posters. One girl's father was even painting a fresco on the wall, a dreamlike space landscape in purples and greens, populated by goofy, friendly looking aliens. I was friends with their daughter, Jenny, and my mother had to drag me kicking and screaming when we moved.

One time when I was in kindergarten my mother scared me by not getting out of bed for several days in a row. We shared a Murphy bed with an electric blanket. I don't know whether she was sick or depressed but somehow I knew enough to call in sick for her at her job. I went to school and when I came home she was still in bed. I made myself a peanut butter sandwich for dinner and crawled in next to her. She revived after a few days and went back to her job but I was still in a panic. I had to stuff myself with Oreos, Fifth Avenue and Clark bars, and M&M's until I was numb enough to sleep.

I spent a lot of time by myself in those days even when my mother was around. She made me a hot dog, or heated a can of soup, or macaroni and cheese from a carton, while she scarfed down a six-pack, a pint, or a bottle of red wine. She was jovial and companionable for a while until she hit the skids and got sick, and then she might pass out for twelve hours or so and I was on my own.

If there was a coin-operated TV in the room, I watched reruns of "I Love Lucy," "Amos 'n' Andy," or "The Ann Sothern Show" until the change ran out, usually after about an hour. Then I looked through a threadbare orange book that was loose at the spine called *The Fairies of Tintendale.* My mother read me the stories so often I knew them all by heart and mumbled them out loud to myself. It was almost like reading. I turned the pages of the black-silhouetted illustrations of elves and fairies and tried to cross over into that world, like Alice in *Through the Looking Glass.*

I looked at the blank wall ahead of me or out the window and thought about my father, and wondered when he would come back and thought about how different everything would be when he finally did. I wasn't clear on exactly where he had gone. I didn't know what death meant in those days, but it was too hopeless to think that I'd never ever get to see him. All I knew was that he didn't live in a skuzzy hotel room like ours, but a lovely mansion somewhere, with an empty space in it for us and I half expected him to show up looking for us one day.

My mother had shown me his house once a long time ago.

She woke me in the dark and took me on a long bus ride. It was so early the tule fog still covered the ground and when we got off the bus, we walked a long ways, and the pavement was wet from the dew. When we got there, we stood staring outside a wrought iron fence at a big white colonnaded house with a wide expanse of grass in front of it. The streets were silent and it felt like we were the only ones awake in the world. We looked at the house a long time and then walked back to the bus to go home without even knocking on the door. She didn't say a word, but she didn't have to. I knew for certain it was where my father lived. Why else would we have gone there?

My father subsisted in a parallel universe that hovered nearby but was inaccessible, but someday the two worlds were bound to intersect. In *The Little Princess* Sara Crewe's father was thought to be dead but actually lived in a hotel kitty-corner to Miss Minchin's School for Girls, where Sara worked as a scullery maid. He had an apartment with Persian rugs and a soft yellow light from the lamp and a monkey for a pet. It was just a matter of time before she met him, and I hoped the same would happen to me one day if I bided my time. I fully expected it to.

When my mother was sacked out, I had my father to turn to. Silence and emptiness weren't silent and empty at all but a whole mysterious world. I went back and forth between them like a child of divorced parents. I had my own fresco on the wall if I stared at it hard enough, filled with curlicue vines, elves, witches, and bluebells—the magical world of Fairie. I conjured it up at will.

Of the two, my father was infinitely more reliable, being gone. My mother was emotional and touchy, and you could never be sure which side of her you were going to get. Sometimes she held me close and said it was her and me against the world, and we had to stick together, no matter what. Other times she lashed out and sent me flying. It was me that was driving her to drink, she said. I had been the ruination of her and one day she might be of a mind to up and leave me God knows where, and I could see how I liked that. She scared me crazy when she talked like that and I promised her anything, mainly to change my ways and start behaving, and to stop being a pest and a brat, at which she said I was becoming very accomplished.

It wasn't an idle threat, because when I was six she left me for a long time with her mother who lived on a little chicken farm on a bare patch of land on the outskirts of Mineola, Texas. It took us two days and nights to get there in the back of a Greyhound bus, eating bologna sandwiches all the way. With her parched face, caved-in mouth, and wispy hair, I thought my grandmother was the oldest person I'd ever seen. But no one had ever made a fuss over me before and I loved it. What was left of her farm was as ruined as her face. The cotton fields had long since yielded a crop, and all that was left were some chickens pecking on the hard-packed earth yard.

The bare earth burned my feet as I padded across the yard, and the sun blinded you when you looked at it. It was amazing how flat and empty the land was, and how far you could see when nothing was on it. My grandmother showed me the frog pond at the edge of her property and how to catch a frog in it. She took me to the local convenience store for candy and let me gather the eggs from the chickens with her.

A week into our visit, I woke up one glaring, sun-filled morning to find the bed empty beside me. My grandmother was sitting stone-faced at the kitchen table with a cold cup of coffee.

"Where's Lilah?" I asked, because my mother was never an early riser.

"I don't know," my grandmother said slowly. "All her stuff is gone. She must have up and left in the night. Your things are here, though."

The news tripped my nerves and I went flying out of the house, determined to prove my grandmother wrong. I scoured her small property looking for my mother. I don't know whether I expected to find her hiding in the barn, or see her departing silhouette against the horizon, but whatever direction I looked, I saw nothing. A cricket chirping in the yard reminded me of how the plague of locusts in *The Little House on the Prairie* had begun. The worst had now happened, and there was nothing I could do to keep it from bowling me over. Grandma Heaney's shadow fell in front of me, and we walked back to the house together.

My grandmother comforted me with warm milk from a chipped crockery cup that she got straight from the teat of the cow. Later, I sat next to her like a pet tabby while she sewed and listened to the revival stations, going through her sewing basket for bits of ribbon and piping. She made me a little stuffed mouse out of gray felt. I still have it in my jewelry box—the bead eyes have long since fallen out, leaving me one blind mouse. I also kept some of her handmade lace and tatting.

Grandma Heaney was a Holy Roller and a powerfully religious woman. She took me with her to the revival meetings of Little Gethsemane Pentecostal that were held outside in the congregation's backyards. That was the first I knew what a real church was and not just a building, because they didn't even have one. She said they did once but Jesus tore it down and built it for them again in three days with no walls or ceiling to it. They got all het up and chanted prayers that sounded like cheerleaders at a pep rally: "Jesus is the standard; Satan is a nerd." Sometimes they did a telephone prayer wheel that put them in touch a couple of times a week, so that the whole congregation would be on the same page about the latest crisis, even if it was as insignificant as someone getting over a cold or a child passing a test at school. Church was entertainment and socializing to them, like other people go to the movies or watch TV, and after attending services a few times, I could see why.

The sermons introduced me to stirring concepts that captured my imagination and rocked my soul, like the Tribulation and the Rapture, when Jesus' chosen would vanish, departing the earth in a gravity-defying vacuum that left their shoes behind, and purges of fire and flood would be leveled against evildoers. I believed these ideas instantly. They explained the turbulence and chaos I had been through, giving it meaning and purpose.

The sermons voiced my deep-seated belief that my father was coming back, a secret so profound I'd never even shared it with my mother. The preacher spoke of a time when he had walked with us in the garden, but we had been disobedient and thrown out of his presence and lost our place in paradise. Hell was the absence of our father, and love and grace were in his return. There was a covenant that if we were good and fulfilled his commandments, he would return—this had been promised since time immemorial. Sometimes they called him our father and sometimes Jesus, but the two were essentially indistinguishable, which was a great mystery, for no one would know the father except through the son. I didn't understand everything the preacher said, but I understood the one essential thing. He was talking about my father coming back and debunking those who said he wasn't.

I was thrilled to be among people who openly celebrated and reveled in my secret, believing it with far greater certainty than I did, actually counting the days till his return. The Second Coming, they called it. They scanned the horizon for signs from

God. Anything else was just a blip on the screen to them, hardly worth notice, and I heartily agreed.

The congregation believed they were chosen to be among the 144,000 to inherit the peace of the 1,000-year reign, and I was elated to be somewhere in that throng. I was put off by the rigors of the Battle of Armageddon and the Judgment Day, but couldn't imagine that they would be that much worse than anything I'd already been through, so I figured I was a shoo-in to survive.

We sang "Do Lord" and "I Got a Home in Glory" and "Holy, Holy, Holy." When someone was possessed of the Holy Spirit and took to speaking in tongues, others signified by falling to the ground in a dead faint. Occasionally during a service the sick would come forward to be healed, awkwardly lurching on crutches or metal braces toward Pastor Everson. The minister had his hands up, channeling Jesus's energy like a lightning rod and laid his hands on them. The force was powerful enough to drive the demons out of them in an instant, and it was glorious to see them throw down their crutches and walk down the aisle as tall and straight as a tree. The church was a hospital and entertainment hub as well as a redemption center, and there seemed to be little point to anything outside it.

I thought long and hard about how to be good, since this was the only way to bring my father back and it couldn't be easy or he would have come back a long time ago. The church was very clear about their standards of behavior. You were supposed to forgive someone up to seventy times seven, almost 500 wrongs, so you would surely lose count by then, which was perhaps how that could be accomplished. The idea of loving your enemies seemed like a contradiction in terms. I thought God might be setting us up for a self-defeating prophecy and perhaps he never was coming back and it was all a shuck.

Although when I thought about it, I must have forgiven Lilah at least 550 wrongs by now, and she me. I certainly never hit her back and I may even have turned the other cheek, because she frequently hit me more than once, and we loved each other anyway, so perhaps I knew something about loving your enemies after all, and it wasn't as far-fetched as it seemed.

Grandma Heaney was amazed that I took to the faith with such enthusiasm, since my mother had turned away from religion at an early age. My mother's real name was Mary, but out of spite and apostasy she changed it to Delilah. Everyone just called her Lilah, though Grandma Heaney never would. Grandma Heaney was proud of me and thought I might have the makings of a child evangelist when I was older, perhaps nine or ten, something I think I would have enjoyed. She took me to hear a few of them preach and I saw how they could hold the crowd as rapt as an adult. I would have liked nothing more than to have stood before the congregation myself, the words streaming from my mouth like fire, but my mother came to take me back long before that ever happened.

My grandmother said she knew I had never been baptized and arranged for it one Sunday afternoon with the preacher. There was a slow-moving, muddy river outside of town and the entire congregation gathered on its banks to witness. The members of the congregation were a lanky, loose-jointed people with big shocks of hair and wide-open faces and missing teeth. Their clothes were made from fabric as coarse and rough as mattress ticking, and they rarely wore socks. They bought their kids' shoes a few sizes too big, so they wouldn't have to replace them as often.

I stood on the bank with the others in a white cotton shift. Pastor Everson was already in the river with the water up to his waist, and beckoned me to come toward him. My friend Marlene Hampton told me she'd seen cottonmouths slither into the river on occasion, but my grandmother had led me to understand that I could never be united with my father unless I went through with it, so I was eager to proceed. The silt river bottom squished between my toes and by the time I reached the preacher, the water was over my chin and I had to gulp for air. Pastor Everson leaned toward me and I thought he was going to pick me up but instead he pressed down hard on my shoulders, forcing me underwater. I must have swallowed a couple of glasses worth, but I couldn't break surface with him holding me down. I couldn't hold my breath any longer, but hard as I struggled, I was unable to free myself from his grip.

There was a moment when I realized he was going to drown me in front of the entire congregation, and that was the point of the ceremony. I was to be put to death like Jesus for the benefit of others. I thought I was scaring myself with the water snakes but never contemplated child sacrifice before. I heard someone call out "Take her, Jesus!" and someone else "Amen!" and they began singing "Holy, Holy, Holy." My lungs filled with water, and I stopped struggling and felt the life begin to drain out of me. Pastor Everson said "Lord, fill this child with your Holy Spirit!" I saw a light emerge out of the darkness and thought perhaps it was Jesus calling me. The congregation was more serious than I could ever have imagined about death and resurrection, and now I understood why Grandma Heaney hadn't told me anything about the ceremony in advance. I would be reunited with my father in the afterlife. It made sense in a way, and I suppose I should have thought of it myself.

My spirit eased toward the light and just as I had made my peace and was finally ready to die, Reverend Everson jerked me out of the water and reeled me in like a prize catfish and flung me on the bank where I coughed and spat out some of the water I had swallowed. I don't remember much more than that because

I passed out, and didn't come to until three days later, on my cot at Grandma Heaney's.

My grandmother appeared pleased with the baptism. She fed me spoonfuls of chicken soup and said it had been a powerful ceremony, just as she knew it would be. I nodded my head uncertainly, thinking now that the whole point had been my seeing Jesus when I was under, and not to kill me after all, but even then I wasn't sure.

Grandma Heaney leaned close and said she had something important to tell me. I thought she was going to explain what had happened at the river, but she had something else in store. Her eyes bugged out of her head as she told me my mother had gone away due to her wickedness which God was punishing her for, that's why life had been hard for us. She accused her of drunkenness and harlotry and said she didn't like to speak ill of family or create enmity between the generations, but there were things that were more important than family, like one's immortal soul, so she was going to say it. My mother may be indistinguishable from the Great Harlot, the Whore of Babylon, that rode on the beast with the seven horns and the number 666 imprinted on its forehead and been prophesied for thousands of years by John in the Book of Revelation. None other. She wanted me to know, because the information could be crucial to my salvation one day. God was punishing her for her drinking and fornication and I was not to follow in her footsteps or I might wind up in Sodom and Gomorrah. She didn't want me to take a wrong turn in life, and if I should come to a crossroads someday, I could get lost forever in a dark and scary forest. She had thought about it long and hard, and come to the conclusion that it was so, and the only reason she was even mentioning it was because she knew for certain we were in the end times.

CHAPTER 5

Grandma Heaney's house was little better than a shack. You could see the dirt through the floorboards and scorpions got inside more than once, though I was never stung by one. There was a front porch from which you could look out a very long way at the empty plains. The shack had a chicken coop behind it and a barn made of the same dull gray wood and there was one shade tree in the yard.

Eunice Heaney hadn't always been scrub poor like that, she told me, and my mother confirmed it after she came to get me, filling in some of the blanks of the story. When my mother was a little girl they lived in a big house with a cleaning lady that came once a week, and they ate dinner every night with the forty men and women who worked on the 500 acres they owned. There were herds of cattle on the land and milking machines in the barn and fields of cotton to be plowed and harvested. They were prosperous and happy, my grandfather was still in the house then, and my mother had no reason to fear for the future.

What happened next was hard to explain. Grandma Eunice was given a revelation from God so beautiful, tears gushed from her poor tired eyes. She wouldn't describe what she had seen, other than to say it was the fulfillment of everything that had been promised in the Bible, going back to Elijah and Ezekiel. It was a glorious vision, but it imposed an incredible burden on her. Seeing was believing, she said, and she got to prophesying about the Rapture. She read scripture and studied the signs and set the date as May 14, 1948, which was to be the birth date of the sacred nation of Israel. She fixed on that date because it had been prophesied since time immemorial that Jesus's feet would touch down on the Mount of Olives at which point all of Israel would rise to meet him like a bride in the miraculous Second Coming.

She had herself a job to get the congregation ready, because while they were ostensibly one flock, everyone was pulling in different directions. Grandma Heaney had the manner of a field sergeant marshaling troops. It wasn't her natural temperament but had to do with the import of her vision and the urgency she felt about conveying it. Sadly, it had the effect of alienating and scattering the fold she sought to draw to her. They mocked my grandmother and ridiculed her theories and wanted nothing to do with her, which mightily frustrated her.

Eunice Heaney tried so hard to convert her vision into reality she completely bankrupted herself in the process. Since love of money was said to be the root of all evil and Jesus said to take everything you had and give it to the poor, liquidating her assets seemed the strongest statement she could make to convince people she was in earnest and not self-serving like Evangeline Brown and Natty Davis accused her of being. While she may have been lacking in charisma and the social graces, she was possessed of a farm of 500 acres, livestock, tractors, milking machines, and a big house and barn and she was prepared to mortgage all of it, if that's what it took to bring the flock to Jesus.

In the end she just earned herself a reputation for foolhardiness, lack of wisdom (which was a sign of the devil's handiwork) and discernment, and vainglory rather than Christian charity. Sister Bartholomew said that she was attempting to buy friends and even the church itself. Grandma Heaney said she was trying to turn herself into a pillar of cloud by day and a pillar of fire by night, but Sister Evangeline said she was more like a pillar of salt, taking them all straight to hell and Sodom and Gomorrah, because she was a bitter, stern, old battle-axe who didn't embody the gospel, which was all about love and God's word fell on barren soil when it landed on her. She quoted Paul, Corinthians 13:1-3: "If I speak in the tongues of men and of angels, but have not love, I am a noisy gong or a clanging cymbal. And if I have prophetic powers, and understand all mysteries and all knowledge, and if I have all faith, so as to remove all mountains, but have not love, I am nothing. If I give away all I have, and I deliver my body to be burned, but have not love, I gain nothing."

Grandma Heaney was undeterred. She sold her farm and liquidated her assets and started making monthly payments to each of the parishioners, including Sister Evangeline, to show that there were no hard feelings and her mission was above petty rivalry, even though Sister Evangeline continued to be her harshest critic and actively proselytized against her. There were knock-down drag-out fights between her and my grandfather who owned half the farm, but there was no talking to her. She said she had to take her cues from reading the signs, and do God's bidding because in the end it was God she would be accountable to.

She said they couldn't take the farm with them anyway, and how better to spend it than on their beloved church, bringing everyone along with them, in a glorious imitation of the parable of the loaves and the fishes? She envisioned being taken up into the Rapture as akin to passing through the eye of a needle.

She became the cash cow of the congregation and money hemorrhaged from her bank account at a dangerous rate. Her generosity led people to believe there was more there than there really was, and they milked it for what it was worth, milking her dry in the process. When word of her generosity got out, others came to her for money, and those she had already given to came back for more. After her initial resistance crumpled, she had no ability to say no. Who was she to deny anyone access to God's kingdom? Wasn't it her job to ferry them across? All that mattered as far as Grandma Heaney was concerned was that the money held out until May 14, 1948, the appointed day of the Rapture. They wouldn't need money after that, anymore than they need fear the heat of the sun or the furious winter's rage. Neither would they hunger nor thirst.

She gave $50,000 to the Browns, and $30,000 to the Davises, and $10,000 to the Dodges, because they needed it, $5,000 to the Cunninghams, $10,000 to the Tuckers, and $20,000 to the Ramseys. She kept not a thing for herself. Some begged her for money, demanded it and accused her of being cheap if she denied it. Others accused her of being prodigal and foolhardy, although people were happy to take the cash off her hands if she wanted them to. After all, it obliged them to nothing.

My mother said that preaching was a rough racket, because a mistake was viewed as character flaw or a sign of God's displeasure. There was little incentive to admit mistakes, and problems tended to get swept under the rug and ignored. That's how things went for some time while Grandma Heaney parceled out her funds and supported the congregation.

When the appointed day arrived, she no longer owned the

barn whose roof was to serve as the launching pad to kingdom come, although the Henderson family that bought it off her said they'd be proud to have the congregation sit on the barn roof all night to wait for Jesus, just not so many of them as to cave it in. My mother said that all of the flock that could fit gathered on the rooftop at sunset. The rest were nearby in the surrounding fields. Midnight was the appointed hour. They had their provisions—their picnic baskets full of ham sandwiches, buttermilk, and fried chicken. The people were wild with excitement. My mother remembered it—she was there, wrapped in a log cabin quilt. She was thirteen years old. Grandma Heaney was wrapped in a crazy quilt, and my grandfather was there too. They had the cat and the dog with them and their suitcases packed. That was all they were taking with them into the next life, only it wouldn't be one of glory, but a trail of tears, hardship, judgment, and poverty.

The skies didn't open. Jesus didn't come. It was a long night. My mother mostly remembered the difficulty trying to sleep on the steep roof and the effort it took to keep from rolling off. By dawn, the excitement began to wane, and one by one people started leaving the hillside and the barn for home. By the end of the third day, even Grandma Heaney gave up hope, and moved into the little shack with the blue gingham curtain fluttering in the window on the dirt patch that would be her home from then on.

Grandpa Heaney left her on account of how she had ruined them both. He'd tried to talk her out of it, initially, but there was no talking to her. He maintained that their biggest mistake was in defying Paul's commandment not to suffer a woman to preach. That was how it all started.

When the Rapture didn't come like she thought it would, she went to the friends and church members she had given everything to and asked for help because she had nothing left. But the church members didn't feel like they owed her anything, because she'd given them the money out of her own free will—except for a few, they hadn't asked for it. It was their money now and they thought anyone foolish enough to give their money away deserved what they got, which was nothing. Some set off for travel and adventure using the money she had given them, to places they'd never had occasion to visit before. Those that stayed made improvements on their property and lived better as a result of her gifts. They didn't like to see my grandmother with her wild eye and scraggly hair; her visage depressed the spirit. They didn't want to help her because she was mean and they'd never liked her, and they were glad about what had happened to Grandma Heaney. God had clearly judged her and she'd gotten what was coming to her.

Then the angel poured out the second vial.

You'd think Grandma Heaney would have turned her back on religion and lost her faith completely because of how it had let her down and ruined her. Instead she clung to it more fervently than ever. She clung to it like an old rugged cross, becoming more rugged and cross with each passing day. I guess it was all that was left to her. The sacrificial lamb and the scapegoat were conventional roles, part of the Christ legacy, and the way of the cross. There was nothing for her to do but endure, and hope never completely eluded her.

God judged her and increased her despair but also her faith because she knew it was the Tribulation, which was something that had to be endured and couldn't be avoided because it had been prophesied since the beginning of time, just as Jeremiah had preached that Israel must submit to slavery in Babylon, which were hard words but they had been borne out and proven true.

The church had her money and their star was rising so it was the Rapture for them, just like Grandma said it would be. They didn't see how they owed her anything because even if she had given with her pocketbook, she hadn't given with her heart. She needed to learn the true spirit of giving and sharing, which was something other than trying to buy friends and power in the church. She had dealt in falsehood and false prophecy, and she could see how God had dealt with her. The church decided that what she needed was Christian School.

The Christian School designed for Grandma Heaney turned out to be sharecropping for Evangeline Brown on a hardscrabble piece of scrub wash that had once been her own land. Sister Brown worked her hard, and grew sleek and fat off her work. She was the acknowledged and unchallenged preacher of the church now. Grandma Heaney was whupped and exhausted when she came home at night, without even the energy to cook dinner or drag herself to bed. In the morning, she picked herself out of the rag heap and cooked my mother breakfast and changed her clothes before tromping out to the fields again for another twelve-hour day.

During her labors she pondered what she had done and how she had been dealt with. If the skies had failed to gather her up, there was a judgment in it. She mustn't seek to blame God for her misfortunes, but find the fault in herself, because God's hand was in it, sure. She had squandered the gifts God had given her and gambled everything away.

They said my grandmother had a mental disorder with her visions and giving money away and they were like to have her committed to the state farm if she did anything else one bit odd. They considered it a kindness to let her stay in the little shack that had been a toolshed before and not good enough for anyone to live in. What's more she was a terrible mother because she had given away her daughter's inheritance and college money, and they were of a mind to take her away too, though they never did.

The only one to show her any kindness at all was her childhood friend Mrs. Finney. She and her old yellow dog came down the dusty dirt road to my grandmother's shack once a week with a pot of soup and one of thin gruel. Mrs. Finney hadn't been one of the ones that my grandmother had blessed with a gift of finance, but she didn't seem to hold it against her. She didn't think it was right how my grandmother had been treated after all the good she'd done.

My mother was pretty much soured on religion for good after that, seeing as how it destroyed her mother, lost her her father, and cost them the farm and her college education. There'd be no going to Baylor now. She was lucky to have a guidance counselor in high school who found out about California State University at Stanislaus, which was in its first year, and helped her land the only out-of-state partial scholarship. She took the first bus out of Mineola as soon as she graduated, and never looked back. She took alternate semesters off to work, paying the rest of the tuition herself.

Grandma Heaney was the first to acknowledge that no one benefited from the Tribulation as much as she. She had me to understand this as we sat on the glider of her front porch and she told me the story. She had been blind to it at the time, but Evangeline Brown had been right about her character. She found this out in trials and travail after she became Evangeline Brown's servant and sharecropper. She learned true Christian love and humility in the school of adversity, and anyone who thought God's love was peace and angel hair and Christmas presents, need only study scripture. Jesus himself had said he came not to bring peace but the sword. One had to be found worthy as the seven seals were opened one by one, because God never meant anything for evil but only good, and how else were the prophecies of John of Patmos to be fulfilled?

Once she was a person of property and had a good and easy life, but she had been found wanting. But now through the trials of the white election, she had inner stores of character that she hadn't had an inkling of before, though she lived as a sharecropper in a shack with a tin roof. She had things that neither storm nor fire nor flood could take away, things that God saw, in here—she thumped her chest with her index finger. Her clothes had been washed so long in the blood of the Lamb that they were threadbare and rusty, but her spirit had quality and merit. She'd lost her house and her rolling hills but she had vast pastures within herself to contemplate and was secure in God's love.

She said, "Who is worthy but the Lamb who has been slain to open up the Seventh Seal? And woe to anyone who tries to take away any of the words of the book. And if anyone tries to alter or add to the prophecies of the pages of the book, a curse on the hairs of his head."

Her eyes were on fire as she said it, and I had no clue as to what she was talking about but I got a tingling in my spine and gooseflesh on my arm. I thought it was a comfort to my grandmother to have me as a witness, even young as I was. Age didn't seem to matter to her. What mattered was that I was a believer, and that she'd finally found a true disciple. She was trying to communicate everything she'd lived through and seen to me, but what was I supposed to do about it? I was only a kid.

CHAPTER 6

Although I was sympathetic to Grandma Heaney and outraged by what so-called God-loving people had done to her, I hadn't cared for the way she talked about my mother being the Whore of Babylon, and it gave me an idea of how she could have run afoul of people. But when Lilah dropped out of the sky one day to take me back, I knew that what my grandmother said about her had been God's truth.

My mother was drunk when I opened the door. One hip leaned into the doorjamb, and a bottle of champagne was wedged headfirst into the back pocket of her jeans. Grandma Heaney was off tending to a church member who was sickly at the time. Lilah was wearing a silver metallic leotard and a red snakeskin jacket that fit her like a second skin. Her hair was teased and bouffant and she wore a bandit mask of eye makeup. She looked trashy—there was no other word for it.

"What do you want?" I asked.

"Is that all I get?" she asked. "After all this time?"

"A lot you cared," I said. "Where've you been, anyway?"

"You wouldn't have wanted to be with me where I've been

the last few months," she said defensively. "It wouldn't have been good for you and I figured you were better off here."

"I probably was," I said. "I probably still will be, too."

"Now don't start with that punishment crap," she said. "If you must know, I was in a whirlwind romance that evaporated into a little poof of dust, but it was a beautiful ride. I had high hopes for it. I really thought it was marriage material and a better life for us, but I was wrong. So it's back to the drawing boards, and I want my little girl back. Is that so terrible? I'm glad you had a good time, but it's time to come home now."

A horn beeped behind her, and a guy waved at us from behind the wheel of a white Impala convertible. His reflector sunglasses looked like metallic beetle's eyes and the short sleeves of his T-shirt were rolled up exposing tan, muscular arms.

That was Buzz, my mother explained, an old boyfriend of hers from high school who'd picked her up at the Greyhound station and was willing to drive us the two hours to the Dallas/Fort Worth airport. She wanted to leave pronto before Grandma Heaney came back. The notion of leaving without saying good-bye to my grandmother threw me into a tailspin.

"Where'd you get the jacket?" I asked.

"In a trade," she said. "A fair trade."

I thought about my meager possessions and wondered what she'd come up with to get someone to part with the jacket. It looked expensive.

"Oh, yeah?" I asked. "What'd you trade for it? My birthright?"

That seemed to tickle her funny bone.

"What do you know about birthright?" she asked. "You've been going to church. You've been learning about Esau and Jacob. Esau traded his birthright for a cup of lentils, a snakeskin jacket. What of it? You got religion now, huh? Even in this short time? Ezekiel saw the wheel, right?"

She started to cackle.

I shrugged. I knew she had traded her immortal soul and the jacket was all she had to show for it. I was glad Grandma Heaney wasn't there to see it. It would have broken her poor heart. Pastor Everson talked plenty about the bargain with the devil, the ultimate losing proposition made for wealth, fame, and the wrong kind of love. Just as Grandma Heaney ransomed everything to build an eternal mansion, my mother had agreed to the other contract and placed her soul on the dotted line.

I stared into the face of evil—my own mother—and I didn't protest or make a fuss. I'd always known she'd be back to pick me up. I went, meek as a lamb, although I had no illusions about what I was getting myself into. I remembered our life together well enough.

She threw my clothes in the suitcase and left my grandmother a note, and we took off on a long, drunken ramble to Dallas, the two of them drinking champagne from plastic cups in the front seat. Buzz weaved in and out of traffic like a cabbie. He got pulled over for speeding and I figured I'd be returned to my grandmother, but the pact with the devil held. He somehow passed through the checkpoint with no more than a speeding ticket and got us to the flight to Bakersfield on time.

On the plane, Lilah ordered more drinks and gave me her packets of peanuts.

"I've got something for you," she said. She always had something for me when she came to get me, no matter how pathetic or tawdry. Whether she'd picked it out of a free box or the trash, it was always something I would want even if it was only a half a stick of gum. She fished a book out of her carry-on bag, and based on her past performance, I figured it would probably be pretty good.

There wasn't a single picture in the entire book except the one on the dust jacket that showed a young blond woman in a state of alarm with a spiral staircase in the background. I wanted my mother to read it to me, but she was already passed out in the aisle seat snoring beside me, and I had nothing better to do than pore over the book by myself. The print was so small I had to squint to make it out and I sounded the words under my breath. I knew more of them than not and even the ones I didn't know I was able to figure out through the process of elimination. The book was called *The Secret of the Hidden Staircase* and was about a girl detective named Nancy Drew, a thrilling story that set the mold for my being hooked on mysteries from then on. By the time we arrived in Bakersfield, I had taught myself to read and worked my way through almost a quarter of the book. It felt as though I had discovered fire.

Our plane landed in the middle of the night and we slept on chairs in the airport till dawn. We stayed in a St. Vincent shelter for three days while she negotiated bus tickets to Fresno with Travelers Aid. We checked into the Monte Carlo Hotel in Turlock, and before long it was as if I'd never left.

Grandma Heaney told me that since I'd been baptized nothing would ever be the same for me again, because my soul had been claimed. No matter what happened in my life or wherever I went, I would always belong to Jesus. But I quickly reverted to my old ways—drinking Coke and eating Cheez-Its and watching TV—and now I was even reading mysteries, all activities frowned on by the church. I lost my religious fervor, and my dedication to pulling my mother out of the flames. Instead, I slid down into them with her.

I didn't have the strength of character to confront my mother every time she drank or cursed. Bit by bit, I lost my devotion to God, and thought about Him only when I saw the red neon "Jesus Saves" signs on the local churches and the Salvation Army kettle. I asked my mother if we could go to church a few times, but didn't put up a fuss when she said no, and I never tried to go on my own. Once I got excited about a sign for a Redemption Center, but my mother said it had nothing to do with religion. It was a place people cashed their savings stamps for toasters, waffle irons, and other rewards they were given for spending money. I puzzled over why they would call something like that a redemption center but never managed to figure it out. We weren't in East Texas anymore, and things were more far gone than I had imagined.

I seemed equally at home in hell and in heaven. Pastor Everson said not to get too comfortable, because once you acclimated yourself to evil, you no longer saw it and it took root in your soul. It became habitual, second nature, and then Satan had his hooks in you. Perhaps that had already happened to me, and for all my promise of being a child evangelist, I didn't have the strength to resist it.

All I remembered of the baptism was how the minister had tried to kill me and flung me on the riverbank like a drowned rat, how nasty the water tasted, and I was over an hour coughing it up. I remembered the miseries that had been visited on my grandmother in the name of religion. Lilah filled in even more of them for me, and told me how she had gotten out of Mineola as quickly as she could and it was only her second trip back in over ten years.

Our life resumed pretty much where it left off, but my sojourn in East Texas had given me the possibility of a life away from my mother and a sense of a separate identity. I had the knowledge that there was someone other than herself and the Department of Social Services that cared about me or even knew of my existence.

I didn't know then, but the Department of Social Services, and Child Protective Services in particular, were to figure prominently in my future. If I thought I was in hell then, I would find out soon enough what hell really was. It wasn't just the absence of our father. It was the absence of our father *and* our mother.

Lilah went on a bender and didn't come back for several days. I woke up to find myself alone one morning in our skuzzy room in the Hotel Essex. There was most of a bag of Cheetos and half a can of flat soda for breakfast, and I had my Nancy Drew book, *The Secret of the Old Clock*, to read, so it was OK by me not to have Lilah on my back about putting my stuff away. I rolled over on my stomach and read my book in my pajamas all day.

By five o'clock it was another matter. She was usually back by then. Having finished the chips, there was now nothing to eat. Plus I had finished my book. Crying and whimpering helped put me to sleep, although I slept fitfully, hungry and worried. When I woke up and she still wasn't back, I started thinking CAR CRASH. If I'd had some Snickers bars, Mars, or Milky Ways, I might have been able to calm myself down. But there was NO FOOD anywhere. When she'd met someone and wanted to stay away, she usually laid on the treats—rewards for being a big girl, on my own. She dropped off groceries or money and the only explanation for why she didn't this time was CAR CRASH. The image of a car hanging over a guardrail, and her upside down, bloodied, and lifeless, was too vivid not to be true.

I gnawed at the skin around my fingernails. I ate some toothpaste and the parakeet and goldfish food from when we still had

Que and Flipper, but they just made me throw up and my stomach roiled and rumbled worse than before. I was getting the idea that you had to cook spaghetti for it to taste like anything, but I wasn't sure how to do that. Besides she'd told me *not* to use the hot plate when she wasn't there, just to fix peanut butter and crackers, but we didn't have either one.

Her gaping absence swallowed me whole, and I flailed on the bed in the empty room like Jonah in the belly of the whale. The slats of light from the venetian blinds looked like a whale's rib cage. I mentally apologized for all the mean thoughts I had about her, and bargained with God to bring her back. I wouldn't run her down and blame all our troubles on her anymore. I would appreciate the comfort of her banter. Kneeling by the bed in my own vomit put me in a mindset to forgive her all the times she'd been passed out by the toilet.

But since the Almighty holds all the chips, He usually drives a hard bargain. He wasn't content to deliver Lilah till I'd been through worse hell, and He'd made sure I appreciated her good and proper. If only I'd been stronger and able to wait it out, but hunger drove me into the hallway on the third day. I didn't know I'd get taken into custody and nine months of hell for both of us. When she didn't come back by that evening, the concierge called Social Services. By the time she got back to the Hotel Essex five days later, I was already in placement and they were looking for her.

I was taken by the courts due to reckless child endangerment, and Lilah wasn't put in prison but in court-ordered rehab. I assumed I'd be sent back to East Texas, but Grandma Heaney was sick now and couldn't take care of me. She was frail even when I was there and walked with a backward list. She looked like she might pitch over if you as much as touched her, and I wasn't sure how much longer she was of this world. Instead I was sent to Mrs. Gannett's foster home in Stockton. I never liked Stockton after that; Mrs. Gannett's gave me what amounted to a permanent hatred of the place.

Mrs. Gannett was a mean, fat lady with swollen legs who padded around in blue rubber zoris. She never went much farther than the backyard. She wore a torn flowered housedress with a soiled apron but she was never cooking anything good. I found a slug in the cabbage once and her stews were watery and tough. She watered even the skim milk till it was weak and gray as ammonia, and her house smelled like the industrial-strength cleaning agents at the SPCA. She described her establishment as a Home for Waifs and Strays. If we ever had a treat it was Kool-Aid or marshmallow Rice Crispies snack, things so sweet they made your teeth hurt. She scared us to keep us in line. If we cried we were scolded, and I learned early on not to, or to keep it to myself.

When Mrs. Gannett showed me to my room the first day, there were two other girls there sitting on their beds. Gigi wore gray slacks and a pink sweater. She had a narrow, tan face and blond hair pulled back in tight braids. Amelia was darker skinned with black hair cut in a pixie. She wore jeans and a purple blouse with yellow dandelions on it. They looked a few years older than me, and I wondered if it might be sort of fun here after all, like having sisters. But as soon as they opened their mouths, I knew otherwise. They started even with Mrs. Gannett in the room.

"What's in the bag?" Gigi asked.

"Her clothes," Mrs. Gannett said, opening a few of the dresser drawers. "Gigi, get these clothes out of here to give her some space."

"She's got her clothes in a paper bag?" Amelia asked incredulously. "She doesn't have a suitcase?"

"Nope," Mrs. Gannett said.

"Why doesn't she have a suitcase?" Amelia asked. "We have suitcases."

"I don't know," Mrs. Gannett said. "Ask her, why don't you?"

"Where is your suitcase?" Amelia demanded.

My mother and I had lived out of suitcases for years, so they were with her, in jail or wherever she might be. Mrs. Gannett refused to tell me. When the police and Social Services took me away, they put my things in a brown paper bag.

"With my mother," I said finally.

This made them all laugh for some reason, Mrs. Gannett too. I didn't think it was funny. It just made straightforward sense. I blushed hard at being made fun of, especially by an adult.

It was just the three of us in the attic room, and the girls played a hateful game called "What I Don't Like about Mimi." They called me Mimi rather than Miami and I didn't bother correcting them, because that was the least of their taunts.

"I don't know," Gigi said. "What don't you like about her?"

"I don't like the freckles on her face or her gray eyes the color of bat guano or the way her hair falls in her face and gets in her mouth while she's eating."

"And I don't like her ratty old clothes she brought in a paper bag. She doesn't even have a suitcase."

"A paper bag," Gigi screamed with laughter. "A paper bag."

I felt sick and faint listening to them. A cold place opened up in the center of my stomach. It felt like my bones had all been broken and everything hurt so bad I couldn't sleep for most of the night.

The next day I told Mrs. Gannett about it.

"They were mean to you?" she repeated. "Well, what do you want me to do about it?"

"Make them stop," I said. "They're picking on me. They gang up on me and say mean things in front of me so I can hear them. They make fun of me on purpose to hurt my feelings."

"You don't want them talking behind your back, do you?" Mrs. Gannett asked. "I always tell my kids how unpleasant and ugly gossip is. If they have something to say to a person, they should say it to their face."

"I'd rather they talked behind my back," I said. "I don't want to listen to it. I can't stand it."

"You're going to have to learn to stand up for yourself," Mrs. Gannett said. "I can't do it for you. And I can't tell them who to like and who not to like, either. It's up to you to win them over. That's not my department. They've been knowing each other for a long time. You just arrived here a week ago."

I didn't have a clue how to make them like me. At this point, it seemed pretty near impossible.

"You don't have your Mama to fight your battles for you anymore. Didn't your Mama ever teach you nothing about standing up for yourself? No? Well, then you can learn it here."

I doubt my mother knew how to stand up for herself, since she was a falling-down drunk, let alone be able to teach me anything about it. I knew there were things I was missing all those times she was passed out. She could have been helping me with life lessons, but this was the first I was ever brought up short as a result. This was the first I knew that there would be gaping holes in my abilities that would haunt me the rest of my life and trip me up. I thought life would get better if only I survived my childhood. I didn't realize it would leave lasting scars.

"They only do it because it gets a rise out of you," Mrs. Gannett said. "If you paid no attention to them, they'd stop it like that. You'll see."

"I didn't say anything," I said.

"No," she said. "But you're coming to me instead. Those girls know they got under your skin. They're no dummies, Gigi and Amelia."

I went out to the backyard to look at the geraniums to try to cheer myself up and to get away from Amelia and Gigi. I didn't understand how the bright red geraniums could be so cheerful at a place like Mrs. Gannett's, but there they were, growing all over the backyard, almost climbing the fence. Up until now, I had only seen them growing in pots, like the ones on our windowsill at the hotel. When the girls came out to the yard, I went up to the room.

Mrs. Gannett said to ignore the girls and they would stop but the opposite happened because I had ignored them and they kept at it. Now it was their favorite ritual before bed every night. They'd long ago run out of my personal characteristics to despise and started making things up—ridiculous things that were so outrageous they shouldn't have hurt my feelings but managed to get to me anyways.

Amelia and Gigi started in on me again, and I tried to ignore it. I didn't have a clue what to do if Mrs. Gannett wasn't going to do anything, and again I got the sick, whirling feeling of falling through space.

I may not have known how to stand up for myself, but I had a scrappy side and discovered I could throw a punch. I earned a reputation for fighting at Mrs. Gannett's Home School and for being a bully and a troublemaker.

"Lookee here," I said. "You better shut up. I don't like the way you're talking to me."

"Well, we're not going to shut up," Gigi said.

"Don't tell me to shut up," Amelia said.

"I *am* telling you," I said.

"Well, we're not going to, are we, Gigi? Things I don't like about Mimi—I could go on forever. Her foul breath, her cocoa farts, and her horrible, ugly clothes, and her lying, cheating..."

She didn't get a chance to go any further because I hopped out of bed and plugged her between the eyes with my fist. I'd never hit anyone before, and I didn't hit her just once either. I attacked her like a dirt devil and kept pummeling her and she flailed back at me like a steamboat paddle. I knew I was getting the better of her, and it felt good after all I'd taken off of them. She called out at the top of her lungs for Mrs. Gannett, who lurched into the room and turned on the lights and pulled me away by the ear and led me downstairs to sleep in the laundry room.

"You little hell-raiser, you'll see what will happen to you. We'll put you out of the way where you can't do any harm."

She hurled me down the cellar steps.

Her rottweilers, Trudi and Gus, barked furiously and the furnace raced and the shadows from the flames licked the walls. I skinned my knee when she threw me down the stairs and there was a dull ache in my right thigh. The dogs stopped barking and wagged their stumpy tails, twitching their rear ends.

I sat in stillness for a long time. The dogs licked my face as if they were lapping up tears, kissing them almost the way my mother used to, although their bared teeth were frightening at close range. The flames licked upward in the furnace and the shadows danced on the wall, illuminating the unfinished basement.

"Sweet Jesus," I whispered.

I waited for Mrs. Gannett to come get me but she didn't. The thought of drinking turpentine or Clorox from the utility shelf crossed my mind. I'd heard of people killing themselves when they'd come to the end of their rope. I was suddenly more tired than I'd ever been and I lay down on the floor. The cold cement went straight through my pajamas and I crawled onto a flattened cardboard box for insulation. I wasn't going to sleep on the smelly blanket with the dogs, and after a while I curled up on a pile of clean clothes in the wicker laundry basket near the washer and dryer. I was about to drop off to sleep when I felt a gentle hand on my shoulder. I thought it was Mrs. Gannett come down to get me and I rolled over but no one was there. I scanned the perimeter of the room. In the far corner next to the metal utility shelves, I saw the shadowy figure of the Gray Lady.

I knew right away she was not a person. She resembled nothing so much as the gray statues in the reliquary outside St. Philip's, the Catholic Church where Mrs. Gannett took us for mass on Sunday. I knew instantly who she was. She was Our Lady of Sorrows, the Virgin Mary, the Mother of our Lord. The slight inclination of her head in a gesture of modesty and grace connoted peace, and I felt a wave of comfort pass over me. She had touched my shoulder. I was suddenly calm and at rest, and I sank into the clean clothes and fell back asleep.

I woke with a start to see Mrs. Gannett red in the face, bellowing at me. I was crumpling her nice clean clothes. When had she told me it was all right to sleep in the laundry basket? The laundry basket was off limits but I was to stay in the basement. She brought down a cot, a sleeping bag, and even a thin pillow. I didn't mind the basement at all. I considered it the Grotto of Our Lady. The dogs were ugly but friendly and affectionate. I certainly preferred to be down there with them than in the attic room with those awful girls.

The next night I looked hard across the room to where I had seen her, but there was nothing but the utility shelves full of paint, varnish, epoxy, Tide and Cheer, and gallon jugs of bleach. She was gone. She was ephemeral, but I knew what I had seen and wouldn't forget it. I didn't think about drinking bleach anymore.

Grandma Heaney had been right about the baptism and how I belonged to Jesus now. I hadn't been much of a believer since I left Texas but as she said, seeing was believing. When I felt the most alone and abused in my entire life, the Blessed Mother had come to give me assurance of God's love. I wondered if my failure to stay with the faith had resulted in my predicament in the first place. But I'd learned my lesson, and vowed not to stray so far afield again.

I lay on the cot in the basement at night and watched the furnace flames and thought of Mary. I remembered Shadrach, Meshach, and Abednego who'd not only survived the trial in the furnace but been seen dancing in its flames.

CHAPTER 7

I had no idea how long I'd been at Mrs. Gannett's. I measured the length of my stay like marks on the wall, against the height of the other kids. I had started first grade now and Gigi and Amelia were in third grade. Charlotte and Huey Clarkson were in junior high already, and I prayed to God I was luckier than them and wouldn't be stuck there for the duration.

If Mrs. Gannett knew my mother's whereabouts she kept them to herself. I knew she hadn't died in a car crash but that was all. When I asked Mrs. Gannett if she had any letters for me, she said that mail was a privilege and my behavior hadn't merited any privileges. I continued on in the basement. When school started, she moved a small desk down there.

First grade at Emerson Elementary was a pleasure and fun compared to Mrs. Gannett's place. I stayed after school every day helping Miss Corcoran wash the blackboards, beat the erasers clean, and run the ditto master. When she said, "Well, I guess that wraps it up," I shrugged and went home. I got an A+ in reading but was just average in everything else.

I was in the backyard looking at the geraniums when I saw my mother standing by the gate looking back at me. Everyone else was inside watching TV and eating snack. It took a few minutes before I grasped who she was. Then I ran over and buried my face in her stomach, practically bowling her over, tears streaming down my face.

"Whoa," my mother said. "What a reception! Could it possibly have been as bad as all that?"

I was too choked up to answer.

She was wearing a gray dress with a Peter Pan collar, and she didn't look anything like I remembered her. Her hair was neatly coiffed and her makeup was subdued. She gave me a prolonged hug and stamped my forehead with a lipstick kiss, and we went inside.

"Why was she sitting by herself looking dazed into space like that?" she asked Mrs. Gannett. "Why is her dress torn? And there's a bruise on her cheek."

She glared at Mrs. Gannett and Mrs. Gannett glared back.

"She's a feisty little thing," Mrs. Gannett said. "Always getting into fights with the other kids. We've had to isolate her somewhat."

"Miami, feisty?" my mother said. "Since when? Never used to be. She's a trooper and a good girl. I can't imagine she'd resort to bad behavior unless it was called for. Unless she was corralled and painted into a corner."

My mother perused the other children suspiciously.

I guess Lilah knew a few things about standing up for herself after all. She was tough and effective and hadn't been reduced to violence the way I was. It was a pleasure watching her berate Mrs. Gannett, but nothing could compare to being out of there completely. I ran down to the basement to gather up my clothes and tugged on her arm, pulling her toward the door.

"Well, good riddance!" my mother said, when we finally set off in the car. "I barely recognized you, you've grown so much. And that tangled mane of hair! She never had it cut even once, huh?"

I told my mother she looked like Julie Andrews in her gray dress. She laughed and said she'd gotten a job at a department store in Modesto, and she had monthly visits with her probation officer, so she was heavy into polyester these days. It was all part of getting her act together.

She was driving a white Dodge Valiant with a push-button gearshift.

"Where'd you get the car?" I asked.

"At a dealership in Turlock," she said.

"It's our car?" I asked. "Where'd you get the money for that?"

"I'll explain," she said. "There's more to come. You'll see."

We stopped at Kentucky Fried Chicken for lunch. The greasy chicken sedated me enough so that I could answer her questions about Mrs. Gannett's. She looked pained to hear what I'd been through.

"I feel like I've just rescued Cinderella from the coal bin," she said. "No wonder I remind you of Julie Andrews. Too bad it was my fault that you wound up in there to begin with, so I guess I'm half fairy Godmother, half evil stepmother."

She looked at me with the woeful eyes of a dog, but I was too grateful at being saved from more ridicule and humiliation to have any interest in recrimination.

"I'll never forgive myself for what you had to go through back there," she said. "I took an oath to God that if I ever got you back He wouldn't have cause to regret it."

This was the first I heard of my mother praying or making promises to God. I remembered my own oath at the Hotel Essex. I guess the experience taught us both what we had in each other, and the Lord had ways of guaranteeing his pledges.

I didn't tell her about the visitation by Our Lady. I've never told anyone about it to this day. I don't think it would be physically possible. They say the secret name of God is too holy to be spoken and that's certainly been my experience.

"I had it easy compared to you, kid," she said sadly. "I was in a residential treatment program with thirty other people—nice folks for the most part. No sex or alcohol, just work, meetings, therapy, Alcoholics Anonymous, housework, and more work, but it was a bed of roses compared to that place. I've been clean and sober for more than six months, so I can't argue with results."

"How long was I there, anyway?" I asked.

"The better part of a year," she said. "And now, I'm afraid I have some bad news for you."

"Grandma Heaney died," I said quietly.

"How did you know?" she asked.

"From the way you were talking—what else could it be?" I said. "Besides, I could see how frail she was. Why didn't you come and get me?"

"I wasn't allowed to," she said. "They didn't call me until the eleventh hour and I had to go racing back there. There wasn't time to arrange for temporary custody. Believe me, she asked about you plenty and was very concerned to hear that you were in foster placement. She gave me hell for it, in fact, even weak as she was. I was at her side in the hospital when she finally gave up the ghost. She had a painless death, slipping away quietly in her sleep, with a sweet smile on her face. I think she'd had enough of this life."

My mother gave me the program from the memorial service, which was prefaced with a quote from the Bible:

"When I was a child, I spoke like a child, I thought like a child, I reasoned like a child; when I became a man, I gave up childish ways. For now we see in a mirror dimly, but then face to face. Now I know in part; then I shall understand fully, even as I have been fully understood."

It was my grandmother's favorite quote from the Bible and the conclusion of Corinthians 13 that Sister Evangeline used to preach at her.

We left the fast food joint and took an hour-long drive on the freeway. Then she got off at an exit and pulled the car up in front of a beige stucco bungalow with white trim. When I looked up the walk at the wide steps, broad porch, and sloping roof, I felt like I'd seen the house before, although it took me a minute to place it. It reminded me of my father's house, the one she had taken me to in the early morning that time, although this was more of a cottage and that had been a mansion. Birds of paradise grew as high as the windowsills and a red leaf maple stood in the yard.

She had a key to the front door and I followed her inside. The rooms were large and flooded with light. As I wandered through the house, it occurred to me that my father could be there and might even be in the next room. There was no furniture in the house except for a double bed upstairs and the suitcases that had been my undoing at Mrs. Gannett's.

"Well, what do you think of it?" she asked. "It's ours. I bought it with the money I inherited from my mother's property. Who would have thought that little shack of hers would be worth anything? But there was more land around it than any of us realized. It turned out some of it had been kept in her name after all. It was the one thing she hadn't lost. I sold it for $5,000, which I put mostly as a down payment on this place.

"I moved in three days ago. It was the final condition of your release—providing a stable home environment—and the social worker approved it, even without a stick of furniture."

My father of course was nowhere in sight. He was dead, I realized, just the way Grandma Heaney was dead. I was seven now and old enough to accept it. It felt as though we had inherited his house. I felt his presence in its spaciousness, just as I had in the mist and tule fog that morning.

My mother said her recovery depended on making amends to the people she'd wronged, a list that began and ended with me. My room was the first one that she furnished. She painted the walls a cheerful yellow and hung light-blue drapes in the window. She bought me a four-poster bed, an antique doll collection, and installed a window seat which she hand painted with tulips and ivy in a Pennsylvania Dutch motif.

Without alcohol taking up every waking moment and sacking her out, my mother turned out to have a lot of energy and a flair for homemaking. She ripped up the carpeting, sanded and varnished the floors, and polished them to a high sheen. She picked up furniture at flea markets, garage sales, and the Salvation Army and varnished and waxed that as well. We eventually had a house full of the stuff, so much in fact that the place began to look like a secondhand store.

She started a vegetable garden in the backyard, and before long we were eating half our meals out of it. Chard, lettuce, green beans, corn, beets, cabbage, and broccoli. She might have even started making my clothes if it hadn't been for the huge employee discounts at Yarborough's. I kept waiting for her old personality to reassert itself, after her initial enthusiasm died down, but it never did. Within a year or so of our arrival at 174 Sycamore Lane, our old life of rolling through hotels receded like a bad dream.

The one constant was that the house and garden had replaced drinking as her passion. I was still lost in the shuffle somehow. She was either at work or working on the house. Perhaps Grandma Heaney was the only one who'd ever really loved me. She and my father, of course.

My father had written a book, it turned out, which surfaced now that we moved, a blue clothbound book without a dust jacket, *Indian Tribes of the Miami Confederacy*, which my mother kept on a refurbished coffee table in front of the sofa. I loved seeing my name in gold leaf on the cover of the book with my father's name, Derek Montague, underneath it.

I couldn't read the text but I pored over the numerous illustrations, the pen-and-ink pictograms and petroglyphs in the book. There was an image of an oak tree divided into quadrants, each depicting one of the seasons, and a picture of a flat-topped mountain surrounded by rays of light. There were shields decorated with an eagle's head, a horse in full gallop, and a bear claw. I traced them and created a few new shields of my own—a pine cone, blue jay, squirrel, maple leaf, and a lizard.

When I was older, I read the prayers and prophecies, as well as my father's commentary, in the book. I leaned against the trunk of the ash in the backyard with the book in my lap and read out loud. I didn't necessarily understand the meaning but the sound of the words alone sent a chill through me and made the hair on my arms stand on end.

Mount the wild horses with only a blanket and they will carry you to a new land. Their whiskered muzzles will be wet in your palm and nuzzling the back of your neck, as they neigh and whinny. Thunder will come, and after that a giant rain, which will wash everything clean. When the thunder sounds in the northwest quadrant, it will be the reverberation of the horses' hooves. This will be the first blessing.

When thunder builds on the northern horizon, it means the

horses have gathered in that quadrant. This is a sign for the people to make themselves ready and prepare for the coming of the next world, for the world we live in will pass away. There have been worlds before this that all passed away, just as this world so seemingly solid, will pass away.

The way to prepare for the next world is not like squirrel—scurrying, gathering, and hoarding—but like otter who dives below the surface and like badger who goes within. We must look at our faults and see how to correct them. If there is anything we can do to improve our character, we must do it now, because there is little time. If we are satisfied with what we see, we should give thanks but refrain from self-satisfaction.

When the thunder sounds simultaneously in all four quadrants, then is the time to pack your belongings and ***leave the coastal areas and take the family and move inland.*** *Contact relatives and tell them you are coming, and if you have no relatives, go anyway because you will be welcome. And if you are already inland, prepare for visitors. It will be a Great Migration. Share what you have, for they are coming to make their home with you. Let no one be a stranger.*

That is what the Thunder said as a prophecy since the time of the grandmothers, long before the white men came.

CHAPTER 8

I attended church only a few times after we moved to La Grange. "Suit yourself," was all my mother said when I told her I wanted to go, but she couldn't stop me, since Calvary Methodist was in walking distance of our house and I could go by myself. Even if she considered it poison pure and simple, it wasn't like I'd started smoking or drinking coffee, but it didn't take me long to tire of it on my own. It didn't have the evocative liturgy of the Catholic Church or the foot stomping energy of the Holy Rollers and was at best lukewarm.

The logo outside the church showed the dove or Holy Spirit diving into an open book. The church is no longer there; it was razed a long time ago, burned down in a freak fire. It wasn't that bad, it was just sort of boring because they seemed to think that everything significant had happened already a couple of thousand years ago, and I figured what was the point? They weren't like the Pentecostals who waited and watched and looked for signs with daily urgency, so after a while I stopped going, and my mother didn't say anything, but I could see she thought I'd finally come to my senses.

I had no reason to think I'd ever pick up with the Pentecostals again, but I did briefly the summer before my sophomore year of high school. They worked their way back into my life through my friendship with Jolene Carpenter. My mother pitched a fit, but there was nothing she could do about it this time either, because I was old enough to make my own decisions, and it would have been hypocritical since she was a strong believer in self-determination. Nonetheless, she carried on as if I'd taken up with a motorcycle gang. She said everyone had to make their own mistakes in this world, that was how people grew and matured. Who would have thought that would be the hardest part of being a parent? But if I'd seen how those people had treated her mother, I wouldn't have gone within ten miles of a revival tent.

I met Jolene Carpenter at the Fantasyland Roller Rink in Turlock. We literally ran into each other out on the floor, knocking each other down. My wrist throbbed so badly I knew I'd really hurt myself, but I couldn't take my eyes off Jolene. She had big brown eyes and a freckled nose and red hair teased into a bouffant hairdo. She was wearing a turquoise velveteen skating skirt with white angora trim and looked like she'd stepped out of a fairy tale or at least the Ice Capades. The other skaters went around us in a big wheel, while Jolene and I stared at each other as if there was some kind of connection between us, although I didn't know what that would be, unless we were polar opposites, which is why we were on a collision course to begin with.

Jolene kept telling me how sorry she was as if it was her fault when it wasn't. She seemed like a beautiful person with a special warmth. She helped me up while my friend Susie called her father and then waited with us outside for him to pick us up. I wound up going to Emergency and getting a soft cast and a sling. I had torn the tendons in my wrist.

I thought that was going to be the end of it, but a week later

Jolene called to see how I was doing and invited me to spend the week with her at her aunt's cottage in Capitola. I was surprised because she didn't even know me, and I figured she thought I was a total dork in my kelly green cable-knit turtleneck and gray cords. I didn't know how much we were going to have in common, but I went anyway. I had the cast on my wrist so I couldn't swim. I waded and sunbathed, and at night we went into Santa Cruz and walked on the Boardwalk.

Her aunt's cottage was a funky place with a linoleum floor and Jolene's little brother and sister and cousins tracked in sand, but her aunt was good-natured and didn't care. Jolene slept on the couch in the living room and I slept on an army cot next to her. We stayed up talking half the night, and she told me about some of the guys she went out with, and I was right we didn't have anything in common, but it wasn't a problem, because I was her confidante, so there was a role for me after all. It surprised me that we liked each other so much, because I'd never been friends with anyone quite like her.

She lived in Ceres and my mother wasn't exactly crazy about driving me all the way over there. I don't think she was too thrilled with Jolene either. She called her "The Raccoon" because of all the eyeliner and mascara she wore. Being friends with Jolene reminded me that I was a teenager too, which was something I could forget living with my mother, who thought of me as her best friend, so I felt like I was going on forty years old most of the time.

It turned out Jolene was a complete David Bowie fanatic. She played his records constantly and never stopped talking about him. Her room was plastered with pictures of him in spacesuits and unisex outfits with his hair dyed purple, orange, and blue, striking a pose in the spotlight. I'd never known anyone who was that into rock 'n' roll before. I'd always thought of it as more of a guy's thing. It turned out she had a fantasy of going to New York or London or wherever he lived, and it took awhile but I finally realized she actually thought she was going to meet him and they were going to get together. I thought she might be a little crazy, but then another way I could see it, because she was the type who could pull it off. Given the range of ambitions, being a groupie seemed fairly low on the food chain, and I didn't know how worthy it was. At the same time, it was so different from my stifled existence with my mother as to be almost glamorous, and I got a vicarious thrill from it.

Jolene put on a record and danced around the room singing, "Turn and face the strain, Cha-cha-chaaaaanges," and I sang with her. She was so obsessed that there was something kind of pathetic about it. Additionally, it got old hearing about David Bowie all the time, so I began to lose interest in her, although I didn't drop her completely. Not then, anyhow.

The other thing was that Jolene was a Jesus freak and was always bugging me to go to a church meeting with her, and I thought, why not? If she didn't see a discrepancy between being a David Bowie fanatic and a born-again Christian, that was fine with me, although if I'd thought about it, it might have tipped me off as to how being a Jesus freak would play out for me.

I went to a Sunday picnic with her down on the San Joaquin. It was more like a sing-along at camp than a revival meeting. There were picnic tables laid out with platters of fried chicken, biscuits, and coleslaw and everyone was scattered on the grass under the cottonwoods and along the riverbank. The Jesus freaks both were and were not like the Christians of Little Gethsemane. Nobody fainted or testified for Christ, but they were into it nonetheless, and they weren't rednecks and country crackers, but freaks and hippies, so it was like the best of both worlds.

People were friendly and nice to each other as befitting the occasion. At the center of it all was a guy with shoulder-length hair who was playing the guitar and leading the singing. Light radiated from his head like a halo, and it seemed like the whole promise of Christianity was contained in his person. I was impressionable enough to believe in the Rapture when I first heard about it in Texas, but I got the grown-up version of the Rapture in Brian Quinn. Like my grandmother used to say, seeing was believing.

The congregation swayed back and forth singing "I Want to Be Ready," "Were You There?" "I Been 'Buked and I Been Scorned," "Good News," "This Little Light of Mine," "Walk in Jerusalem," and "A Closer Walk with Thee." The whole time I couldn't take my eyes off the singer, Brian Quinn. He was tall and graceful with big blue eyes that rolled over the crowd and up at the sky like they were taking everything in and reflecting it all back at you. I stared at him but it wasn't because he was so good looking—it was more that he made you want to see things the way he did, because he looked like he could see about five times as much as anyone else.

A light radiated from him and a flock of geese flew up off the river all at once, and a wave of emotion went through me. It was like a second baptism right there and I joined the Holy Order of Man on the spot. My hair was full and fluffy that day and I was wearing a red-and-yellow cotton print skirt and a Mexican peasant blouse. I had no way of knowing if he had noticed me or not, but I probably would have taken my clothes off and jumped in the river to get his attention. I don't know if I found religion or just fell in love with Brian Quinn, but in the end maybe I was saved. Because before, I was hanging out at the magazine rack and makeup counter at Long's Drugs with people like Jolene; but after I fell in love with Brian, I became friends with K.D. and got my camera, things that really changed my life forever.

I was on fire with the spirit and sang the songs from the riverbank around the house, and my mother rolled her eyes and acted like the end had come. I couldn't sleep at night thinking about him and mooned over him during the day. Brian was different from the guys I usually got crushes on and was the first one I actively followed up on. I usually frittered them away in daydreams and considered them too hopeless to give chase, but I was convinced Brian and I were fated. I was as bad as Jolene in that respect. I went back to meetings of the Holy Order of Man and signed up for the newsletter and Bible Study, and thought I was bound to see him again, but I never did. The Jesus freaks without Brian Quinn was an empty bell for me, but I was helpless to do anything about it. It felt like I'd been lured into a trap with live bait. He mysteriously disappeared from the group and after a few months I stopped going too. That was also the end of my friendship with Jolene Carpenter. She faded out of my life completely after that. Years later, Glenda said she heard she'd gotten pregnant and had to drop out of school and was living at the Starlite Trailer Court with her husband and baby, checking groceries at the Safeway.

I lost the faith and dropped out of the Holy Order of Man but mysteriously found it again a few months later in an unlikely place—the orchestra pit at Alamo. We were in the middle of the second movement of the *New World Symphony* when it occurred to me that Katy Quinn was Brian's sister, and I put down my bow and stared at her across the orchestra pit. It was as if she had stepped out of the fog and I was seeing her for the first time. Mr. Stephenson glared at me and Katy looked up from her music stand and saw me staring at her fiercely, and who knows what she thought? She had long black hair and a big slow white face but her eyes were as quick and changing as a river.

After class I asked her if she wanted to get together and play duets. I was usually too shy to approach someone I didn't know, but my passion for Brian made me fearless.

"OK," she said slowly but she looked skeptical. Not only was it the first time I'd ever spoken to her, but she was first viola and I was only fifth seat on the cello, so we weren't exactly a match.

Saturday I hauled my cello over to Katy's house in the back of my mother's car and we set up down in her basement. Katy's father was a civil engineer and her mother a housewife, but they were nonetheless highly eccentric types and the house was dark and cluttered with books and magazines. I perused the place for signs of Brian, but didn't see any. The wall-to-wall shag carpet was speckled with lint and the old furniture was covered with bedspreads to hide the holes in the upholstery and frayed edges. The place was a mess but passed muster anyway for its bohemian qualities.

Katy wore a pleated skirt and a mangy beige sweater and I wondered if she was someone I would want to be friends with if it wasn't for Brian, but I chalked it up as another aspect of being from an offbeat family and decided she was cool. He didn't show up that night so I arranged to go over the following Saturday, but he still wasn't there. I figured if I hung around long enough I'd eventually get to see Brian and I did, but it was almost two months before that happened. Meanwhile Katy and I *did* become friends because she had a quicksilver mind and was an incredible musician, better than I'd ever be that was for sure, so it almost didn't matter about Brian anymore. Of course it wasn't until I felt that way that I finally got to meet him.

One afternoon I went home with Katy after school and Brian

was sitting on the sofa playing "Abilene" on the guitar. Light poured through the doorway into the darkened room and I stood still staring at him. His hair was long and parted in the middle like before and he looked up and smiled at us. Meanwhile he kept strumming the guitar.

He moved over to make room for us on the sofa and gave me a wink and my heart started pounding and I smoothed my hair and sat on my hands, because I was so nervous I didn't know what to do with them. I couldn't tell if he was just being friendly or he thought I was cute or what.

I didn't even know him and I already liked him, but he turned out to be a lot of fun—full of personality with a good sense of humor—in addition to being nice. The next time I went over, he was playing basketball in the driveway with a friend and his eyes lit up when he saw me.

"All right!" he called out. "Miami's here! Miami's on my team."

He bounced the ball right at me and we played basketball all afternoon—him and me against Katy and Jim Jakes. I only made one basket the whole game, but he wasn't even mad at me. He actually ran up and hugged me when I did it. It wasn't romantic—he just treated me like a friend of his kid sister's, but I was thrilled anyway and made as much of it as I could. Afterward we went inside and sat around the kitchen table and drank apple juice, and he got out his guitar and started singing "Blowin' in the Wind." He looked right at me while he sang and for a minute, it almost felt as if he was playing just for me. So then I thought he *did* like me, because he was paying five times as much attention to me as he needed to just to be nice.

I figured Katy knew something she wasn't telling me, so the next time I was over I asked her outright. We were sitting on the living room floor watching *General Hospital*, and she was wearing a bright red corduroy jumper that set off her eyes and hair.

"So tell me about Brian," I said, hugging my knees to my chest.

"What is it you want to know?" she asked. She looked puzzled and I wondered if it was possible she hadn't picked up on my feelings this whole time, because I thought I was so obvious.

"Well, does he have a girlfriend, for instance?" I asked.

Her eyes were big and round and she nodded her head.

"I thought you'd met her already," she said. "It seems like she's over here all the time, although I guess they're usually up in his room listening to records or something."

She grinned at me.

"What's she like?" I asked and heard my voice getting small and faint, almost fading away.

"Well, her name is Susan," she said. "She's a senior at Alamo and she has brown hair in a long flip. I don't think she's particularly deep but Brian seems to be crazy about her anyway. Maybe that's what he wants—she's bubbly and seems to have a constant case of the giggles. He's been walking on air ever since he met her. Haven't you noticed?"

I nodded my head because I hadn't noticed anything else, only the whole time I thought it was because of me, so I'd just been living in a dreamworld. Meanwhile Katy kept staring at me and I figured my face was probably giving it away, because I felt like I was about to cry. *General Hospital* was over and *The Days of Our Lives* started. I looked around and suddenly it occurred to me that they could come in at any minute, and if they did, I couldn't be there, because there was no way I could handle seeing them together at that point.

"I've got to go," I said, jumping up. "I just remembered I've got a doctor's appointment. My mom's going to kill me, because she told me to come right home after school and she took off work to take me."

I was gone before she had a chance to say anything. I got a block from the house and started running and crying at the same time and didn't stop until I got to Bailey's Crossroads. I felt better once I was inside KMart. There was something numbing about the neon lights, the linoleum, the racks of cheap clothing, and all the junky gadgets. There was a camera display at the back of the store, and I went over and picked up a Nikon. It had a lot of attachments and I started fidgeting and playing with the levers, and I figured out how to adjust the light meter and the aperture. I was surprised I could do it because I'd never had anything other than a cheap Instamatic before.

There was something satisfying about figuring it out, and I was so engrossed I didn't notice at first, but there was a commotion on the other side of the store. I looked up and a crow was flying overhead in a zigzag course. It hit the ceiling and brushed its wings against the light trays and then dropped down and hit the shelves, knocking some merchandise to the floor. It circled the store and butted its head against the glass over the doors trying to get out, and then it turned and flew back in the other direction, creating a general uproar. One of the store clerks chased it with a butterfly net on a long bamboo pole, and the cashier yelled for someone to open the windows. The crow looked like it was going to beat its head bloody if it didn't get out of there pretty soon. Everyone was over on one side of the store, and it looked completely lopsided like a boat that was about to tip over.

I looked up at the bird and back at the camera. It was a Nikon F2S and it cost $240 and I figured I'd never be able to afford anything like that in a million years. There was a minute when everyone was completely distracted and I only had a split second to decide, and I didn't even think. Suddenly it was just under my coat and I walked out with it.

The crow or raven or whatever it was and I got out of KMart at the same time. I was walking back to the highway when I heard people clapping and cheering behind me, and I turned and the store clerks and customers and everyone stood in the doorway watching the crow fly off southwest over the parking lot and out over Dekins Woods.

CHAPTER 9

My birthday fell on Labor Day that year, the same as the day I was born. It was the 87th Labor Day in U.S. history, commemorating a big strike in Chicago that eventually put the eight-hour workday in place, although it took another forty-four years before that ever happened. There had been riots and a bomb in Haymarket Square, and four of the labor leaders were eventually hanged, although it was later widely believed they were wrongly convicted. The original Labor Day was May Day but President Cleveland changed it to September to break with the more radical, socialist holiday.

I'd had these facts drummed into me since my mother was a die-hard, union activist. If the retail clerks at Yarborough's had never unionized, she'd be at minimum wage and never able to afford the mortgage payments on the house, and we'd still be living in the rotting walk-ups and welfare hotels in Fresno and Turlock. All courtesy of Local 16—with its credit union, cost-of-living increases, negotiated union contracts, and grievance procedure. She was the local shop steward and had even passed up a promotion to management in order to stay with the rank and file.

We'd put up a family for a couple of months once that had lost their own place when the strike dragged on. I helped make picket signs with stencils and black spray paint—"Local 16—On strike for a living wage" and got to join the picket line. It was the highlight of my sixth-grade year and probably contributed to my tendency to confront authority and hold out for a better deal.

I was born at 6:03 a.m. at Mercy Medical in Modesto, California, on September 6, 1957. I was finally delivered by C-section after twenty-four hours of labor—it was labor day for Lilah, that's for sure, and she probably would have appreciated an eight-hour limit to it, but no such luck. I was pleased with the omen of being born on Labor Day. It automatically conferred on me the status of a working-class hero, compounded by the C-section delivery fulfilling the prophecy of the witches of *Macbeth*. If I'd contemplated it more thoroughly, I would have realized in all likelihood it meant I was workhouse bound, not to mention being stabbed in the back by my friends.

Lilah surprised me by giving me a zoom lens for my birthday. I asked for it, but it never occurred to me she would actually give me one because they were really expensive, and it was the first time she'd ever given me anything for my camera. She never came out and said anything but she'd always been suspicious about it. I told her I got it at the Tulare County Flea Market but I could tell she didn't believe me. It didn't look in the least bit old or used, but I wasn't about to scuff it up just for her sake.

In the afternoon I rode my bike over to the old train tracks on the other side of town. The remains of the station were nothing but pilings and a concrete platform covered with morning glories and crawling with geckos. Bits of broken track lay in the grass and I practiced zooming in on them from a couple of different ranges. Then I lay down on the platform and looked up at the sky and out to where the grass blew in the wind so the fields waved like bolts of burlap tossed into the air, and the earth looked like it was about to rear up and break free of its moorings. I rolled over on my stomach and started shooting. I knew I wouldn't be able to catch it all but I was determined to get whatever I could.

For my birthday, Glenda, K.D., and Jane took me to see *Gaslight* in the film noir series at the Luminette. We got out of the movie around ten and the four of us walked arm in arm down the middle of the street. Ingrid Bergman was the niece of a big opera star and Charles Boyer played a jewel thief who had murdered her aunt and only married her to get at the aunt's jewels. He tried to make her think she was going crazy, so he could have her committed and walk away with the jewelry. It was excruciating to watch him torment her, but in the end Joseph Cotten showed up to save her, and it was such a relief, you were almost beyond caring that she had to be rescued by a man.

The shadows from the streetlights fell over my friends' faces, and it looked like the movie was still playing and projecting over them. We talked about it for a while, and then I surprised everyone by telling them about my mother's marriage and that we would be moving soon. I'd saved the news until we would all be together. Glenda was the only one who knew my mother was even seeing anyone.

"You're going to be transferring out at the beginning of your senior year," Jane said.

Jane had long brown hair and a thick fringe of bangs covering her eyes so you never knew what she was thinking. Her eyes were big and green and she had a full pouty mouth and rosy cheeks.

"That is seriously messed up," K.D. said. "Why can't they just wait?"

"I get the impression love blooms anew at their age, and they just can't," I said. "Also she implied that she needed to sell the house to have money to send me to college."

"I hope this doesn't totally screw you up so you wind up going to Modesto J.C.," Glenda smiled.

"It better not," I said.

Modesto Junior College was a standing joke of ours. It was our worst-case scenario that we'd be stuck in the Valley the rest of our lives, because we were bored to death by the place and college was our big chance to get out. K.D. wanted to go either to Julliard or the San Francisco Conservatory of Music and Jane wanted to go to one of the Seven Sisters. It wasn't for the prestige but she thought they were really Mystery Schools in an old priestess tradition, and it was code for the Pleiades, the place of origin of some of the native tribes. Jane was so weird. She was always drawn to the least plausible, most far out explanation for things. Glenda was the only one of us who wasn't interested in college. She wanted to be an actress so she was going to go straight to New York or Hollywood when she graduated. I used to want to go to Santa Cruz, but now that I was into photography I wanted to go to either Berkeley or the San Francisco Art Institute.

"You've left out a pretty important piece of the story, haven't you?" Glenda said. "Tell them about the boys!"

"Ben has three sons in high school," I said. "I've only met two of them so far. The third one I haven't actually met yet, but he's the one I think I would like the best."

"How do you know?" Jane asked. "Did you meet on the astral or something?"

"Something like that," I said, because it was actually the fact that Marvin *didn't* want to meet us that made me feel even closer to him than his photograph had.

"Or did you just like him best because you didn't like the two you actually met?" K.D. said, smiling.

"I liked them fine," I said.

"So how do you feel about moving in with three brothers?" K.D. asked.

"OK, I guess," I said. "I think I'll be able to handle it."

"Handle it?" Glenda said. "It'll be fun. Why wouldn't you be able to handle it? You're making it sound like some sort of ordeal."

Her tone of voice made it sound like a preposterous idea. Glenda had always had a lot more self-confidence than I did, so it was easy for her to say. I tended to go in for worst-case scenarios, so this was a familiar standoff between us. Of course if you looked like Glenda, the only problem you were likely to have with boys was fending them off.

Glenda was wearing jeans, a green T-shirt, and a denim jacket. She had platinum blond hair that nobody believed was natural but it was. She was the clotheshorse of the four of us, K.D. was on the other end of the spectrum, and Jane and I were somewhere in between.

"So what are they like, anyway?" Glenda asked. "You haven't really told us anything about them."

"Here's what I know," I said. "They're into The Wailers and William Burroughs. One of them's a photographer. The two I've met are really good looking, and they seem pretty nice. Except for being these heavy-duty sports fanatics."

"It might not hurt you to be more of a sports freak yourself, you know," K.D. said suddenly looking straight at me. She had penetrating black eyes and I felt suddenly stung. Was she implying I was a bad sport? K.D. was very psychic and I never knew if she was trying to tell me something or I was reading too much into it, which put me at a loss as to how to respond.

"You'll have to have us over to meet these guys," Glenda said. "So we can see for ourselves."

"Of course," I said. It would be great if she wound up with one of my stepbrothers. I could see her with Cal, actually.

There was a break in traffic and we all ran across the highway. A giant red neon Stuckey's sign loomed up ahead and we started walking toward it. Then we took a shortcut through the Hennessey almond orchard. Across the way, an A-frame Pentecostal Church was lit up and voices from inside carried over the field. I couldn't understand a word they were saying, and it occurred to me that maybe they were speaking in tongues.

"You're so quiet all of a sudden," Jane said.

"I'm listening to the testimony," I said. "I'm trying to understand what they're saying."

Glenda grinned.

"I don't think you have to be a genius to figure that out," she said. "Praise Jesus! Hallelujah!"

My mother wasn't home when we arrived at the house. She'd already started packing and sold a red velvet rocking chair and a Chippendale table, and there were fade marks on the wall where she'd taken down the Maxfield Parrish poster and a Gauguin print. She left a lemon cake out on the kitchen counter and there was ice cream in the freezer. She'd written "Vive la Huelga!" on the cake in blue icing and in that spirit they sang "There Once Was a Union Maid" instead of "Happy Birthday" before I cut the cake. I got Joni Mitchell's *Miles of Aisles* from Glenda, K.D. gave me a book of photography by Imogene Cunningham, and Jane had written up a five-page horoscope of my natal chart.

"So Miami's a Virgo," Glenda said. "Stickler for detail, nose to the grindstone. Focus on detail to such an extent they never really see the big picture. That doesn't sound like Miami. Except for the virgin part, of course."

Glenda gave me a sly smile.

"I'm beginning to think the world just has it in for us," I said. "Have you ever heard one decent thing about Virgos? It's like we can do no right."

"That's true," Jane said. "It's a sexist stereotype because Virgo is mutable earth which is the sign of the Great Mother. Actually, the truth about Virgos is that they're generous, creative, and fair minded—just like Miami."

"So are you going to change your name to Beasley now?" Jane asked me.

"Of course not," I said. "It's not like he's adopting me or anything. Besides I'd never give up Montague, you know that."

"Not even when you get married?" K.D. asked sarcastically.

"That would be Ms. Montague to you," I replied.

"What's this going to be, *Romeo and Juliet*?" Glenda asked after a while. "Not the Montagues and the Capulets, but the Montagues and the Beasleys?"

"Or perhaps *West Side Story*," K.D. said. "The modern sequel."

"When is the wedding, anyway?" Jane asked.

"November first," I said.

"The Day of the Dead," Jane said. "El dia de los Muertos."

"And All Saints Day," K.D. said.

"Not to mention the day after Halloween," Glenda said.

Halloween was a big deal with us, the High Holy Day of the pagan New Year, and we usually celebrated with a ritual.

"So what's the astrological forecast for the event?" I asked Jane. "Any predictions?"

Jane's face lighted up.

"Saturn and Jupiter are conjunct," she said. "The sacred kingship and the changing of the guard. That's a very good omen."

"Isn't there a drag strip over in Coombs or something?" K.D. asked. She looked straight at me but the lamplight blinked off her glasses and I couldn't see her eyes.

"Yeah," I said slowly. "I think there is."

That's where Marvin had been the day of the barbecue but I didn't know what K.D. would know about any drag strip. But like I said, K.D. was the most psychic of any of us, so she had all kinds of ways of getting her information.

Then Mrs. Richter honked outside and they all got up to leave.

After they left, I looked over the chart Jane had given me. I wasn't surprised that each planet was out of its element and in its least auspicious place the hour I was born. I had Mercury Void of Course, which meant that if misunderstandings and miscommunications *could* take place, they were likely to. Neptune was conjunct my sun, which implied a close identification with my dreams and ideals, that I would always be reaching for the stars. But Jane said Neptune was also the planet of intoxication and oblivion, which made it easy for an idealistic agenda to get derailed under the guise of wishful thinking or going unconscious about it. Worse still, my moon was close to the Nadir in Capricorn, so the seat of the emotions which wanted to flow freely were out of their native element, water, and placed not only at their lowest possible ebb but in a rigorous, uphill ascent. Lacking the agility and sure-footedness of a mountain goat, I would stumble and fall. But then I had Mars square Jupiter in its Exaltation, so perhaps I would eventually land on my feet again. That was the one bright note and it sounded truly powerful. All but two of my planetary aspects were in the western hemisphere, which indicated that the balance between what I had to achieve outstripped what had been given to me to do it with. The whole thing seemed like a baffling combination of the best and worst (mainly the worst), and I would have to get Jane to go into greater detail about it. The forecast supported my sense of being a dark horse, against-the-odds long shot, all about striving and identifying with the underdog.

My mother still hadn't come home and I didn't know where she was. I don't know if she was spending the night with Ben, but if so, she might have mentioned it. I stayed up for a while listening to my new album before going to bed. I was happy to have it, but it wasn't going to replace *Blue* as my favorite.

I woke up in the middle of the night from an astounding dream. A big train pulled into a station somewhere, I don't know exactly where, but some central place, like Chicago. The train rumbled in, and I knelt down to try to get a picture of it, and for a minute I thought it was going to roll right over me. But it braked and finally screeched to a stop, and steam and smoke billowed out of the smoke stack, and behind it was the most beautiful pink and gold sunset I'd ever seen.

CHAPTER 10

Alamo started the next day and it turned out my classes were so bad I was almost glad we were going to be leaving. My algebra teacher Mr. Schumacher was an android and my English teacher had the false warmth of a Gerald Ford or Ronald Reagan, which was even worse. It was going to be hard to get used to him after Ms. Richmond, who taught almost at college level, but then third period I had the school paper, *The Record*, which was pure magic and I didn't care about anything after that.

The office was on the second floor and the walls were covered with old posters for the Farm Workers and Stop the Draft Week and *Les Enfants du Paradis* and *Black Orpheus*. There were eight-and-a-half by eleven glossies of demonstrations as well as a lot of art photos. I recognized a couple by Man Ray and Cartier-Bresson but the rest might have been taken by students. It wasn't like being in school anymore and it wasn't like the Valley either; it looked like someplace up in San Francisco or Berkeley. The darkroom was in a little booth in the corner, and there was a drafting table with T-squares and X-Acto knives, and even a couple of ashtrays sitting around, and I figured they were a daring crew if they actually smoked in school. It was hard to believe that in this bastion of pod people and fodder for American Empire, I had finally stumbled onto an enclave of freaks, artists, and subversives.

There were a total of eight of us on the paper. The editor was an enthusiastic redhead named Stephanie who gave an inspiring talk about how everyone was free to be creative and follow his or her interests, and she hoped *The Record* would be a place where we could fulfill our potential. She said the paper set the cultural and political standard for the school, and there was no point underestimating the impact it could have. We could be as influential or as inconsequential as we wanted to be—it was up to us. The other photographer was a guy named Kevin whose blue eyes sparkled when he looked at me. He was tall and blond and good looking and flirted with me like crazy, so between him and Stephanie's talk, I was buzzing when I got out of there. I couldn't believe that everything I hoped to find in college had been here at Alamo all along and now that I'd finally stumbled onto it, of course we were leaving.

My friends were slouching against the wall outside the cafeteria waiting for me, and they seemed relieved when I showed up. Glenda wore a pink blouse and navy blue skirt and sandals, and K.D. and Jane were both wearing shades and T-shirts and patched jeans.

"What took you so long?" Glenda said. "Come on. We want to go outside so we can smoke."

They all had their sandwiches already and I got a carton of milk, some potato chips, and an apple, and we filed out of the cafeteria and climbed the crest of the hill above the school and sat down in the tall grass.

"I think I just had the worst class of my entire life," Glenda said. "My chemistry teacher comes on like a complete hard-ass. She says we're going to have at least ten to fifteen hours of homework a week, and if we aren't serious and can't make a commitment to that, we should drop the class right now. Wouldn't you know she'd be a woman, too? It really pisses me off when women act like that. What do they think they're doing—trying to outmacho the men?"

"So get out of there," K.D. said. "I don't see why you're taking it in the first place. Chemistry. Yuk."

"What's going on with you?" Jane asked me. "You look happy."

"I am," I said. "I just had the greatest class. It's not a class really. It's the school paper, *The Record*."

"How'd you happen to luck onto that?" K.D. asked.

"I signed up for it because they have a darkroom," I said. "But now that I know what it's like, I'd take it anyway. It's a whole different scene in there. It's not like being at Alamo at all. It's more like college."

Glenda's jaw went slack and her eyes lit up as she listened to me.

"I know," she said. "Maybe I'll drop chemistry and transfer onto that instead."

She took me totally by surprise when she said that. I tried to compose myself but my face must have fallen, and as usual she picked up on it right away.

"What's the matter?" Glenda asked.

"Nothing," I said. "I'm just not sure there's room on the staff, that's all. There might be a limit to the number of people who can work on it. There's already eight of us."

"So there'd be nine," Glenda said. "Big deal. Well, you can put in a good word for me anyway."

"Sure," I said. "I'll ask Stephanie tomorrow."

But I hesitated again.

"Another thing," I said. "Even if they do need someone, it would probably be for pasteup or layout, so I don't know if just *anyone* could get on."

"I think I'm intelligent enough to learn pasteup, don't you?" Glenda asked.

She looked hurt and I gulped.

"Of course you are," I said. "I only meant that most of the people have been drawn to it by some special skill like writing, reporting, graphic design, or photography."

I didn't know what I was talking about and she seemed to sense it. The truth was that it would probably be fine if Glenda came aboard *The Record.*

"Maybe they could use someone to sell advertising space," Glenda said. "Ask her anyway."

"I'll talk to Stephanie tomorrow," I repeated.

"Well," she said. "Either you will or you won't."

I did a double take when I heard that, because now it occurred to me that I didn't have to ask Stephanie if I didn't want to, and she'd never know. Because the truth was I *didn't* really want Glenda on *The Record* although I wasn't exactly sure why. *The Record* had felt like my special discovery when I stumbled onto it last period, and already I could feel it slipping through my fingers. Glenda always met a lot of interesting people through drama, and this was the first time I'd met a group of far-out people on my own.

I didn't think of myself as selfish and I was surprised at this unexpected proprietary streak about the paper. It went counter to the hippie ethos of inclusion that drew me to it in the first place, and I was embarrassed to feel this way. I don't know if it was because of Kevin or just her general personality, but Glenda was such a live wire she always got about five times as much attention as anyone else. I was kind of shy anyway, so I would be in her shadow if she was there, and it wouldn't be the same as it was last period. No one would notice me. The sun beat down and sweat broke out on my forehead, and now there was an awkward silence between all of us because of this thing about the paper.

Jane was the only one still eating her lunch. She sat cross-legged on the grass and tore her tuna sandwich up into little pieces and chewed them slowly.

"Guess what?" she said after a while. "I'm going to change my name."

"What to?" K.D. asked. K.D. used to be Katy, Brian's sister, but she had changed her name to K.D. in honor of Katherine Dunham, a black modern dancer who used voodoo in a lot of her dance pieces. K.D. was never into the Jesus freaks like Brian.

"Goody," Jane said. "You know, like Goody Putnam in *The Crucible*?"

She had a mischievous smile on her face, and it was impossible to tell if she was serious or not, because *nobody* would call themselves Goody but Jane was actually weird enough to do it.

Witchcraft was a really big thing with all of us. It had been for a couple of years now, even before Ms. Richmond taught us about the Salem witch trials when we were discussing *The Crucible*. They were part and parcel with paganism and Goddess worship and our whole feminist thing, but I was interested in witches even before that. My involvement dated back to the books my mother read to me as a child with their black-silhouetted illustrations of vines and elves and fairies. They populated my imaginary world when I was alone and had to entertain myself. Later I initiated my friends into my private world and was delighted that they were as enchanted by it as I was. It was more fun playing with friends in the fields outside La Grange than being alone in a sorry hotel room. In the spring the fields were a vibrant green, and you could practically see the activity of the little people animating them and bringing them to life.

We would dance from tree to tree and say, "This is my house, from this tree to that rock," and witches and fairies would whisper spells and give us secret charms and tasks full of ritual and meaning. They were usually from the Good Witch but there was a Bad Witch too who sometimes made demands on us.

We played the Queen of the May and Mistress of the Principalities of sunlight, grass, and rain. There was a Lily Pond Princess and a Frog Prince. Once I got in trouble for pushing a friend into the pond. But I had only done it because the Good Witch said to because the girl had touched the sacred sundial and birdbath that we had all agreed were off limits.

The sun went behind a cloud and the rays caught the right side of K.D.'s face. There was almost a radiance about her for a minute and I picked up my camera and thought I was able to catch it. Glenda and I exchanged glances briefly and I lowered my eyes. It was a small thing maybe, but I realized I still didn't want Glenda on *The Record.* It felt almost like a betrayal that she expected it of me, but then I remembered *I* was the one betraying her, and started sweating again. Now for sure I would talk to Stephanie tomorrow, because it would be too fucked and selfish not to, because Glenda was one of my best friends, and Stephanie had struck a high tone in her talk. The other thing was that I was going to be leaving in a month and a half anyhow, so what difference would it make then? But it still pissed me off because she had drama and K.D. had music and Jane had astrology and the occult, and we didn't all go and get into each other's trips and compete like that, so I didn't see why she had to start now.

"Welcome to Los Alamos," K.D. said suddenly.

I looked up and her black eyes bored into me. The sun was blinding behind her and I squinted into it. I didn't know why she said that or why she was looking at me, but she didn't say anything more. No one else said anything either. Then the bell started ringing and we all got up and ran back down the hill for fourth period.

CHAPTER 11

We got into witchcraft through feminism to begin with, except for Jane who had sought it out because of her family. Her father was an alcoholic who went on rampages sometimes, and we figured she developed her sixth sense to protect herself from him. But we didn't meet her until later, and it was indirectly through the Craft—Wyrd, Faerie, Wicca, the Old Religion, whatever you wanted to call it—that we got to be friends with her, and she probably knew more about it than all the rest of us put together.

I don't remember when Glenda and K.D. and I first read *Dialectics of Sex* and *Combat in the Erogenous Zone*, but it was right around the time I first met K.D. and got my camera and had my heart broken by Brian Quinn. I'd lost my faith in God and was primed for something to replace it. Glenda's sister was studying Women's Studies at San Francisco State and tipped her off to the books, and we started passing them around between us like contraband—they were that powerful. We sat up in Glenda's room with the blinds drawn and our eyes gleamed like marbles because it felt like we'd stumbled onto the biggest mystery of all time. We'd broken the code, and nothing was ever going to be quite the same again.

The books gave me an idea of how we'd been ripped off as women and our legacy stolen from us just like blacks or Indians or any other oppressed group. Now I could see why I always identified with their struggles so much, because I'd been blind to my own. We'd been encouraged to give our power away and it left us incredibly vulnerable to rejection or abandonment, even when it was accidental, like my father's death or the fact that Brian already had a girlfriend when I met him. I saw for the first time that I had unwittingly participated in my oppression by overevaluating my father and underestimating my mother.

Suppressed herstories were legion once we started uncovering them. There were buried legacies of Mother-Daughter religions that predated the Father and the Son, and the Christian trinity was little more than a throwback to the Mother-Maiden-Crone, the triple Goddess. I treated my mother with newfound respect, though the feminist concepts I introduced her to didn't interest her much, even Demeter and Persephone, the goddesses of grain and spring vegetation. She gave them a passing nod but wasn't actively hostile to them as she had been with the Christian ones. She turned out to have a lot more sense than I had given her credit for.

I remembered my grandmother calling her the Whore of Babylon, and how I had inherently reacted against it. The whole concept was sexist and specious and reeked of women hating and women blaming, all the way back to the Garden of Eden. It was the basis and bedrock of the whole religion, and I disavowed my association with it there and then. I'd been interested in fairies, gnomes, dwarves, and witches before I'd known anything about

Christianity and I was happy to return to them. I had some innate sense too, as it turned out.

The worship of Diana, Brigid, Venus, Kali, and a hostess of other goddesses had covered the globe at one time. We had lost a lot in empowerment and self-esteem by not having access to this information, but more important was the adverse effect on social institutions, world governance, power, and authority. Private property, organized warfare, and hierarchical power structures all had their origin in patriarchy, as it turned out. Warfare, starvation, pollution, overreliance on technology were all due to a lack of balance between the masculine and feminine principles. The only thing that could heal it would be the Second Coming of the Sacred Feminine, with a return to egalitarian tribal societies, equal distribution of wealth, and worship of nature as a divinity, rather than a resource to be harvested.

Mother's Day wasn't meant to be a sentimental celebration of debased motherhood and apple pie, but was a call by Julia Ward Howe for women to pick up their power and put an end to war, to civilize the world and actively mother it. Women hadn't raised their sons to be fodder for the American Empire to be shipped off to Vietnam, Laos, and Cambodia, not to mention all the secret places they were waging war that we didn't even know about. What kind of mother would be willing to sacrifice her son, to let him go out and kill and be killed? Feminism wasn't some limited agenda designed merely to put women on an equal footing with men. Men stood to benefit from it as well. We wanted to transform society and the entire world. The implications were incredible—just as staggering in their way as the Second Coming—and we had to get to work to turn our vision into a reality while we still could.

Glenda whispered, "It's a brotherhood," and K.D. mumbled

something about "a gentlemen's agreement" and "a good old boys network." It was like a big conspiracy that had been running the world so long they'd forgotten about it themselves, and they were on automatic pilot or cruise control.

We had to wake them up too before they inadvertently blew up the world, and we didn't have much time because there weren't that many of us who even knew what was going on. We didn't know what we were going to do, but Glenda dropped out of JV cheerleading and I quit the Honor Society, and K.D. even left orchestra for a while. All we knew was that we had to form a psychic and spiritual sisterhood.

We read what we could and tried to piece together the legacy of how the Old Religion had been practiced before it was stamped out. We made things up as we went along and set up altars with old snakeskins and owl feathers and whatever else we could find. We concocted spells using oils and candles and circles of protection and fasting and made up rituals to celebrate the equinoxes, solstices, and the cross-quarter days and tested our powers of divination, scrying, and astral projection. We went out in the woods looking for leopard's bane and chamomile, and K.D. took us to an old stone circle she had stumbled upon in a clearing in the woods. Who knows where that came from? Who knows if it was made by Indians or early settlers or people from other cultures? Because we knew that people had been circling the earth in canoes and rafts a long time before Columbus ever got here.

It was during this period that I got to know Jane. She was a serious girl with long sandy hair and big iridescent eyes in my English class, but I never paid much attention to her until one day the teacher had her read an essay she had written out loud in class. I thought it was going to be the typical boring piece about what she had done on her summer vacation. But it turned out she had been a Junior Archeological Associate with the California Historical Society and the Society for the Preservation of the American Indian and spent most of the summer excavating an old Modoc campsite on the San Benito River. She herself had personally found four arrowheads, some pottery shards, fragments of an old weaving, and a couple of pieces of benitoite, which she brought with her to class. While she was reading, the sun shone behind her like a halo, and I almost thought she was a visitation of some kind.

For all my adulation of my father, it never once occurred to me to go on a dig myself. I didn't think of it as something kids could get into, but she'd actually had the gumption to seek it out, and I felt like I'd just been wasting my time while she was this bright light. I took triple steps to keep up with her on the way to her next class. I was reluctant to let her out of my sight, and I arranged for us to get together as soon as possible.

Jane's house was a rickety old two-story building with the paint peeling off and weeds proliferating on the front lawn. Her room was cluttered with *National Geographics*, books on Egypt and the treasures of King Tut's tomb, a microscope, a piece of jasper, a cross-section of a meteorite, and fossil of a fairy shrimp. She was a prodigy of some kind with a genius IQ and an encyclopedic mind. She was also a fountain of information about occult phenomenon. She talked really fast because she had so much to say and being around her was a crash course on the subject. She'd actually read the Egyptian *Book of the Dead* as well as Aleister Crowley and Kevin Gardiner and Dion Fortune. She told me the Tarot deck at one time had been a book of sacred knowledge, but was broken up into cards and disguised as a game when it was declared a heresy. She was knowledgeable about the Masons, the Rosicrucians, the Illuminati, and other secret mystical societies.

I introduced her to K.D. and Glenda posthaste and they were equally impressed with her. She told us about the fifty-year hell cycles of the Mayan calendar and the prophecies of the Popul Vuh that placed the end of the world in 2012. In Western culture time was viewed as a thief, eroding property, beauty, health, and life itself, but the Mayans worshipped time, probably because it promised them deliverance from the Spanish conquistadores, although their beliefs predated the conquests themselves.

Jane's grandmother actually *was* a witch with an uncanny knack for locating lost objects. Farmers paid her to dowse for water with a willow wand on their land, which was what witches in Europe did in the Middle Ages, along with making up herbal remedies and counseling people before there were doctors and priests. But men had wanted their positions, land, and money, and the rest was, literally, history—the rise of the medical and legal professions, the priesthood, and the bourgeoisie. It was almost a reversal of the battle between the sexes going on today.

Jane said the four of us could form a coven because we had all the directions covered—K.D. was East, Glenda South, she was West, and I was North, which was Earth, the directions corresponding with our astrological signs. She picked up on them psychically even before we told her what they were.

Our zodiac signs corresponded closely with the four beasts in the Book of Revelation, which were also the four evangelists—the ox, the lion, the man (sic), and the eagle. She said this was really an old circle casting spell, because they took the power of the matriarchy for their own and devoked what went before, but we were going to reclaim that and devoke them. Jane said we were working on the astral and etheric planes in a place Between the Worlds, where acts of real Spirit and Power happen. What mattered most was right intention—"Do what you will and harm none."

What they called science was really a form of black magic. Because they had taken away the psychic and spiritual properties of the Earth and Earth Mother a long time ago—Magna Mater becoming inert, lifeless *matter*. And they defined the smallest unit as the atom, and split it in two, bombarding it in a cyclotron and particle accelerator. Now they were going to destroy the physical universe and they thought God and Jesus and the Rapture would come and establish some hokey kingdom, which was 100 percent spirit, on a vaporized universe after the nuclear winter. You'd have to be in kindergarten or else totally lobotomized to believe that, and I *had* been in kindergarten when I believed it, and it was a major embarrassment to me. Now it was midnight on the nuclear clock, and both hands were joined together in prayer.

We thought if we hooked up psychically with enough like-minded people, we might be able to neutralize the effects of the bomb and save the Earth. We had a bonding ritual where we braided our hair together. We all looked pretty weird after we cut off the braid, but part of the initiation was to break away from obsession with our appearance and fitting in, which had traditionally fractured women and stripped them of power. Jane wanted us to make a pilgrimage to Ceres to bury it, so we got up before dawn one Saturday and started walking over there. K.D. had her period and put a dab of menstrual blood on her forehead as a tribute to the goddess, which Jane said was likely the origin of the Indian bindi.

Jolene Carpenter used to live in Ceres and it was hard to believe I had ever been friends with her and into the Jesus freaks or Brian as recently as a few years ago. We wound up hitchhiking part of the way and finally got there around three. We walked along the side of the road for a while and then ducked into a cornfield. The field seemed to go on forever and the sky arched over it in a big dome. It was the end of the season and the plants were tall and swayed slightly in the breeze. Glenda wove in and out of the rows and we followed although I almost couldn't see her anymore because her flaxen hair was the color of the corn silk.

"Hey, stop," I called out. "Isn't this far enough?"

But she kept going.

"It's a *maze* dance," she called back laughing.

The sun was high overhead and the sky mottled with clouds and finally we stopped and made a circle. We each took a stick and dug a hole in the ground for the offerings we'd brought. The earth was harder than it looked and it took the better part of an hour to do it. I buried a roll of film to dedicate my photography to the Goddess. Glenda buried her lipstick, Jane a quartz crystal, and K.D. a copy of *Don Juan Speaks.* We wrapped our braid in corn silk and cornhusks, binding it with calico scraps and fashioning it into a corn doll. K.D. drew eyes and a mouth with markers and attached strands of black yarn for the hair, and we buried the doll in the center of the circle. Jane broke off an ear of corn, husked it, and passed it around, and we each took a bite. It was so ripe and sweet it was like sugarcane and in the sacred space of the ritual I thought it was the most delicious thing I'd ever tasted. We lay down on the ground and Jane led us into a past life regression.

I didn't know if I was going to have one or not, I didn't think I was the type, but I actually had two of them. In the first one, I was a priestess in Delphi and sat on a three-legged birthing stool reading prophecies left by a python in the patterns in the sand. The sea shimmered in the distance, and other priestesses danced around me in flowing white Grecian robes. The second one was dark and chaotic, and I could barely make it out. I was in the Middle East somewhere, probably ancient Israel. There was an upheaval, perhaps a revolt against the Romans, and soldiers were chasing people, and there was blood on the sand. I was a priestess of the Old Religion and I cut a deal of some kind with the priests. I think I even sold out the matriarchy. I don't know why I did it. I can't tell if it was out of greed or delusion, or I even thought of it as a last ditch attempt to save the matriarchy. Or there was no choice and I was forced into going along with it. The picture in my mind was surrounded by the beating of wings and a feeling of the Virgin Mary and Jesus, not in their blessedness but their agony at the crucifixion.

Clouds had appeared from nowhere when I opened my eyes and there was a quick patter on the leaves of corn. It only rained for a few minutes and stopped. Jane brought us gently out of trance and we went around the circle and shared our journeys. Glenda said she went back to Avignon where she had been burned as a witch in the early Renaissance. She looked dazed and scared, and Jane put her arm around her shoulder and told her she had come through a terrible trauma but it was over now. She said Glenda had done deep trance work, and those were the portals Glenda had to pass through to reclaim her power, the Gates of Fire.

K.D. said she had been a court musician in ancient Egypt, playing the zither and the lyre. In the end, she and the pharaoh's entire entourage had been buried alive in the pyramid to accompany him to the afterworld. Jane had been a Zuni Medicine Woman Rainmaker. She was the one who first delivered the news that the Spaniards were coming, and the kachinas danced in the pueblo as the tribe prepared to enter the new era. That's why she stood where she did in the West, at the Gates of Water.

"Watergate!" Glenda said and we all giggled, but she stared straight at me when she said it because now it was my turn.

They all laughed but I didn't because it *was* like Watergate and wouldn't you know *I* would be the one to sell out, and I was just going to tell them the one about the Delphic oracle, no way was I going to tell them about selling out the matriarchy. I don't know if the past life signified some holdover from my days as a born-again Christian or a conflict between the two belief systems. I caught Glenda's eye and gulped. I hoped I hadn't had anything to do with her being burned at the stake. I didn't see how I could have if she was in France and I was in the Middle East, but who knows what to make of it because I didn't know if it was past, present, or future anymore. It was Between the Worlds, outside time and place.

The whole time I was hearing a rattle coming from somewhere. I didn't know if it was a snake coiled around one of the corn plants or just the wind in the husks, but nobody else said anything and I thought I might be the only one who heard it. I figured if I did betray the matriarchy, then the diamondback or whatever it was could go ahead and bite me, because I deserved to die. In the end it didn't, and perhaps it wasn't a snake at all but a rattle from one of the kachina dancers in Jane's past life regression. I flicked my eyes and caught a glimpse of a dancer wearing an owl mask. But I knew it wasn't over yet because the past life regression put me on notice of a capacity for betrayal in myself that I never knew about before. At the beginning of the ritual, Jane burned sage and copal like we always did, only who would have thought there would be *that much* to purify? We thought we had enough enemies in the patriarchy, but then we came to find out we had worse or at least deeper ones within ourselves, and who would have thought that?

We held hands on the way out and Glenda cut the same meandering path, but it seemed to take only half the time it did going in. There was a lavender sky over the cornfield, and when we got to Ceres we sat at an outdoor table at the Frostee Freeze while K.D. called her mother to come pick us up. Nobody talked, and they all looked dreamy and peaceful, but I felt the opposite of that and didn't know how I was going to regain my footing. I'd had a revelation of some kind, but it wasn't what I was expecting.

After that ritual we really were bound, and if I didn't feel it then, I found out for sure when I got in the argument with Glenda over *The Record*, because I felt an inner wrenching that was more than if it was just me. Because if it was me, it was the same as if it was her, so it was like there was no difference between us anymore, and I couldn't keep her off *The Record* even if I wanted to, because it would be like I was doing it to myself.

CHAPTER 12

There was going to be a big women's march called Take Back the Night in San Francisco next weekend and K.D. was hot for all of us to go. She said it was a demonstration against violence and the sexual exploitation of women and it would march through the Tenderloin and North Beach where all the topless and bottomless clubs were. There was also a Diane Arbus exhibit at the Museum of Modern Art, and I was even more excited about the show than the march. I had a poster of Arbus's albino sword swallower up in my room along with a quote about her choice of subject matter: "Freaks was a thing I photographed a lot. It was one of the first things I photographed and it had a terrific kind of excitement for me. I just used to adore them. I still do adore some of them. I don't quite mean they're my best friends but they made me feel a mixture of shame and awe. There's the quality of legend about freaks. Like a person in a fairy tale who stops you and demands that you answer a riddle. Most people go through life dreading they'll have a traumatic experience. Freaks were born with their trauma. They've already passed their test in life. They're aristocrats."

It was like poetry and almost as compelling as her photographs, which seemed to pose a riddle too. I knew she had committed suicide in the end, so perhaps she hadn't passed her test in life after all. Her death implied that art wouldn't be enough to save you, which was a depressing thought, and made me wonder if I'd hitched my wagon to the wrong star.

We all showed up at the Greyhound bus station in Alhambra early Saturday morning. My mother drove me over and Glenda came with K.D. and her mother. The two of them sat together on the bus and I settled myself in the window seat behind them and Jane sat by the aisle next to me. Someone was listening to Watergate on the radio. I didn't know what was left to discuss now that Nixon had resigned, but I guess it wasn't over yet. Up ahead of us, I heard Glenda tell K.D. she was going to try to write an article about the demonstration for *The Record*.

It turned out that it was fine with Stephanie for Glenda to work on *The Record*. I thought it would be, and I figured it would be different with Glenda there, but I didn't really notice because I was in the darkroom 90 percent of the time anyway. I probably spent more time in the darkroom now that Glenda had joined the staff, almost as if, if she was going to be there, then I wouldn't.

We'd had our rivalries and tiffs over the years but none in a long time. She had been a JV cheerleader for a while and went to the junior prom and homecoming dance, but jealousy and competition hadn't really surfaced till our fight over *The Record*. Maybe it was the first time I had something I wanted and thought she would take it away from me.

I shifted in my seat. What a nasty cuss I turned out to be! There was obviously room for both Glenda and me on the staff and it should have been more fun for me to have her there. That's how any normal person would have seen it. Why couldn't we just enjoy it together? I'd better get a grip on myself before I destroyed my friendship with Glenda and all the rest of them. Just because I was leaving didn't mean I had any intention of dumping them, least of all her. I didn't know how I had let things get to such a pass and vowed to reverse it. I would miss her terribly if anything happened to our friendship.

When I looked out the window we were just past Manteca. We left the flat, agricultural plains behind and the landscape was hilly and the bus began to climb. The rains hadn't started yet, and the flaxen grass looked like it was being spun into gold around the occasional live oak.

I'd only gotten about three or four hours of sleep the night before and felt like I was coming down with a sore throat. Jane was reading an astrology magazine and I glanced over her shoulder at my horoscope. "Watch it, Virg," it said. "That stony virgin silence could get you into trouble." I didn't know what that meant, whether I was supposed to be making conversation with Jane, but I didn't have anything to say and she seemed totally absorbed in her reading. Perhaps it was a general nudge in the direction of reaching out and friendship, echoing my own thoughts on the subject.

I didn't think I was going to be able to sleep but I must have dropped off, because the next thing I knew the air had cooled off and the city skyline rose up ahead of us out of the fog. I loved San Francisco and I was usually excited to see it, but today I felt a measure of dread, as if I were riding into an ambush among its tall buildings. We crossed the bridge and the bus barreled down an off-ramp. Steam rose out of a manhole and the air was full of the rich, oily smell of gasoline.

We stopped at a Greek greasy spoon near the Greyhound station for souvlaki, coffee, and baklava and then went to the Museum of Modern Art. I walked by myself a little ahead of the rest of them.

The Arbus exhibit included a lot of photographs I'd never seen before, both of freaks and the so-called normal people that were my favorites. The state of the world was such that what passed for normal *was* freakier than the freaks, but nobody else saw it, which was what was so great about her. She captured the denial of heartless, commercial Americana and put it on the same playing field as circus freaks and transvestites. Her photographs of pro-war demonstrators with their Yankee Doodle hatbands went right alongside the dwarfs, midgets, and mental retards, making clear what she thought of them. She threw their abnormality into relief even as she integrated the others into the mainstream.

My friends finished before I did and waited in the lobby while I went through the rest of the exhibit by myself. I stopped in front of her photograph of the hermaphrodite. He was different than I remembered and less feminine and glamorous than the one I had seen at the County Fair. He was a chubby older guy wearing a silver sequined bra and bikini, and a dog rested its chin on his bare thigh. I had my own photos of a hermaphrodite now but I hadn't even developed them yet. I finished the rest of the exhibit and joined my friends in the lobby. As we walked down the steps of the museum, K.D. linked her arm through mine.

"I feel like I've barely seen you all day," she said giving me a big smile, and we crossed the street to the demonstration.

A crowd was already gathering in the Civic Center Plaza. A purple banner with a crescent moon and a "Take Back the Night" sign reached across the back of the stage, and a young woman tested the microphone for feedback. A couple of girls in leather jackets and white armbands called out directions to the crowd over their megaphones. Policemen milled around the edges of the crowd and some very obvious plainclothes men took pictures of everyone. I take it they didn't think they were fooling anyone.

The sky darkened and shadows lengthened, and everywhere I looked there was a picture, but I didn't take any. Their presence muddied the stream and I decided to leave the field to them.

We finally ran into Glenda's sister and her roommate with whom we were going to be spending the night. Linda was wearing a leatherjacket and looked like she'd gained maybe ten pounds since the last time I saw her. I'd always liked Linda and Ruth, the roommate, was nice too. She had frizzy red hair and a friendly smile. The speeches started and I fazed in and out of them. A woman with a long ponytail spoke on domestic violence, saying that three women were killed in family disputes every day in the U.S.

The next speaker was Margo St. James, from COYOTE, Call Off Your Old Tired Ethics, a radical prostitutes' group. She talked about the need to legalize prostitution and we agreed with that, but I'd heard all this before and the speeches seemed to be going on and on, and I felt restless and antsy. I looked across the plaza from city hall to the main library, and it occurred to me that I could run over there real quick and see if I could find any information about my father.

I usually looked up my father anytime I went to a new library, and the San Francisco Main was bigger than any library I'd ever seen but I'd never been inside it before. It was only 6:15 and the march didn't start till 7:00, so I figured I could make it over and back in forty-five minutes without a problem, and the more I thought about it, the better an idea it seemed. I told K.D. I was going for a walk and I'd meet them by the fountain before the march began, and I started across the plaza as the speakers' voices faded behind me.

The library ceiling was high and arched overhead and the floor was black-and- white checkered marble like a giant chessboard. There were over thirty aisle-long cases in the card catalog and a whole drawer full of Montagues. I found a blue hardbound edition of *Indian Tribes of the Miami Confederacy* in the stacks and checked out the *Anthropological Index* and the *Who's Who in Anthropology* at the reference desk.

There was nothing in the first one but there was a listing in the *Who's Who*, and my heart started pounding when I saw it. It was the first time I'd ever found any information about my father in the all the times I'd looked him up. The entry cited critical acclaim for *Indian Tribes of the Miami Confederacy*, his only book among numerous articles but it had carved him a place of such prominence that twenty years later it was still the seminal work in the field. Its unique contribution was the speculative notion that the Miami were descendants of the ancient mound builders of the Mississippi. My father had been educated at Harvard and Oxford and taught at Boston University before devoting himself full-time to research in 1952. He died at home in New Brunswick, Connecticut, of heart failure in 1965 at the age of 60, and was survived by his wife, Jeanette, and sons Avery and Philip.

I must have read that last sentence over ten times. My vision blurred and the page was swimming, because I couldn't figure out why they didn't mention my mother and me and who these people were that they talked about instead. It was the first information I'd ever found about my father and it was completely wrong.

My vision cleared and I looked up and could see almost every detail of the wood squares and gold rosettes on the ceiling that must be at least thirty-feet high. I was trying to figure out the mistake in the *Who's Who* when I suddenly remembered my friends. By my watch it was almost 7:30, so I was already a half-hour late. I didn't care about the march anymore but if I didn't get back, I'd have a hard time finding them again. I took the reference books back and caught my reflection in the window as I pushed open the library doors. My eyes looked wide and flared like those of a horse that was trapped in a burning barn.

A church bell rang as I clattered down the steps and ran across the plaza, but the fountain was already deserted. The whole demonstration had moved on. I heard them chanting "WOMEN UNITE, TAKE BACK THE NIGHT!" a few blocks away. The plaza was empty and the wind blew some flyers around, and I headed up Larkin Street after the march.

It was cold and getting dark and I was walking through a down-and-out neighborhood. Welfare hotels and single-occupancy residences lined the block—the Royal, the Ritz, the All Star, the Albion. I'd grown up in places like these although they looked even more run-down than the ones I remembered.

I could think more clearly about the *Who's Who* now. When I first saw it, I thought the *Who's Who* must be wrong, but now I knew it was the other way around. Everything I'd heard about my father my whole life had come from my mother, so she was the one who was wrong, and she wasn't just wrong, she was *lying*.

At first I couldn't figure out why she would lie about something like that but then I understood. I was standing at the corner of Eddy and Jones in front of a sleazy nightclub when the truth came to me like a shower of cold moonlight. Because the truth was that Derek Montague wasn't my father, but she could never bring herself to tell me. She'd never married my father and she might not even know who he was. It was completely obvious now, but it was still as ugly and hard to look at as the neighborhood itself.

Grandma Heaney tried to tell me in Texas a long time ago, but I'd been too young to understand and dismissed it as the confused ramblings of a fanatic or attributed it to a mean streak. I was too young to know what a whore was in those days, but I knew now. Everything my grandmother told me about my mother was true. Granny had tried to protect me, but I'd paid her no heed and followed my mother right into Sodom and Gomorrah against all warnings.

I caught up with the march, and all around me women were locking arms and chanting slogans. Old people and Vietnamese immigrants watched us from the hotel windows, and a couple of guys heckled us from the sidewalk. A drunk with a grizzled beard and bloodshot eyes teetered on the corner and staggered toward me. I stepped out of the way and he stumbled into a parked car. There was a San Miguel bottle in the gutter next to me, and I kicked it hard and it shattered against the curb. We marched into North Beach and passed the topless clubs on both sides of Columbus. Red lights flashed on and off the nipples of a giant neon nude above the Condor Club, and police patrolled every intersection. The crowd jostled me and someone grabbed me by the shoulder. I didn't know if it was the old drunk again or one of the cops, and I had a fleeting fear of being mistaken for Patty Hearst, but when I turned around it was Glenda. She looked overjoyed to see me and I was equally happy to see her.

"There you are!" Glenda said tightening her grip on my arm. "God Almighty! We've been looking for you everywhere!"

"We didn't know what to do when the march started and you weren't back," K.D. said. "So we decided to go on and hoped you'd catch up with us sooner or later. Where have you been all this time?"

"I went to the library," I said.

"The library? In the middle of a big demonstration like this?" Glenda asked. "Talk about a bookworm! You just decided to up and do a little research, eh? Are you working on a term paper, or something?"

"Right," I said, hoping she wouldn't pursue it.

"Well," Glenda said. "You have an odd sense of timing, but then again you always did march to a different drummer."

She gripped my arm again.

"Isn't this great?" she said excitedly. "Isn't this wonderful? Look where we are and what we're doing! We're changing the world!"

K.D.'s and Jane's faces glowed. Behind them the crowd chanted slogans and roiled like a giant, slow-moving dragon. They were caught up in the magic of something bigger than themselves that connected them to all humanity. Meanwhile, I didn't think I'd ever been so miserable in my life and felt even worse by comparison.

CHAPTER 13

The demonstration exploded around us and women went by with picket signs saying, "Pornography Is Legalized Pimping" and "Get Our Bodies Off the Line!" Hecklers jeered at us from the sidewalk and women screamed "pigs" and "male chauvinist pigs" back at them. Men came out of the clubs to gawk at us as if we were competition for the floor shows. Linda got into an argument with a barker outside of the Tit-for-Tat Club. They screamed at each other, and for a minute I thought they were going to get into a fistfight, but then Glenda and Ruth pulled her away and we moved on.

It was after eleven and the demonstration finally broke up, so we started back to the Civic Center to look for Linda's car. The light from the streetlamps was ghostly and pale and the buildings were shrouded in fog. The library looked like a sphinx with its granite steps thrust forward like giant paws.

When we got back to Linda's apartment I was ready for bed, but they were still excited and hopped up, so we stayed up talking around the kitchen table. Linda lit candles and poured us glasses of Burgundy and Ruth brought out her guitar and we sang "Oh, You Can't Kill the Spirit," "I Still Ain't Satisfied," and "Ain't I

A Woman?" The wine made my throat feel worse, and they were still going strong when I stumbled off to the living room and rolled out my sleeping bag. I didn't bother to undress. I got in with my clothes on and fell asleep right away.

When I woke up, my throat ached worse than ever and for a minute I didn't remember where I was. Glenda and Jane were stretched out on either side of me and K.D. was asleep on the couch. The blinds were drawn and the room was dark. Finally I realized I was in Linda's apartment and with a groan I remembered my discovery in the library the day before.

When the world is at its lowest point and the lights have all gone out, and the world has been tipped on end like a saucer, so that the world itself appears to be running out, that is the time to take heart.

Miami prophecies from "my father" Derek Montague's book. Old habits die hard. But now they were more of a taunt than a comfort.

I'd forgotten my toothbrush, so I gargled with toothpaste and water and went out for a walk around the neighborhood. I took a couple of pictures of some guys working on an old two-tone Buick up on cinder blocks. One was wearing a leopard-skin vest and had muscular arms and the other was wearing a leatherjacket and a hairnet.

When I came back, everyone was sitting around the kitchen table drinking coffee. The Sunday paper was strewn about and their tortoiseshell cat, Guru, lay stretched out on one of the place mats and Jane was rubbing her stomach. There were oranges and Mexican pastries on the table, and Linda and Ruth were deep into an argument about the effectiveness of consciousness-raising groups versus direct action as an organizing tool.

Glenda and K.D. put in their two cents worth from our activist days at Alamo, and then Ruth got up to go to work and

Linda went to her room to finish a term paper on Elizabeth Cady Stanton and the Women's Bible. We had the rest of the afternoon free before our bus left. I would have preferred to take the early bus home, but they all wanted to stay longer. We were divided as to whether to go to North Beach or the Haight Ashbury, but K.D. broke the tie and said she wanted to go to North Beach after all. We got on the 30 Stockton and went to Cafe Trieste and drank espressos and K.D. played a selection from *Rigoletto* on the jukebox. I'd barely said a word all day and K.D. leaned over and asked me if anything was the matter. She had deep, soulful black eyes and I almost felt like telling her what I'd found out about my father. But I just blinked and shook my head, and after a while we got up and wandered over to Chinatown.

Smoked duck and plucked chickens hung in the storefront windows, and bok choy, black mushrooms, garlic, and ginger filled the wooden bins on the sidewalk. We looked around a couple of souvenir shops and K.D. bought some embroidered silk scuffs and a Quan Yin statue, and Jane bought rope incense, ginseng tea, and a book on Chinese astrology. We were all born in the Year of the Rooster, so according to our horoscope we were colorful, optimistic, grandiose, temperamental, vain, and opinionated, which somehow managed to be true of all of us, different as we all were. We went to the Suet Lee on the corner of Broadway and Stockton for dinner and sat in a dark wooden booth in the basement.

The only other people in the restaurant were Chinese, which meant that the food should be good, and it wasn't just for tourists. I spaced out, half listening to my friends and half thinking about Derek Montague's sons Philip and Avery and imagining their house in Connecticut. I pictured a small Tudor cottage full of books and tribal artifacts out in the country someplace. By now they would be grown up and probably have families of their own, and I imagined them building ably on their father's legacy, not necessarily stellar careers but sound, sturdy ones, like the little pig who built his house of bricks.

When I tuned back into their conversation, Jane was raving about Linda and Ruth.

"Linda's OK," Glenda said slowly. "A little on the bossy side, maybe."

There was a pause and then she looked around at us. "They're lovers, you know," she said. "Did anyone figure that out?"

It took me a minute to realize who she was talking about. My breathing got shallow and my back was so stiff it felt like there was a poker going through it.

"It occurred to me," K.D. said. "But I sort of put it out of my mind. Oh well, that's OK, I guess."

Then she started laughing.

"What's so funny?" Glenda asked.

"I was just thinking of all the times last night those guys called us lezzie's and shit and we got mad, and now it turns out they were right!"

They giggled and meanwhile my foot pressed into the floor, like I was braking, because I wanted them to stop talking about it. It was too much on top of the thing with my father, and I couldn't handle it. I couldn't believe Glenda had brought us there without telling us, and I for one don't know whether I would have come if I'd known. I didn't want to feel that way, but I did. I looked over at Jane and K.D. but they didn't seem to have a problem with it.

"They seem happy enough," Jane said. "It's a little weird but I don't really see anything wrong with it."

Glenda rolled her eyes and let out a long low whistle.

"My parents sure do," she said. "You should have seen my

mother the night Linda told us. She was hysterical. She said it was the worst disgrace that had befallen our family, and maybe we'd always had problems but we'd never had a *pervert* in the family before, so Linda had brought us all down. They didn't see the point in sending a pervert to college; and they weren't going to spend any money on her until she came to her senses. But you know Linda, she's stubborn and besides she can't change her essential self just to please my mother, so she had to get a job and now she's got to pay the tuition on her own. This is the first time I've seen her since the big blowup. They never would have let me come if they'd known where I was going, let alone bringing my friends. I told them we were staying with Jane's cousin."

She looked around at all of us and smiled. Meanwhile I thought, They were right, she should have told us. There was no problem with any of us knowing what it was—we all knew that. Lesbians. My mother once insinuated that that's what Ms. Richmond was, and I thought she was crazy, but she could be right about Ms. Richmond, who knows? I know I dreamed about her and the hermaphrodite the night after the County Fair, although I couldn't remember those dreams anymore.

The waitress set a big porcelain soup bowl on the table and it was so hot the mirror at the back of the booth steamed up. I wasn't hungry anyway but the soup looked completely gross. It had black elephant ear mushrooms and sea kelp and squid, all tangled together. I wasn't going to eat that and I couldn't figure out why Glenda ordered it. She was always showing off, trying to be theatrical and sophisticated.

K.D. giggled and said, "I wonder what they *do*."

Glenda grinned and said, "You know what they *do*."

Then she turned to me and said, "What's the matter? Cat got your tongue?"

She doubled over as if she'd said the most amusing thing imaginable. I held myself so stiff I practically shook from the strain and blushed as if I was bleeding under my skin.

"Don't take me seriously," Glenda said. "You know I can't resist a joke."

The waitress brought a platter of fried bean curd and prawns in black bean sauce. I usually loved Chinese food, it was my favorite, but I'd lost my appetite completely. When she came back with the check, I took one of the fortune cookies off the little tray.

My fortune said, "You will find the courage to go against the grain," and I groaned. I didn't want to go against the grain. I was always going against the grain—I needed to go *with* the grain for a change.

"What'd you get?" Glenda asked. Her eyes caught mine but I didn't answer.

"Mine says 'You will make someone very happy,'" she said raising her eyebrows up and down. "I wonder who that could be?"

K.D.'s was "Hard work and perseverance will pay off in big bucks," and Jane's was "You think it is a secret but it has never been one."

The waitress cleared the plates away, and Glenda looked at her watch and slipped out of the booth.

"Come on," she said. "We'd better get going if we want to get back in time for the bus."

When we got back to Lapidge Street I waited on the front steps while they went in to pick up our sleeping bags. I thought we'd walk to the bus station from there but Linda came out to give us a ride. I tried to smile but ended up just squinting into the sun and couldn't think of anything to say.

The bus was already half full when we got on, and they all

scooched into the back seat. I told them I had a sore throat and was going to sit by myself so I could get some sleep.

It smelled like someone had been sick in the bathroom, and the kid in the seat in front of me was listening to "Mr. Bo Jangles" on a transistor. I'd always hated that song and I hated it more than ever now. I couldn't sleep but I didn't smoke because of my sore throat and because I didn't want them to know I was still awake. I didn't want to talk to anyone and I didn't want to hear any more about Linda and Ruth either. I already knew what they were thinking. They thought I was uptight and prejudiced like Mrs. Richter. Maybe I was, but it was easy for them to say because Glenda had always been popular and had a lot of boyfriends, so she didn't have to worry. Of the four of us, K.D. and I were the only ones who were still virgins.

I don't know what my problem was, but it seemed no matter how hard I tried, nothing ever worked out for me with boys, like with Brian and probably nothing was going to happen with Kevin either. I just couldn't get along with guys for some reason. I wasn't exactly sure why, but I thought it might have something to do with never having had a father. As a result, I was ill at ease around them or overeager and desperate. Or else I was picky and had too high a standard, because of my grandiose ideas about who my father had been, which had turned out to be a crock. All of them not only had fathers but brothers as well, so it felt perfectly natural for them and they were comfortable with boys, while I was squirrelly and uptight. Now it turned out even Derek Montague was a sham, so who knows what was going on with me or how I was going to end up? And it seemed like no matter what happened, everything was always my fault somehow.

Glenda once told me that my problems with boys weren't due to my looks but my personality, which was at least five times more serious. It wasn't something that clothes, diets, makeup, or hair dye could ever fix. My personality was my essential self and it was horrible to think of it as defective in some way. It was dubious whether years of psychotherapy could even alter it substantially.

It bothered me that I liked those girls so much, and I didn't know what that meant except that it would have been better if I didn't, and I liked their apartment too. I wanted one just like it someday with the Dorothea Lange poster and the four-drawer file cabinet and the big ficus and philodendron in the bay window.

I still remembered Linda as the bossy older sister from the days when I used to spend so much time at Glenda's. I didn't particularly remember anything from early on that would have earmarked her as a lesbian. She had been kind of a tomboy, but then so had I, I thought queasily. I remembered her as particularly wholesome, fresh- scrubbed, and all-American looking—blond, blue-eyed, sun-burned, and freckled. She was an avid tennis player, horseback rider, and a drum majorette. She was attractive enough but never quite the cutie-pie or blithe spirit that Glenda was.

Everybody had thought of it at one time or another, but no one really did anything about it. But those girls actually had, and I still couldn't imagine why anyone would take it that far. I was thinking about that when the picture of the hermaphrodite came back to me and I shuddered. I knew he was connected to me from the first; I just wasn't sure how.

All my life I'd had a feeling there was something wrong with me, and if people knew what I was really like they would never accept me. The only reason anybody liked me at all was because I suppressed my feelings and tried hard to be different from the way I really was. I gulped and looked out the window where a strip of gold sun was setting between the horizon and the bottom of a dense black cloud bank. The band of light shrank as the two dark masses moved closer together, and I felt like I was being squeezed between them and would die if they ever finally met.

CHAPTER 14

I didn't know what to say when my mother came to pick me up at the Greyhound station. I'd barely talked to her all week because she was mad when she found out I had dropped orchestra to take *The Record.* She'd spent a lot of money on my cello lessons over the years and thought it at least earned her the right to a consultation before I ditched it. She was late coming to get me so I had an extra half hour to mull it over, sitting on the curb under the red neon Greyhound sign, but I still hadn't come up with anything when she pulled up. I looked at her suspiciously, and I didn't say much during the ride in the car. I barely answered her questions about the march and the exhibit, and when we got home I stared at the house for a minute because there was something different about it. Then I realized it was the big "For Sale, Ewing Realty" sign planted on the front lawn.

The deadline for the California Arts Council's Young Photographers' Contest was at the end of the week, so I was in the darkroom more than ever. It was my sanctuary and I was like a mole in there. I stayed late after school every day because the realtor was showing the house all the time, and I was still trying to avoid my mother. I developed anything and everything I'd ever shot, both for *The Record* and for myself and hung them on the clothesline like Tibetan prayer flags. They were my offerings and my links to sanity.

I had little fantasy vignettes about my real father while I worked. In some, he was a janitor; in others an Amtrak conductor or a police officer. But he was never an important or famous man, and he always looked somehow bland and inconsequential. It occurred to me that he was probably still alive and I might even get to meet him someday if I wanted, but it wasn't a prospect I had much interest in anymore.

When the last leaf on the last corn plant in the last field is about to expire from lack of rain, and people have given up hope, then is the time to dance and chant for the five directions. For the rain will come again, drenching everything with renewing water.

I couldn't stop the words coming back to me; I needed them more than ever, although I didn't see the point now that they had nothing to do with me anymore. They just seemed to be mocking me. The shields in *Indians of the Miami Confederacy* flicked through my mind like I was flipping through the pages of the book—starburst, cricket, moose. They had been my allies and talismans, but that had all turned out to be a shuck. When I became a feminist, I realized I'd made too big of a deal out of my father, but I wasn't ready to have him totally revoked either. I had lost my greatest magical protector and now anything could happen to me.

All that was left to me was exploring the darkroom in *The Record* office, which fortunately turned out be full of potential. Developing your own prints increased the possibilities of what you could do with your photographs exponentially, and it also provided me ample opportunity to completely lose myself. You could cultivate an idea and refine it until it came across loud and clear, and yet it was done so subtly that no one could follow your tracks. The greats like Edward Steichen, Edward Weston, Alfred Stieglitz, and of course Diane Arbus—now I could see how they were able to do some of what they did, and before it was all a big mystery.

Kevin was the one who showed me everything—how to eliminate distractions by burning in and how to protect areas by dodging and using a mask, and the different effects of fiber-based and resin-coated paper. He showed me how you could alter the perspective, either purposely distorting it or just correcting an error by tilting the angle of the print while you exposed it. He seemed just as excited by it as I was, and I never quite knew if it was because he was turned on to me or because he was turning me on to something really great or what. I was still interested in him, but when I got back from San Francisco, I just wanted to be alone and didn't even want Kevin in the darkroom with me.

I looked through my contacts from the County Fair and came upon the shots of the hermaphrodite and printed one. There was a leer on her mouth as she held up her dress and with a groan I remembered her saying, "You may be headed the same way yourself" with a hissing, sibilant *S*.

The pictures held a secret, forbidden excitement for me, probably the same thing that lured me into the tent to begin with, and it transferred nicely to the prints. The sign for the Holy Roller arcade and Gospel Singers was in the background. They came out better than I thought they would, and I wound up printing them all. One of them was still in the bath when I heard Kevin hammering on the door. He said he had to rush something through by deadline, and I thought, Shit, wouldn't you know it? That was all I needed was to jinx things with Kevin because he thought I was some kind of pervert, although if he was half as cool as I thought he was, he would have been intrigued by the pictures himself.

"Wait a minute," I said. "I've got something in the bath."

I pulled the print out of the tray and pressed it between two sheets of blotting paper and stuck it in the bottom drawer and waited until after school to pick it up. The football team was the cover story for the forthcoming issue, and Kevin's photos were hanging on the clothesline, but he was nowhere in sight. I held my breath as I reached in the drawer and groped around for the print and was relieved to find it was still there.

The following day I printed an entire contact sheet of what looked like double exposures. I took them completely by accident over the summer when I thought I'd lost a roll because the film hadn't advanced so I rewound the film and reshot it. Now the original images hovered beside the newer ones like they were haunted by ghosts. Some of the pictures looked almost magically composed, and I enhanced them with my newfound darkroom skills. I printed one of a bathtub covered with morning glories; another of a forest with a white convertible moving through it; and the hull of an old motorboat crawling with ivy. The images reverberated off each other with a mysterious quality and reminded me of a Sufi prophecy Jane had talked about that there were two worlds coexisting in time, and at the Judgment Day they would finally merge into one.

I submitted the best ones to the California Arts Council under the title of *Between the Worlds*. I got them mounted and shipped off to Sacramento, and when I came back from the post office the phone was ringing. I heard a twinge of a Southern accent on the other end of the line and stiffened as I recognized Ms. Richmond's voice. I didn't think she'd ever called me before. I was always the one calling her.

"I haven't seen you in a while, Miami," Ms. Richmond said. "I keep wondering when you're going to come over for a visit. Huffy and Shasta miss you too."

Huffy and Shasta were her two silver-haired shelties. There was almost a wistful sound to her voice.

"Why don't you come over on Saturday?" she asked. "And stay for dinner?"

Ms. Richmond was my English teacher from last year, and normally I would have been ecstatic to be invited to her house. But I was haunted by the hermaphrodite and my mother had insinuated a couple of times that she thought Ms. Richmond could be gay, so at the moment she was the last person I wanted to see.

"I have a couple of new books I'd like to show you," Ms. Richmond said. "Besides, I'd like to see some of your recent photographs. I don't think I've seen any for at least six months. I'm sure you've been up to some interesting things."

I was working up to turning down the invitation when I heard myself accept it. After all, Ms. Richmond was my beloved mentor and it would be completely chicken-shit to suddenly drop her.

"*Pretty* interesting," I said. "Not all that interesting. I'll show you Saturday."

The hill up to her house was steep and I made myself pedal the whole way. I zigzagged slowly up the slope and was out of breath when I got there. Geraniums grew from coffee cans along her front porch, and Ms. Richmond came out wearing jeans and a Western plaid shirt with a turquoise scarf around her neck. She had a heart- shaped face and short black hair and thick eyebrows. She cupped my face in her hands and gave me a scrutinizing look.

"Have you been sick or something?" she asked. "You don't look quite like yourself."

I shook my head.

"Is anything bothering you then?" she asked.

"No," I said. "Really, I'm OK. Just tired, I guess. All the work getting ready for the CAC contest."

I pulled away and followed her inside.

Ms. Richmond's house sat high on a hill, commanding spectacular views in all four directions, and the whole place was flooded with light. The walls were lined with books and the rooms were furnished with Mission furniture and two amber Tiffany lamps. I sat in a Morris chair with wide armrests with my feet up on an ottoman, looking at the framed photo portrait of Virginia Woolf over the fireplace. Her hair was swept up off her long swanlike neck and her eyes were slightly downcast, in an expression of grace and keen intelligence.

Ms. Richmond came in with a tray of tea and cookies and saw me looking at the picture. She picked up a book off her desk and handed it to me. It was a slim paperback called *Revelations: Diaries of Women.*

"A wonderful book," Ms. Richmond said. "Excerpts from all kinds of women's diaries. Famous writers like Woolf and Katherine Mansfield, alongside everyday women that nobody's ever heard of that otherwise never would have made it into print. The wonderful thing is that the excerpts from their diaries are every bit as interesting and well written as the ones by the famous writers. Go figure, huh?

"Have you heard the saying 'What would happen if one woman told the truth about her life? The world would split open'?" she asked.

I shook my head no but smiled because it rang true.

"It's from a poem by Muriel Rukeyser about Kathe Kollwitz.

It's become popular in feminist circles. Like 'Women hold up half the sky.' Perhaps the diaries are a spin off from that."

I looked out the east window where a snowy egret landed its long stilt-like legs in the pond of a neighboring cow pasture.

"Have I ever showed you any of Christina Rosetti's poetry?" she asked.

I shook my head and she handed me a blue hardbound book.

"It contains 'Goblin Market,' her longest poem and the one that made her famous. Take it with you, and we can discuss it the next time you come over. She was Dante Gabriel Rosetti's sister, the famous Pre-Raphaelite painter. Most of her poems were addressed to an unnamed lover, and there's a lot of speculation about who he might have been. "

I finished drinking the warm, milky tea that Ms. Richmond always made and we went outside for a walk.

The dogs bounded ahead of us along the path, and we got to a bluff where the trees parted onto a spectacular view of the San Joaquin. The river must have been a quarter of a mile wide and was quite shallow. The light filtered through the beech trees and reflected off the fast-moving water as it rippled over the stones, and a flock of starlings took off out of a thicket.

We followed the path down to the river and sat on a bank in a grove of willow and beech. I took the prints out of my backpack and watched Ms. Richmond's face as she looked through them. A breeze blew off the river and the air was thick with pollen and flax from the milkweed pods. The leaves were beginning to yellow, but it was still Indian summer.

I got up and took off my shoes off, and Ms. Richmond smiled at me.

"Going wading?" she asked and I nodded.

"Good idea," she said. "Maybe it will help you relax. You

seem kind of on edge, like you might be giving yourself a hard time about something."

I rolled my jeans up to my knees but the water only reached my ankles. It was the first time I'd been in the river all summer, and it was September but it was still freezing cold. The sun was in my eyes and the stones were slippery but didn't hurt my feet. A hawk dipped into the water right in front of me and took off again at a steep angle and I couldn't see if it had caught anything or not. That was the first I knew of hawks being some kind of fisher bird. I made it over to the other side and sat down on the bank and watched my feet turn white from the cold. Tears filled my eyes and I convulsed into sobs. I was far enough away that I didn't think Ms. Richmond could see, and it was a relief to finally cry—it had been building up since the trip to San Francisco but it was the first time I'd actually been able to.

Across the river, Ms. Richmond sat on a rock with her feet curled under her, carefully looking through my prints. Sunlight splashed on her through the trees and I was moved to see her take such an interest in my work. She made it possible for me to take myself seriously too. She was more encouraging than any of my friends or my mother. She had turned me on to the things that meant the most to me—Arbus and Plath and Frida Kahlo. My mother could insinuate all she wanted about Ms. Richmond, but my mother was the one with the problem, as far as I was concerned, not Ms. Richmond, and if I didn't watch out, I was going to be just like my mother. I didn't care what Ms. Richmond was or might be and I didn't care what I might be either. There, I had said it.

It could just be sour grapes and my mother might be envious of Ms. Richmond, because she had an intellectual career and my mother didn't. Or she could have been jealous, because I liked her so much. In that case she didn't have to worry. Just because I followed in Ms. Richmond's footsteps didn't mean I valued my mother any less. I thought she had charm, grace, and fluidity. For all I liked about her, Ms. Richmond could be a bit arch and academic at times, and I suppose I could too. After all, the world wasn't just black and white like a photograph or the printed page.

Ms. Richmond waved at me across the river and I got up and started back. She smiled when I sat down next to her on the bank.

"There's something about the river that's good for the soul," she said. "Can you feel it? 'Wade in the water,' like the song says. This is my own personal power place, you know, but they say it was sacred ground to the Miwok and the Yokut originally, so it comes from an age-old sacred tradition."

Her black eyes looked ancient and wise. Her nose was beaklike and with her straight back and steady gaze she looked momentarily like a medicine woman. I remembered about my father and had to remind myself that that had nothing to do with me anymore.

"I think these are the best pictures you've ever taken," she said pointing to my prints. "Don't you?"

"Yes," I said. "But it's not me. It's because I have access to a darkroom now which gives you about ten times as much control of the image. You can manipulate it like crazy. It's a whole different level of photography."

"Yes," she said. "But it's still you that's doing it. You're acquiring a new skill. I think it's very exciting."

I gave her a print I had mounted for her of a crescent moon superimposed on a rain slicked city street and she seemed genuinely pleased.

"We went to the Diane Arbus exhibit at the Museum of Modern Art in San Francisco last week," I said after a while. "Glenda, K.D., Jane, and I."

"What a treat that must have been!" she said. "How are those girls? I haven't seen any of them in a while."

I said they were OK. I didn't bother telling her about the Take Back the Night march. Instead I regaled her with what I'd learned about Diane Arbus.

"Did you know she started out as a fashion photographer?" I said. "Her grandparents owned a fur emporium in New York City and her husband worked in the advertising department there, which is how they met. They married when she was really young and he gave her a camera for a wedding present. I think the fur emporium explains a lot about why she looked on the dark side of things. I bet it predisposed her to it."

"Count on you to zero in on that," Ms. Richmond said. "But who knows, you may be on to something, and it could be the subject of a dissertation one day. 'Diane Arbus: Conscience of a Furrier' or 'Prototype of a Vegetarian.' God bless academia, people have certainly succeeded with less to go on than that. "

She laughed and I dangled my fingers in the water and the cold traveled up my arm.

"My mother's getting married at the end of the month," I said. "We're moving to Coombs and I'm going to transfer to Mission High."

"So this is good-bye, is it?" she asked. "I knew there was something going on. No wonder you're tense. That's a lot to be happening all at once. How do you feel about it?"

"I'm beginning to think it'll be a good thing," I said. "I need a change."

"It's not so far that you won't be able to keep up with your friends, I hope," she said. "K.D. and Glenda and Jane. You'll make new friends of course, but not like them. Those girls are for life."

She said that and I felt myself tensing up again. The way I'd been feeling lately, I was looking forward to getting away from my friends and thought I might actually feel better after we moved. She could say I was giving myself a hard time, but she didn't know the way I had been about Glenda getting on *The Record* or with Linda and Ruth in San Francisco, or that I almost hadn't come there today. Now she was admonishing me not to leave my friends and break the Circle, so she'd pretty much dashed my hopes about how much better I would feel as soon as we moved.

CHAPTER 15

Friday after school Denise Hayes was having a party for *The Record* staff and I decided to go. I'd hibernated in the dark-room so long I needed to get out or pretty soon I would start to grow a coat of fur. The other reason had to do with the charge I felt between Kevin and me since the beginning. I figured if anything was ever going to happen between us, it would be at Denise's party.

Glenda and I got a ride over with Phil Wiedens, one of the layout artists. Glenda had the car window open and the wind was blowing in her face and she looked like she was up for a party. We started out in the living room. Phil went out and came back with a couple of bottles of wine and a quart of Jack Daniels from his folks' house, and gradually everybody drifted down to the basement to listen to music.

The ceiling was painted neon blue and covered with gold and silver stars, and strands of blinking Christmas tree lights were strung along the walls. Denise had covered her parents' old furniture with Indian bedspreads and arranged it around a brass tray coffee table. Kevin wandered around looking at the mosaics she had made on the walls, and Phil flipped through Denise's LPs and put on an old Doors album.

Denise danced by herself and Glenda got up to join her and the two of them slid across the floor in perfect synchronization like mirror images. Glenda wore black jeans, a purple leotard, and an old army jacket, and the rest of us sat on the sofa and chairs watching them.

Phil passed a joint and I took a toke and the Jack Daniels came around and I took a hit of that too.

"We've really got to do something about this paper, you know," Kevin said shaking his head.

Kevin was tall and thin with blue eyes and sandy blond hair parted on the side, cut relatively short.

"Why?" Denise asked. "What's the matter with it? I think it's great the way it is."

"Well, it has no political content for one thing," Kevin said. "It's just a high school rag. What exactly do we cover? The football games, the homecoming dance, Mr. McGuire's retirement dinner, the pros and cons of fraternities. If we can't come up with something better than that, we should just pack it in and put the whole thing in the toilet. That's all it is, anyhow, toilet paper. We could actually be doing something, you know. Saying something. Having some kind of an impact."

I caught a peek of Stephanie looking at him coolly over the rim of her paper cup. I'd never heard him carry on like that before and it seemed somewhat tactless in front of her, since she'd made it clear from the beginning that we were free to follow up on our ideas, and she obviously harbored high ideals for the paper.

"Aren't you forgetting Glenda's article on the Take Back the Night march?" Stephanie asked.

"That's true," Kevin said. "That was a serious piece."

"Maybe we could do a special issue on the farm workers," Denise said. "We could drive over to Delano and interview Cesar Chavez."

Kevin had his feet up on the coffee table and tipped his chair back.

"He's never going to give us an interview," Kevin said. "For a high school paper? Get serious. The man is very busy. He's got more important things to do than provide fill for our rag. He works around the clock, he's invested every penny he has in that union—he's even mortgaged his family's home. And if the farm labor bill doesn't pass the legislature, it's going to be a big setback for everything he's worked for."

"Maybe he would welcome it," Stephanie said. "He might view it as an opportunity to publicize the bill."

"I doubt it," Kevin said. "Not for a high school paper."

There was a pause in the conversation and Glenda looked around at everyone with a slight smile on her face.

"You know what I think would be a really *crackerjack* idea?" she said. "A 'Dear Abby' column. Everyone could write in their personal problems, advice to the lovelorn, that sort of thing. Only we wouldn't call it 'Dear Abby.'"

"We wouldn't?" Denise said.

"We'd call it 'Dear Glenda,' right?" Phil said.

"OK," Glenda said. "That'd be fine with me. I've always wanted my own column."

"How about 'Glinda the Good'?" Denise asked. "And you could tell whomever just to click their ruby red slippers together."

"'Dear Glenda,'" Glenda said in a singsong voice, rolling her eyes at the ceiling. "'When my boyfriend comes over to our house all he does is talk to my mother. My mother's great and I'm glad he appreciates her, but I'm beginning to feel left out. What can I do to get him to pay more attention to me?'"

"Dear 'Left Out,'" she said looking right at me. "That *does* sound like a problem. Then again, maybe you'd have better luck if you tried someone your own age. That's what you get when you go out with your American history teacher!"

Everyone laughed and I joined in too, only I didn't quite know what I was laughing about or why she looked at me hard when she said it. I wasn't going out with any of my teachers. Next thing I knew, she'd accuse me of being interested in Ben. I certainly qualified as lovelorn and she was always full of advice, but I didn't know what she was getting at. Kevin was laughing too, and of course *he* was the one complaining that the paper wasn't serious enough, so I didn't know where he was coming from anymore, except that he was staring at Glenda like he couldn't get enough of her. And I thought, Uh, oh, here we go again. Here was whimsical, playful Glenda, the center of attention and Kevin certainly wasn't immune. In fact, he looked completely charmed.

"Here's one for you, Glenda," Kevin said in a mock maudlin tone. "'Dear Glenda, big problem. I'm in a terrible funk and frequently have trouble getting out of bed in the morning, but I have no idea why. Do you think I could be depressed?'"

He straddled the chair with his chin resting on his hands and looked flirtatiously at Glenda. He appeared anything but depressed, and she looked back at him sternly.

"My advice is to get out of yourself, Kevin. Do the piece on Cesar Chavez and stop bitching about it. Get off your duff and take a chance instead of being so negative all the time. It sounds like you know enough about the bill to write the piece yourself. Can I go ahead and assign it to him, Stephanie?"

Stephanie laughed and nodded her head enthusiastically, and

Kevin's eyes sparkled. Glenda had his number, and he looked like he'd been waiting for someone to come along and bust him for some of the shit he'd been getting away with his whole life, so I guess the two of them were made for each other. Glenda really *should* write a pop psychology column, because it looked like she had it down cold. The next thing I knew, they were up dancing together and laughing and chatting like long-lost friends.

I felt like I was sitting in a boat that was slowly sinking. I knew something would happen when Glenda got on *The Record*, and if I'd thought about it for two minutes I could have predicted this would be it. A faint beam of light came through the window at the other end of the basement, and I reached for the glass of wine on the table next to me. I didn't know whether it was mine or not, but I didn't care.

"Break On Through to the Other Side" was playing on the stereo and I lay back on the sofa and looked up at the sky Denise had painted on the ceiling. She had the whole zodiac up there, and I recognized the constellation Virgo off to one side and tried to remember what Jane had said about my horoscope. I had a hard time seeing the implied, connect-the-dots pictures in most of the constellations. I certainly didn't see the maiden in Virgo. It just looked like a collection of rhomboids and trapezoids to me, and I felt like a rhomboid or trapezoid right now myself, not to mention a complete square. Denise had painted Neptune oversized in a blue-green haze nearby. I had my sun conjunct Neptune in Virgo, Jane had told me that, but I couldn't remember exactly what it meant except that Neptune was the planet of dreams and ideals. Meanwhile the wine and whiskey and grass were making me dizzy and the ceiling was spinning around, so that the planets looked conjunct now.

Kevin and Glenda disappeared together into one of the dark

recesses of the basement. I thought they were on the bed over in the corner but I couldn't see them. Someone had turned the lights out and they were swallowed up in darkness. It looked like everybody else had paired off too and the party was rapidly becoming a full-scale nightmare. There was a similar scene in *The Bell Jar*, which was supposed to have laid the groundwork for Esther's eventual suicide attempt, and I hoped this wasn't an omen of some kind.

I noticed Barry Hansley looking at me from the other side of the room. Barry was the one person on *The Record* staff I didn't know yet, who was possibly even shyer than I was. He was tall and skinny and pale and the Christmas tree lights blinked off the lenses of his wire-rimmed glasses. It occurred to me that if everybody was paired up, that left him and me. I'd felt left out before but now I was in a panic thinking, Oh my God no, not with Barry. Because I couldn't, I just couldn't. And I hoped he didn't feel obliged to make some kind of move just because everybody else was doing something.

I reached over to the coffee table and poured myself a big glass of Jack Daniels. It had an antiseptic, medicinal taste I didn't like but it numbed and warmed me and after a while I had a sense of such well-being, I couldn't remember what I'd made such a fuss about. The amber liquid looked magical and potent and sparkled like a semiprecious stone, and when it was gone I poured myself another glass. Meanwhile, I studied the mosaic Denise had made on the wall with pieces of colored glass, pottery, shells, and stones. It reminded me a little of the Watts Towers and I wondered if Denise had been inspired by them.

My mother had taken me to see them when I was twelve on a vacation in L.A. Eight webbed towers rose out of Watts in a gravity-defying testament of hope, one of them over 100 feet tall. They had been built single-handedly by an Italian immigrant in his spare time over a period of thirty years. He covered them with mosaics he made out of broken tile, glass, and bottle caps.

They stood as a graphic demonstration that you could make beauty out of anything, even garbage and trash. You could do the same with your feelings too, which was the premise of magic and witchcraft, overcoming ugly emotions with love and beauty, transforming yourself into a better person. I thought there was something about that in my horoscope too. Self-transformation, the essential challenge of life.

The Rolling Stones' *Black and Blue* was playing, and I didn't think I'd had that much to drink but suddenly I felt sick. My eyes lost their focus and the room was swimming in front of me. Footsteps and voices came down the stairs and Denise appeared from nowhere and said, "Come on, you guys, hurry up. My mom's home. Come on, put the booze away, will you? She's coming down here in a minute and she's going to be really pissed." She ran around picking up glasses and hid the bottles under the sofa and opened the windows to air out the smell of pot.

Mrs. Hayes poked her head downstairs and called out "Hi, kids," and everyone got up and Denise turned on the light. Glenda reappeared out of nowhere, patting her hair into place and arranging her jacket.

We went upstairs and everyone started to leave. Phil Wiedens was waiting for us in the car but before I could get in after him, Glenda was at my elbow asking if I wanted to walk home with her. I was weaving and tipsy and afraid a ride in the car would jostle my stomach, so I started off down the street ahead of her. I walked fast with my head bent forward and she had to run to keep up with me.

"Wait up," Glenda called. "What is this? Road Runner or something? What's the hurry?"

"I think I'm in love," she said, pulling up along side me. She sucked in her breath and wrapped her arms around herself and sighed ecstatically. "Isn't he great?"

"Kevin?" I said, letting out a little belch. "He's very nice, yes."

The only thing I had to be grateful for right now was that I never told her I was interested in Kevin myself.

"I wondered if he liked me, but he was really flirting with me today."

"Yeah, and you flirted right back," I said, belching again. "We all noticed that."

"What's the matter with that?" she asked defensively. "It's the only way I can think of to let someone know you're interested in them. What else are you going to do, stand on your head? He's not a mind reader, you know."

Something clicked when she said that. I thought that might have been where I made my big mistake with Kevin. Perhaps he was waiting for a signal of some kind, but I was so retarded I didn't have a clue how to go about it. Those long weeks licking my wounds in the darkroom were pretty antisocial, and today I had held back while Glenda had been playful and provocative.

"Did you have a good time talking with Barry?" she asked.

"I didn't talk to Barry," I said clenching my teeth.

"He's a little on the stiff side," she said. "But after you got to know him, he'd probably loosen up, and he could turn out to be a lot of fun. Who knows?"

"Please," I said slurring my words a little. "I was just the fifth wheel at a party and it was uncomfortable enough without being paired up with someone I have absolutely no interest in."

The street drifted off into inky blackness broken up by islands of light under the oily streetlamps. I'd slowed my pace but on an impulse I lurched forward again, taking off in a zigzag path. I was almost half a block ahead when I heard Glenda clattering down the street after me.

"Hey, wait up," she called. "What's the matter with you? You act like you're mad or something."

I glared back at Glenda.

"What are you so mad about?"

I kept on running this time and didn't turn back. I just wanted to be home and away from her, and she should have let me go, but she had to keep after me. I was out of breath and began to slow down and she grabbed my shoulder and pulled up next to me. We stopped under a streetlamp that dumped artificial yellow light on us that was as bright as a midnight sun.

Glenda wasn't smiling anymore. She looked tense and angry.

"Wait, I get it," she said. "It's Kevin, isn't it? You were interested in him yourself. So why didn't you say so? How was I supposed to know there was a big sign on him saying 'hands off'?"

I didn't answer.

"You haven't said boo to a ghost since our trip to the city. What've you been ignoring him for if you were so interested? It seemed like you just went on a two-week sulk."

I considered telling Glenda what I'd found out in the library but held off. It might have explained my behavior, but I was too vulnerable to risk bringing it up in the middle of an argument.

"What difference would it have made if I had?" I asked. "What was I going to say, anyhow? 'I've got first dibs on him, keep away.' If I'd told you I was interested in him it would probably have been an incentive, knowing you."

"That's not fair," Glenda said.

"You, it's always you. You have to have everything. You get to be the JV cheerleader and go to all the dances. You get to be the star of *The Doll's House* and *The Fantasticks,* and of course you're the one that gets the boyfriend. What next? The silver screen? I can see it now."

"You hate me," she said staring at me wide-eyed and backing away. "You actually hate me."

"No, I don't hate you, Glenda," I said. "I'm just trying to point out that all you ever think about is yourself, something I don't think you've ever examined before."

The Jack Daniels was acting like a truth serum, bringing up old grievances I'd suppressed, and it felt good getting them off my chest. Now that they were out in the open, maybe we could finally clear them up.

"Yes, you do," she said. "You're jealous of me, pure and simple. Listen to yourself. You're bringing up things that are years old. All this time, resentment has been festering."

A spurt of bile gushed into my throat. My stomach convulsed and the liquid that was sloshing around as I ran came up, and I started puking and retching into the gutter.

"You are not well," Glenda said hurriedly. "You are not yourself. You're completely drunk. You know what, I'm going to do my best to overlook some of this hateful talk."

The heaving stopped and I looked back at her bleary-eyed. I had a bitter taste in my mouth and wiped my chin on my sleeve. I was so relieved not to be sick that I wasn't even angry or jealous anymore. Anger and jealousy seemed like the least of my problems.

"Make a memo to yourself," Glenda said. "'Never mix, never worry.' Remember? From *Who's Afraid of Virginia Woolf?*"

I didn't remember but I nodded anyway.

“Sounds like a plan,” I said limping along beside her. I walked gingerly trying to fend off another attack, but my vomiting had elicited her sympathy and probably warded off a worse blowout between the two of us, so maybe some good had come of it after all.

“Thank you, Glenda,” I said, leaning on her slightly. “You really are a good friend.”

“Well, we’ll just see,” she said. “We’ll just have to see about that.”

She walked me to my door and turned to go without saying good night.

CHAPTER 16

I woke with a dull headache in a pool of self-recrimination the morning after the party. I had a vague, uneasy feeling I might have seriously blown it with Glenda, but my memory of what I'd said was fuzzy. Besides I didn't have time to obsess over it, because our house had sold, and my mother was on my back every minute about packing now, because escrow was closing and she'd already set the date for the movers. She wanted us to be packed and out of there, so that when we left for the wedding, we wouldn't have to look back. It was a lot of work, but I got a sick Virgo satisfaction out of sorting through my stuff and packing it up and giving a lot away to the Salvation Army and Good Will. The only thing that was hard to let go of were my thirty-six Nancy Drew books I'd kept since elementary school. I still remembered the thrill of reading *The Secret of the Hidden Staircase* by myself for the first time.

The people who bought the house were a washed-out looking family with blue eyes and sandy-colored hair from Boise that had the earthy-but-beaten-down look of Van Gogh's "The Potato Eaters." They had three kids and it was hard to imagine how they would all fit into the place, because there had barely been enough room for my mother and me. But that was their problem, and they should have thought of it in the first place, and what did I care if it was going to wind up paying for me to go to the Art Institute or Berkeley?

Saturday night, Jane was having a slumber party. I got to Jane's house around eight and thought there was an unnatural hush when I walked in. I figured Glenda had told them about my drinking binge and our fight, and they had all taken her side and I instantly regretted my decision to come. I could have been home reading *Tess of the D'Urbervilles*. Glenda looked different to me too—like she'd changed her makeup base and she was wearing darker colors than usual, a burgundy sweater and black boots—but she could have just been mad.

We hung out in the living room for a while, and then K.D. suggested a walk down to Saginaw Creek so she could collect specimens of the local flora and fauna for her biology class. We frequently went for walks in the woods at night, sometimes by candlelight or flashlight, for rituals and full moon risings over Landers' Peak. The night was cold and foggy and we walked arm in arm down the middle of the road with Glenda singing "Blue Bayou" at full throttle. It was completely dark and all you could see was the raggedy outline of trees up ahead, and the asphalt was as wet as if it had been raining.

"Sylvia Hamlin's having a Halloween party next Saturday night, you know," Glenda said. "And we're all invited."

"Halloween," K.D. said to me. "That's the night before your mother's wedding."

"Yeah," I said. "Are you coming? You're all invited, you know."

K. D. and Jane nodded. Only Glenda looked away and didn't answer, and I realized she *was* angry after all.

"El Dia de los Muertes," Jane whispered.

"I think I'll go to the party as Marie Antoinette," K.D. said. "Can you get me some kind of costume?"

Glenda nodded. Since she was in Drama she could get anything she wanted from the Theater Department. Jane said she thought she'd go as a railroad conductor, and called out "All aboard!"

I would have preferred the four of us having a Halloween ritual for my last night but nobody had consulted me. Now the party seemed like a done deal, and I felt vaguely hurt.

"Guess what?" Glenda said. "Guess who I went out with last night?"

"How would we know?" Jane asked. "Who?"

"Kevin Sanderson," Glenda said. "We went to see *Klute* at the Globe. And we're going to Sylvia's party together next week."

"Moving pretty fast, aren't you?" K.D. smiled. "Two dates in a week?"

"Who is this guy, anyway?" Jane asked.

"Kevin?" Glenda said. "He works on *The Record.* Miami knows him."

"So what's he like?" Jane asked.

"Kevin's a great guy," I said. "She totally lucked out. He's the other photographer for *The Record*, and he taught me everything I know about the darkroom. Plus he was a blast to work with. Other than that, I don't know much about him."

Jane shone the flashlight in my face and I squinted into the beam like I was in a lineup. I didn't see why she bothered asking me when he was Glenda's boyfriend.

"So what happened?" Jane asked.

"How should I know?" I said. "Ask her, why don't you?"

The four of us stood in the middle of the road, but when

headlights appeared over the crest of the hill, we scattered to one side. Glenda and K.D. walked ahead and Jane and I followed about twenty paces behind, and we turned away from the road down a path to Saginaw Creek. When we got down to the creek bed, K.D. and Glenda walked over to the creek while Jane and I waited for them by the bridge pylon.

"Was there ever anything between you and Kevin?" Jane asked.

"Not really," I said, squirming a little. "I had a crush on him for a while. I wanted there to be, but he wound up getting together with Glenda instead."

"Oh, too bad," Jane said. "What was that like for you?"

"Messed up," I said.

"How'd you take it when you found out?" Jane asked. "Jealous?"

"Yes," I said, "of course I was jealous."

"They say jealousy is a green-eyed monster," Jane went on. "Well, I hope you managed to hide it OK and put a good face on things. You don't want to jeopardize your friendship with Glenda over some guy you barely know."

I didn't answer. Glenda obviously told her what happened and she was taking the occasion to counsel me about my behavior. I felt like a problem child and the troll under the bridge that had just been given his comeuppance.

K.D. and Glenda let out a cry of excitement and K.D. ran toward us waving the specimen jar in one hand and the flashlight in the other.

"Look what I caught!" she said.

I thought she would pick up lichen or moss or at most a minnow, but when she shone the flashlight on the jar, a good size frog blinked its bulbous eyes into the glare.

"You're not really going to take that into your biology class, are you?" I asked incredulously.

"Yeah, I am," K.D. said.

"They'll make you chloroform it and dissect it, you know."

"That's our assignment. What do you think, I want to flunk the class?"

"That's disgusting," I said. "I'm going to liberate it during the night so you can't."

"You better not," Jane said. "I don't want that slimy thing hopping around my bedroom."

Jane giggled along with the rest of them. I tried to pull Glenda aside to offer an apology for the other night, but either she didn't see me or was purposely ignoring me.

The path up to the road was slippery and steep, and I pulled myself up on handfuls of skunk cabbage and the roots of an old madrone. I was almost at the road when my right pump slipped off my foot and slid down the hill.

"Wait up," I called out. "I've lost one of my shoes."

Jane came back with the flashlight and they started looking for it through the underbrush.

"Look at you balancing on one foot," K.D. said. "Like Cinderella."

"Maybe Prince Charming will show up with it in the morning," Jane said.

"Prince Charming," K.D. said. "Kiss the frog and he'll materialize, isn't that it?" She pushed the jar with the frog in it in my face. "Voila!"

"Here it is," Jane said, holding my shoe up in the torchlight. "I found it."

"Eureka!"

I reached for the shoe, but she held it just outside my range, and for a minute I didn't think she was going to give it back. When she finally did, it was so wet and spattered with mud, it looked like it had been gone for a week. I put it on and lagged behind them on the way back to the Stokes' house.

When I got out of the shower they were already in bed. Glenda and K.D. shared one bed and Jane was in the other one with the covers pulled back for me to get in. We chatted for a while about Kevin, the Halloween party, and my pending departure. Then K.D. regaled everyone with a story about coming upon her brother and his girlfriend unexpectedly in the middle of the night a few years ago when their family rented a ski cabin in Lee Vining. They were on the sofa bed in the living room and she stood mesmerized watching before she figured out they were actually doing it.

"Sure," Glenda said. "Then you were really mesmerized."

"No, of course not," Jane said. "At that moment you modestly dropped your eyes and hurried back to your room."

"I think it was that girl Susan," K.D. said. "You remember her, don't you, Miami?"

"I remember who she was," I said faintly. "I don't think I ever met her."

I figured they were exacting revenge for my treatment of Glenda, and had chosen to torment me with a recollection of my failed loves. The conversation lagged, and they must have drifted off to sleep one by one, because I heard them breathing deeply. It wasn't unusual for me to have trouble sleeping and I was wide-awake.

The clock on Jane's dresser flashed a fluorescent green light on and off, and across the room I saw the frog sitting placidly in the glass jar. I considered releasing it in the backyard but I was hesitant to jeopardize any more of my friendships. I thought of it soaked in formaldehyde, cut open and exposed to a classroom of high school seniors, and felt cowardly for not taking action. It looked so pathetic and doomed that I started to cry. I was afraid I was going to wake Jane up, until I realized I wanted her to see how miserable I was, but she slept like a baby.

I don't think I slept all night and as soon as it was light I went downstairs. Jane's mother was alarmed to see me sitting on the sofa when she came down. I assured her I'd had a good night's sleep and it was nothing for me to wake up early; I did it all the time. She brought in the paper and gave me the Comics and Entertainment section. I went out to the patio and sat on an old chaise lounge with the paper on my knees. The dew went straight through my nightgown, but I didn't go back inside. The backyard was narrow and elongated and overgrown with weeds, some the size of saplings. I sat shivering as the trees emerged through the fog at the back of the yard and listened to a cacophony of larks, wrens, and sparrows sparring for seeds among the dried husks. An old bicycle rusted against the back fence and an opossum waddled past me and clambered over the fence into the next yard. A mockingbird sounded like it was mimicking a phone ringing, and I thought it was a sign that the end had come when nature imitated technology.

I thought by telling Glenda what was bothering me we would be able to fix it, but I just opened up a Pandora's box. Now words had been spoken that couldn't be taken back and it seemed evil spirits had been let out into the world. It struck me as ironic that I was afraid I was so shy and mousey that no one would notice me. Now it seemed that self-effacement was my strongest social asset, the glue that held it all together. Keeping mum all those years had allowed me to develop and maintain my friendship with Glenda.

The rest of them came downstairs around ten, rested and

cheerful. We divided a pecan coffee cake into quarters and polished off a half gallon of orange juice, and went back to Jane's room to listen to records. She put on *The Harder They Come*, and everybody got up to dance. I was depleted from lack of sleep and dancing was the last thing I felt like doing but I joined them anyway. I didn't want to attract further negative attention by separating off. Glenda shimmied and did an assortment of exotic movements so that she looked like a many-armed Indian goddess. Meanwhile I was like a zombie. I caught my face in the mirror, and it was so stiff and rigid, it looked like a man's.

I finally heard my mother downstairs and grabbed my overnight bag. I barely said goodbye to Jane or the rest of them and forgot to thank Mrs. Stokes for her hospitality, nice as she'd been to me. I flew down the stairs and followed my mother out to the car like I was being let out of a cage.

CHAPTER 17

My last day of school Kevin blew my mind by giving me an old enlarger from *The Record.* He said they'd replaced it over a year ago, and it was hanging around collecting dust doing no one any good. I blushed at the thought of Glenda describing the scene I had made. More likely he had ferreted out my secret and felt sorry for me, but I took it anyway. I couldn't afford to be proud. I tried to think of it as a good deal and that I'd somehow come out ahead in the bargain. I looked for another opportunity to apologize to Glenda but she was nowhere in sight. I juggled the enlarger along with a bag of stuff from my locker, and ran into K.D. as I was getting on the bus. She said she and her parents would be coming to the wedding, but she'd see me at Sylvia Hamlin's party the night before anyway.

My mother said she could drive me to the party, but we had to go to a dress rehearsal for the wedding in Coombs first, so I figured I'd just wear my bridesmaid dress to the party. My mother's wedding dress was draped and long, made out of clingy white satin. True to form, I chose something trim and tailored and as far away from hers in spirit as you could get. My dress was a bright red silk Shantung sheath with cap sleeves, a Mandarin collar, and frogs over the left shoulder blade. I put my hair in a French twist and tried to make my eyes look almond shaped with pencil eyeliner. I stuck a yellow chrysanthemum in my hair and figured that would have to do it in the costume department.

It was dusk when Lilah and I set off for Coombs. The sky was striated in bands of orange, lilac, and charcoal, and the clouds seemed to shepherd the clusters of children already out trick-or-treating by the side of the road. A group of miniature pirates, tigers, and ghosts carried orange plastic jack-o'-lanterns up ahead of us, and she slowed down as we passed them.

"Your girlfriends are coming to the wedding tomorrow, aren't they?" my mother asked.

"I don't know," I said. "I think K.D. and Jane are. I'm not sure if Glenda is coming."

"Why wouldn't she come?" she said, sounding genuinely shocked. "Glenda's one of your best friends."

"Who knows why?" I snapped. "She's not sure she's coming, that's all."

She gave me a quick look.

"I know it's been hard on you," she said in a softer tone of voice. "Leaving your friends and making a big move like this, all in your last year of high school."

The sympathy in her voice irritated me but I figured I'd let her think what she liked. The truth was that we couldn't get out of there soon enough to suit me, and when I *had* been upset about it in the beginning, it hadn't mattered to her then.

"That's not what's hard," I said suddenly. "What's hard is finding out you've been lied to your whole life."

My voice was tight and sharp and there was a silence for a minute and then she whispered, "What are you talking about?"

"I'm talking about finding out your father isn't your father," I said. "Why? Have you been lying about something else too?"

I'd been waiting for the right time to bring it up, and this wasn't it, I knew that. It was probably the worst, but I hadn't planned it. It just popped out, and now it was too late to do anything about it.

"I'm talking about your deceased husband, the illustrious Derek Montague," I said. "Who's survived by his wife, Jeanette, and his sons Philip and Avery. In New Brunswick, Connecticut, if I'm not mistaken."

I heard her gasp. Her face looked thin and haggard and her knuckles were white from gripping the wheel.

"Aren't you going to ask me how I found out?" I asked, but she didn't answer so I went on. "I looked him up in the library the weekend Glenda and K.D. and I went to the city. I found a biographical sketch in an anthropological reference book.

"Imagine my surprise when I read that. I didn't know quite what to make of it, I can tell you. I still don't, actually."

She didn't say anything. It was so dark now I couldn't see the horizon anymore, and the earth and sky were completely indistinguishable.

"Well," I said. "Aren't you going to tell me who my father is? Is it really as bad as all that? Is he in prison or something?"

She shook her head deliberately and finally said, "No, nothing like that."

I practically had to pry the words out of her mouth. I waited for her to elaborate but she wasn't forthcoming.

"So, are you going to tell me who he is, or not?"

"I'm afraid I can't," she said flatly as though that put an end to it, but I wasn't going to let her off the hook that easily.

"What do you mean you can't?" I asked venomously.

"What do you think I mean?" she said. "I can't, that's all. I don't know who he was."

She turned and glared at me fiercely, and for a minute I was afraid she was going to drive us off the road.

"Look, I understand it was upsetting to find out the way you did, but that's all I'm going to say on the subject right now. I'm sorry about the whole thing, perpetrating a falsehood and such, but this is the night before my wedding and I'm not going to let you ruin it for me. You're going to have a father now, OK? For the first time in your life, a stepfather. Maybe it doesn't make up for this but it should mean something, and if it doesn't right away, well, it will in time. You're going to have to trust me on that. Now that's all I'm going to say about this."

We were both quiet for a minute. It was pretty much as I'd figured on the street corner in the Tenderloin, but it felt worse having it confirmed.

"Well, you sure know how to overcompensate," I said after a while. "Why did you bother cooking up that whole story? Why didn't you just tell me the truth in the first place?"

"It wasn't something I ever planned," she sighed. "It came about entirely by accident. When you were six years old you started asking a lot of questions about your father. You seemed to have an obsession with the subject. It was probably just a developmental stage, but it caught me totally off guard and I didn't know what to tell you. You may recall that I had impaired judgment about all kinds of things in those days, and it was probably the least of my mistakes. I thought you were too young to hear the truth. He had our same last name, and it was true that I named you after the Indians in his book, so one day I just came up with the story about Derek Montague and you liked it so much I never had the heart to tell you the truth after that. You needed a father figure, and I'm sorry, but that was the best I could come up with."

"A lie," I said, and she flinched.

"Yes," she said, "a lie. But a fortunate one, in a way. A constructive one, perhaps. You were always so serious, so good in school. I never had to get after you to study. You thrived on it. I thought it was all because of him, this fiction I had concocted. It seemed to do something for you."

"It's probably genetic," I said. "Besides, it's all gone now, isn't it?"

"Yes," she said. "But then you don't need him anymore either. Look at you. You're a budding artist, an avid photographer. You make practically straight A's. Who knows what you would have been like without him?"

"At least it would have been real," I said. "I don't know who I am anymore."

My eyes filled with tears. I saw her grimace and she looked at me sympathetically. Then she slowed down and made a sharp left turn into the church parking lot.

The church itself was an old-fashioned Spanish mission-style with a sloping red tile roof and a clock tower. The clock said ten after seven, and there was a quote from the Bible underneath it: "Son, heed the time and fly from evil." The quote was from Ecclesiasticus/Ben Sirach 4:20, which sounded like a book of the Bible although I didn't recognize it from Mineola when I'd memorized them all.

Ben and his friends were gathered on the steps talking. My mother and I sat in the car for a few minutes but neither of us had anything further to say, we'd basically finished our conversation, so we got out and joined them. Ben introduced us to his brother, Bucky, who was going to be the best man, and the priest,

Father Ignatius, a dour-looking man with a grizzled beard and iron-gray hair.

"The boys didn't come tonight," Ben told me. "They're just going to usher tomorrow, so there's nothing for them to do until the guests arrive."

"What's with you?" he asked Lilah. "You look like you've seen a ghost. Did you run into some spooks out on the road?"

"You might say that," she said. She was pale and wide-eyed and I probably didn't look much better.

I felt vaguely guilty about bringing it up the night before her wedding, but it wasn't exactly easy on me either when I found out in the city that time, so I tried not to feel too bad.

The interior of the church had a red tile floor and beamed ceiling and staggered tiers of votive candles flickered in front of three different altars. The crucifix on the wall looked like it was a hundred years old. It was small and primitive and the figure of Jesus was stylized and nonnaturalistic. He had ocher-colored skin and his head was turned to one side and his knees to the other. I always wondered why the Church had chosen the crucified rather than the risen Christ as its logo, although this one had a particular pathos about it that touched me, and maybe that's what they were after. I stared at it for a while and walked down the aisles studying the retablos and paintings depicting the Stations of the Cross.

I stopped in front of a large painting of the Virgin de Guadalupe surrounded by tongues of golden flames suspended against a turquoise sky. A vase of nasturtiums and geraniums rested on the altar below it. I dropped some coins into a metal box and lit a couple of the votive candles. I tried to discharge some of the tension I felt from our talk in the car and whispered a prayer for protection, sanctuary, and safe harbor in our new home.

My mother had been meeting with Father Ignatius on Saturday mornings for the past several months in preparation for being married in the Catholic Church, and occasionally she passed his words of wisdom on to me. She said the Catholic Bible was more comprehensive than the Protestant one, including the Apocrypha, and I figured the reference on the church tower must be to one of them. I was never clear on the exact distinctions between Protestantism and Catholicism, except for the belief in the Virgin Mary. I had a limited exposure to the Catholic Church while I was at Mrs. Gannett's and it never occurred to me that *the Bible itself* would be different. It made me feel even more at sea, as if I was entering a world that played by a new set of rules and I had no way of even knowing what they were.

I joined Ben and my mother and Father Ignatius at the altar and we went through the service relatively quickly. I'd never even been to a wedding before, let alone been in one, but my part was small and easy to master. My mother looked at me hard when Father Ignatius called for anyone with an objection to speak or forever hold their peace, but she didn't have to worry. I wasn't going to make trouble—I'd already said my piece in the car. The ceremony began and ended with the organist playing and when it was over, I went out and stood in the foyer with Lester Ferguson and a man in a soft-brimmed hat. Then my mother came out and told me she could take me to my party.

It was after nine by the time we got to Sylvia's and "Black Magic Woman" was blaring out of the windows. I opened the front door and bumped into a guy with a stocking over his head and his face squished in like Jack the Ripper. In the front hallway a couple of Hells Angels types stood talking to some kids that looked like they were straight out of a Special Ed class. I don't think they were wearing makeup, and I didn't know Sylvia very well, but I couldn't figure out what they were doing there or where she would know them from. The door clicked shut behind me and I shivered, because I got a sudden flash that everything was going to be ugly and out of sync like this from here on out.

I looked around but didn't see anyone I knew. Fish skeletons dangled from the ceiling and a coiled plastic snake was glued to the mirror over the fireplace. A pig's head with an apple in its mouth lay on a platter in the center of the refreshment table, and a fish head floated in a bowl of chartreuse green punch. I ate a few Cheetos out of a stainless steel bowl. The whole place appeared to have been decorated with fiendish delight and looked like a Hieronymus Bosch vision of hell.

"Take Me to the River" was belting out of the giant speakers in the living room. There were only a few couples on the dance floor and I leaned against the wall and watched them. In front of me, a belly dancer was dancing with a guy wearing a three-cornered hat and powdered wig. I guess he was supposed to be Thomas Jefferson or some early-American type. It must have been a full minute before I recognized them as Glenda and Kevin. After that, I tried to get away before Glenda noticed me. In my hurry I bumped into a guy wearing a black mask, a yellow chamois cowboy shirt, and a Stetson hat.

"Whoa," he said gripping me by the shoulders. "Not so fast. Where do you think you're going, little lady?"

"How about a dance?" he asked. His big topaz eyes smiled at me from behind his mask and I nodded my head.

"The Tracks of My Tears" was playing when we got out on the floor. Glenda caught sight of me, but I didn't care anymore. I just didn't want her to see me standing around like a wallflower.

"What's the matter?" my partner asked. "You look like you've just lost your best friend."

I did a double take at his perceptiveness and felt as if I was caught in an instant feedback loop.

"You might say that," I said.

When the song was over, I saw that K.D. and Jane had arrived and went over to join them.

"Who was that?" Jane asked and I shrugged.

"I don't know," I said. "The Lone Ranger, I guess. Who do you think? Maybe Gene Autrey?"

K.D. was dressed as Marie Antoinette in a pale blue silk dress and powdered wig and was holding a sequined harlequin mask on a stick. Jane was wearing a green turban, a blue leotard, and a red felt skirt and was probably supposed to be a fortune-teller. She looked like she'd just thrown something together at the last minute like I had.

"Have you ever seen anything like this place?" K.D. asked enthusiastically. "They must have been decorating it for a month. Have you been out in the backyard? There's a whole cemetery out there with tombstones and everything. You should go see. One of them might even have your name on it."

"It's like hell, this place," I said shuddering.

"Hell Night," Jane smiled.

"Hell Night?" I repeated.

"Yeah," Jane said. "You know, like when you get initiated into a sorority or a fraternity? Adelphi, Adelphos. That's what they called the initiates in the Eleusinian Mysteries."

A shadow played over Jane's face and I couldn't read her expression. I didn't know what she was talking about, because this wasn't a sorority party, at least not as far as I knew.

"Have you had any of the punch?" K.D. asked. "There's a rumor going around it's been spiked with Windowpane."

"Not that I remember," I said. "But it would explain a lot if I had."

"Doesn't Glenda look like a million bucks?" Jane asked smiling. "It must be fun having a nice, handsome boyfriend like that."

"Is that your bridesmaid dress?" K.D. asked and I nodded.

"'Always the bridesmaid, never the bride,'" Jane tittered.

"You know, someone could think your outfit was sort of racist," K.D. said. "With the eye makeup and all.'

"Maybe so," I said. "But I didn't mean it that way."

Jane's eyes were a luminous green like the punch and she leaned close and whispered, "No rest for the wicked," and I gave her a sharp look. Her eyelids flickered as if she was going into a trance, and I didn't know what she was getting at, Jane was so weird. I was about to answer when I looked up and the Lone Ranger stood in front of me again. I hadn't expected to see him again this soon.

"I was wondering if I could have this dance?" he asked. He held out a yellow-gloved hand, and I followed him onto the floor. It felt like the second time that evening he'd showed up in time to rescue me from something.

"That's a nice dress," he said. "I've been trying to figure out who you're supposed to be. Susie Wong? Or maybe Madame Nhu?"

"I hadn't thought about it," I said. "But you can call me Tonto, if you like."

I didn't mean it as a come on—I don't know what I meant. It was just one of those off-the-wall things you say without thinking. But I guess it was, because his arm began to tighten around my waist and his lips brushed my forehead and he whispered in my ear, and the next thing I knew he was trying to make out on the dance floor. And I thought, Whoa, who is this jerk? Because he was OK for a while but this was going too far, and I was just about to push him away when I looked up and saw Glenda and Kevin dancing cheek to cheek. I felt a sudden stab of jealousy, and after that I just let it happen.

He pulled me off the dance floor and over to a corner of the room. I didn't know what was going on, but his mouth was wet and it surprised me how good it felt, and I decided I didn't mind anymore and not to fight it. I craned my neck up so he could kiss me. His tongue was in my mouth, and he unbuttoned the frogs on my dress and lightly touched my breast.

"Come on," he said breathing heavily. "Let's go upstairs."

I stiffened.

"Come on," he repeated. His voice was low and husky, and I felt the warm pressure of his body leaning into mine. I whispered, "No," and pushed him away, but he pressed back against me. In the background I thought K.D. and Jane might be watching, and then I thought, why not? It was almost a separate voice I heard saying it. Because for all I knew, this was how I had been conceived myself, some funky scene like this, so what difference did it make? I thought of Jane's "No rest for the wicked," and I didn't care, because it wasn't as if I had anything to live up to anymore. It sounded like my mother was a bit of a slut when she was my age, so it was in my gene pool anyway. The Whore of Babylon, just like my grandmother said. It was the perfect place for me to lose my virginity and I don't know why I was hesitating for a minute. I let him guide me out into the hall and we made our way upstairs, past clusters of people talking in the stairwell.

We went into an upstairs bedroom with athletic pennants on one wall and bunk beds against the other. It looked like a kid's room and I figured it must be one of Sylvia's brothers'. I don't know how she'd gotten rid of everyone for the evening, but I hoped they wouldn't come back unexpectedly. The Lone Ranger sat down on the lower bunk and unzipped the back of my dress and pulled me down onto the bed next to him. I'd barely even made out with anyone before except Terry Taylor back in the tenth grade and there was a part of me that was distanced and removed watching myself specter-like from the ceiling. He had his boots and mask off and wriggled out of his jeans and his T-shirt and writhed on top of me in nothing but his jockey shorts. His breath was warm, and his cock pressed into my crotch. His tongue was in my mouth and his hand slid under my dress and up my thigh. He was breathing heavily and now I started getting excited too. In spite of the circumstances, I was warming up pretty quickly.

Someone knocked on the door. We ignored them and I thought they would eventually stop and go away. Instead, they hammered louder and turned the doorknob and I finally recognized K.D.'s voice calling my name.

"Miami," she said. "Are you in there? My mom's here and we've been looking all over for you. Come on, if you still want a ride. It's almost one o'clock."

It was hard to extricate myself from the warmth of the guy's embrace but I looked at my watch and came to my senses. I looked from the Lone Ranger to the door and wriggled out from underneath him, tumbling onto the floor.

"OK," I called to K.D. "I'm coming. I'll be right with you."

"I've got to get dressed," I told the Lone Ranger. "That's my ride leaving."

"Please don't go," he whispered. He was still breathing heavily and caught hold of my wrist. "I'll give you a ride home later. I've got a car."

"That's OK," I said. "I've got to go now. Really."

I struggled with my dress and he had his mask off now, but it was so dark I couldn't see his features.

"I wish you weren't leaving," he said. "I'd like to see you again."

"Yeah," I said. "That would be nice. I'd like to see you too."

I wrote my name and phone number on a piece of paper and gave it to him.

"We're going to be moving," I told him. "But the phone company can give you our new number. I don't know it yet."

I kissed him goodbye and blinked into the bright lights of the hallway. K.D.'s wig was off and she looked ghostly in her white makeup with her damp hair matted down.

"Who is that in there?" she whispered. "Is it that guy?"

I nodded and she gave me a funny look and turned, and I clattered down the stairs behind her and grabbed my coat from a pile on a chair by the door. The Rambler in the driveway had its engine running, and I figured Mrs. Quinn was behind the wheel because that's what K.D. had said, but it turned out to be Brian instead. I hadn't seen Brian in at least a year, and he looked completely different with short hair and a beard. It was a shock to see him, and I didn't know why it had to be now exactly, and I flashed momentarily on the quote on the church tower.

"Brian," I said. "What are you doing home from school?"

"Hi, Miami," he smiled at me. "What's doin'?"

"Not much," I said. I was so stunned I didn't know what to say.

"What are you kidding me or something?" he said. "I hear your mom's getting married and you're going to be moving tomorrow. Why do you go and say that?"

"I don't know," I said. "I guess I'm pretty underwhelmed by the whole thing. How are you? How do you like Chico State?"

"I love it!" he said. "I'm signed up as an Econ major, and living in a house with a bunch of people over in Paradise. There's a big spiritual community up there and I'm part of Victory Outreach trying to draw in new members all the time and teaching Sunday school."

I muttered, "Whoopdedo," softly enough to make sure that neither of them heard me. I remembered the flurry of excitement during the period when I'd been in the Jesus freaks myself and reflected on how far apart Brian and I had grown since then. For all his sacrosanct talk, he hadn't mentioned doing anything that really helped anybody, and it all sounded like vain proselytizing to me. I'd had high hopes down by the river bank that day, but I'd come a long way since then, and for all I knew, they were a bunch of anti-abortionists with a right-wing agenda like a lot of other Christians.

I sat in the back seat with the window open and the air blowing in my face, and we rode in silence until Brian asked how the party was. K.D. shrugged and said it was OK—the decorations were the best part. My cheeks were chafed from the stubble on the guy's chin and there was a musky smell of sweat and cologne in my hair, and I realized with a start that I didn't even know his name. It had been an off-the-cuff encounter—needy and on the rebound from Kevin. I hadn't been able to see what he looked like in the dark. I only knew that I had been attracted to him, and he was nice and his comment about losing my best friend was uncannily sensitive, and I hoped to hear from him again.

CHAPTER 18

My period started the next morning accompanied by cramps, and I slouched in my seat on the way to the church. I'd only gotten four hours of sleep when my mother woke me up, and there was no coffee because everything was packed and gone. We closed up the house and I turned for one last look as we drove off. It looked at once cozy and forlorn, a little beige bungalow nestled behind the beds of pyracantha.

We were the only car on the road and Lilah drove faster than usual, straddling the centerline. She wore a trench coat over her wedding dress, and her bouquet of lilies of the valley lay on the seat next to her. She had chosen them as a symbol of purity, which was a bit of a joke in the light of what she'd told me last night. Mine was a nosegay of forget-me-nots from our garden. The back seat was stacked with gladioli, lilies, chrysanthemums, and birds of paradise. She'd denuded the backyard to provide bouquets for the altar and the reception. We didn't talk much on the way over, and I figured she was probably still mad at me. She asked about the party and I said it was fine, and that was about it. I was doing a great job of alienating my support—first Glenda, now her.

She pulled into the parking lot across the street from the church and we went into a white stucco Italian restaurant where the reception was to be held. The jukebox was playing "Blueberry Hill," and we crossed the bar and went upstairs to a private room. Card tables circled the brown linoleum dance floor and there was a bandstand in the corner and a solid bank of windows against one wall. Clouds raced by and the sky looked twice as big as usual. It felt like something momentous was going to happen, like the water was going to break and the horizon was about to give birth to some whole new phenomenon.

I attached the wide-angle lens and framed a couple of shots but didn't take them. I had a feeling *I* would be in the picture this time and someone else would be taking them. I heard what sounded like a shutter click and turned around, but it was just the door closing behind the women from the kitchen with the plates and glassware to set the tables.

The parking lot across the street was beginning to fill and my mother and I headed over and slipped in the back of the church. It was about two-thirds full. Jason and Cal stood in the center aisle, and Jason waved when he saw me. I figured the tall guy on the far aisle must be Marvin. He had a ruddy complexion and brown hair brushed back from the side of his face in little wings. He was good looking but I was drawn by something familiar about him that I couldn't place, and he looked back at me just as hard. Meanwhile, my mother pulled on my arm that it was time to go forward as the organist started playing.

Bucky and Lester Ferguson and Hector Lopez were already at the altar with Ben and Father Ignatius. Ben wore a charcoal suit with a light-gray stripe going through it, and he looked handsome and distinguished with his weathered face and bright blue eyes. He looked like one of the Founding Fathers.

If I ever got married I would have the wedding out in nature somewhere, some Robin Hood/Maid Marion affair, with harps and homemade mead. The bridesmaids would wear velvet dresses and cloaks of emerald, ruby, sapphire, and amber, and light bonfires on the surrounding peaks in synchronized succession. At the appointed time, I would arrive bareback on a roan steed wearing an ivory satin dress. My groom would be waiting for me under a spreading oak where the ceremony would take place. Afterward, general carousing and merrymaking would last the weekend.

The only part of my mother's ceremony that departed from tradition was that I was the one that gave her away. I was father, bridesmaid, and flower girl all rolled into one. When Father Ignatius asked if there were any objections, I looked briefly at Marvin and was shocked to find him staring back at me with a fire in his eyes that took my breath away. I gave my mother Ben's ring and Bucky handed Lilah's to Ben and they exchanged their vows—"To love and to cherish, forsaking all others. For better or for worse, in sickness and in health, for richer or for poorer, till death do us part." They entwined their fingers and looked into each other's eyes with an expression of joy and sincerity, and it was impossible not to be moved. Then he lifted her veil and kissed her. Father Ignatius gave the Benediction and the Blessing and the organist started playing again and before I knew it, it was over.

Things started to get busy for me after that, because I was the official wedding photographer, my first paid assignment. I took a shot of the pile of hats on the church porch. Then I positioned myself at the bottom of the steps to get pictures of everyone coming out the door. They must have been the worst shots I'd ever taken in my life, but my mother said she just wanted straight pictures, nothing artistic. This was probably how I would be making my living one of these days, so I figured I might as well get used to it.

I got a picture of my mother throwing her bouquet. One of the boys' friends reached out and caught it, and then they started horsing around, tossing it amongst themselves before finally throwing it to one of their girlfriends. I lugged my tripod out of the car and took pictures of the reception line. I took a bunch of posed shots of Lilah and Ben; Lilah, Ben, and Father Ignatius; and Lilah, Ben, Bucky, and Lester Ferguson. Then I took some pictures of the boys mugging, arm in arm in their white tuxedo jackets.

I tried to get a reading of what the Beasley's friends were like, but they didn't seem to fall into any one category. There were couples in shiny polyester suits as well as grungy trailer trash types and big Mexican families with kids dressed to the nines, the little girls carrying flowers. I saw some of our neighbors from La Grange—the Bethlewaites, the Sandhursts, and Toby Taccone, as well as Agnes, Mabel, and Inez, my mother's friends from Yarborough's.

I'd taken maybe forty-five shots when K.D.'s face appeared in the center of the frame. She stepped out of range and ran down the stairs and the next thing I knew she was standing next to me and Jane was smiling behind her. Jane wore a peach taffeta dress with puff sleeves in the style of a flapper from the twenties, and K.D. was wearing a brown chiffon evening dress and brown velvet headband.

"Hey, old buddy, long time no see," K.D. said. "How are you? Do you feel any different or anything?"

"Not really," I said. "I wasn't the one getting married, after all. At least as far as I know, anyway. I could use some coffee, though. We got up at seven."

Jane noticed me looking around for Glenda and smiled apologetically.

"Glenda couldn't make it," she said. "She said she had too much fun at the party last night and was totally wasted this morning."

I shrugged it off but it still hurt my feelings. The "too much fun" was probably a reference to me at Denise's, and it looked like there was going to be hell to pay over that outburst. Jane was too polite to say "I told you so" or ask if I'd ever apologized.

The Beasley boys were hanging out in the parking lot. Jason had his foot on the fender of an old salmon-colored Cadillac, and Marvin and Cal leaned against the church and stared back at us. Marvin looked somewhat hostile so I figured he was still pissed about the wedding.

"So those are your stepbrothers?" K.D. asked and I nodded.

I was going to take my friends over and introduce them, but the boys didn't smile or seem friendly, so we bypassed them and headed for D'Anuzzio's by ourselves.

I took more pictures at the reception. The only interesting ones were of a couple of albino-looking kids playing in the corner. After a while the boys came in and sat at a card table on the other side of the room. Marvin had his tie off and draped one arm over the back of Jason's chair. He was drinking a glass of wine and a smile hummed around the corners of his mouth and his face was flushed. He had a dark complexion and in spite of myself I got a little thrill when I looked at him.

I took three shots of the serving table. There was a lasagna casserole, garlic bread, a platter of cold poached salmon, a scored ham studded with cloves, potato salad, green salad, tomato aspic, three-bean salad, deviled eggs, artichoke hearts, fruit salad, and pitchers of iced tea, lemonade, and cranberry nectar, and carafes of red and white wine. I didn't think I'd ever seen so much food in one place in my life, and my mouth was watering by the time I joined K.D. and Jane in line. I loaded my plate with vegetarian lasagna, three-bean salad, and artichoke hearts, and led my friends over to my stepbrothers' table.

"Mind if we join you?" I asked and Jason gestured toward a couple of empty chairs.

"Hi," I said to Marvin. "I'm Miami. I don't think we've met before."

Marvin had a bemused, supercilious expression on his face and completely ignored me.

"This is K.D.," I said. "K period, D period. She's a friend from Alamo, and this is Jane. These are my stepbrothers Jason, Marvin, and Cal."

Marvin grunted inaudibly, Jason passed his hand across his face in a long fade-out wave, and Cal got up and made an exaggerated courtly bow.

"So are you like her?" Cal asked K.D. "A camera freak and you make really good grades?"

"What makes you think I make good grades?" I said, because I knew Cal didn't think I was smart. He was implying I was a grind.

"Am I wrong?" Cal asked. "Don't you make good grades?"

K.D. nodded her head and laughed.

"Bingo," she said. "No, I'm not into cameras. I play the viola and like to draw."

Marvin tipped his chair back and looked over our heads at the rest of the party. I thought when I finally got together with Marvin, we'd go crazy talking about photography. His picture from the County Fair was great, so I figured he would be pretty amazing, but now I didn't know what to make of him. He'd seen me taking all these pictures and my camera was sitting on the table and he didn't even mention it. I didn't know where his camera was or why he wasn't taking any himself, and I finally realized he was totally drunk. I still remembered the putrid taste in my mouth from my binge at Denise's party, and I wasn't touching the wine myself. Besides, I didn't have any more friends I could spare.

"Jane is an astrologer," I said.

"Maybe you can do my chart for me some time," Jason said.

"I'd be happy to," she said. "Off the cuff, I would guess Aquarius with Taurus in the ascendant."

Cal and Jason raised their eyebrows.

"That's pretty good," Jason said. "I don't know my ascendant, but you're right about being an Aquarius. February 2 at 6:30 a.m. How did you know?"

"Well," Jane said. "You have the light blue eyes of a lot of air signs, a high forehead, which is a standard for intellect, and sloping shoulders like you're carrying something, which is why I selected Aquarius. Also, you're fairly short with a low center of gravity—that's where I got the Taurus ascendant."

"'Beyond the obvious fact that you are a bachelor, a solicitor, a Freemason, and an asthmatic, I know nothing whatever about you,'" I said.

"Who's that?" Jason asked. "Sherlock Holmes?"

I nodded.

"Observant," Cal said. "Want to take a stab at mine?"

"Sagittarius," Jane said promptly.

Cal and Jason smiled at each other and I knew Jane had nailed it again.

"That horse face," Jason said. "How true. It's written all over him. Not to mention a bit of a satyr."

"Two out of two," Cal said. "A perfect score. Maybe you can do my chart sometime too."

"So what are you guys' interests?" K.D. asked.

"Actually, we're heavily into methamphetamine," Jason said and there was a ripple of laughter.

"No, I'm serious," he went on. "We've got a lab set up in a shed in the backyard. Dad made us take it out of the house after the explosion. We've got Dad running the stuff to the teenyboppers at Alvarado Middle School. As the football coach, he's got one hell of a cover. Our biggest fear about these two moving in is that they're going to shut us down and end our discretionary income. That's why Marvin here is in a blue funk, ain't you, Sport?"

Marvin barely grunted again.

"He's an expert on Kennedy assassination conspiracy theories," Cal said gesturing to Jason. "He's like a terrier with it."

"Ditto," I said pointing to Jane, and the two of them smiled knowingly at each other.

On the other side of the room, Ben and Lilah were cutting the wedding cake. It was a classic moment and I went over to document it. It was a three-tiered angel's food cake with lemon frosting decorated with crystallized pansies, violets, and nasturtiums. Lilah's veil was pulled back off her face and she looked flushed and pretty. She'd been to the beauty parlor and her hair was styled and sleek.

"It's going to be different having her for a mother," Jason said.

"She's OK," I said. "I'm sorry about your mother. She's dead, right?"

"Yeah, well, we're all sorry about her," Cal said. "Yeah, she's dead. But it's not that different than when she was around, somehow.

"She was kind of out of it," Jason said to me.

"She was a drunk is what she was," Cal said levelly.

Marvin pushed his chair back from the table and stood up, his face flushed with drink.

"What do you want?" Marvin said. "She knocked herself out for us, cooking and scrubbing and cleaning the house. I don't believe you're sitting there talking about her like that. Where's your sense of appreciation? She was our mother after all. Have a little respect."

"Sorry, pal," Cal said. "You make her sound like fuckin' Cinderella. Yeah, I guess she cleaned the house pretty good. I just never thought she was that affectionate, that's all."

"Why should she have been affectionate to you?" Marvin leered at him. "Listen to you. The way you're talking about her."

"The favorite," Cal said to me. "The mama's boy."

Marvin glared at Cal. He was all worked up and I wondered what he was going to say next, but he just sat down and shut himself up with another glass of wine.

"Maybe you should watch it with the booze, you know," Cal muttered but Marvin ignored him and slugged it down.

K.D. glanced at Marvin and rolled her eyes at me like, this guy's a real jerk. I didn't know what to think because I'd never had a real family before, and I was surprised at how fierce their loyalties were. Housekeeping didn't look like it had been high on their mother's agenda from what I had seen, but I knew enough to stay out of it.

A three-piece band started playing the theme song from *Casablanca*, and Ben and Lilah were the only ones on the dance floor. They barely moved and looked like they were embracing as much as anything else. The train of Lilah's dress was hiked over her arm and she leaned her head against Ben's cheek. Gradually a few other couples joined them. I got up to take a few pictures and when I got back to the table, Marvin was still putting them away like Bogie in the movie.

"You look familiar to me somehow," I said finally. "Could I have met you somewhere before?"

"Yeah," he said drawing on a cigarette. "You look familiar to me too. You didn't by any chance go to a party last night in Centenaur, did you?"

His question caught me off guard and I blushed. He'd been avoiding me all afternoon but now he stared at me so intently, it was hard to break his gaze.

"Yes, as a matter of fact I did," I said slowly, holding my breath. "Where do you know Sylvia Hamlin from?"

"I think you were wearing that same dress in fact," he said.

"Oh, yeah?" I said, a generalized panic mounting in my chest. "Well, I don't remember *you*."

"Why would you?" he said. "It was a costume party, wasn't it? You might not even recognize me."

He pulled his chair upright and leaned forward so close his cheek grazed mine.

"Who was that masked man?" he whispered into my ear and I caught the sour smell of wine on his breath.

He didn't take his eyes off me, and now I recognized them from the night before peering at me through the mask like golden topaz. Jason and Jane were analyzing the Zapruder footage of the assassination, and K.D. was watching the dancers, and I don't think any of them heard him. There was a hubbub across the room and the band started playing "Strangers in the Night." I sat stiff and rigid in my chair, barely breathing. There was a tap on my shoulder and I looked up and Ben stood in front of me.

"May I have this dance?" he asked. Then he looked over at Marvin. "Or are you otherwise engaged?"

I didn't think I would be able to move but I watched myself get up and follow Ben out on the floor. My feet were like blocks of ice and my palms were sweaty.

"Well, how are the boys treating you?" he asked. "This is the first time you've met Marvin, isn't it? He's really something, isn't he?"

I nodded.

"I give him a hard time sometimes, but I'm really proud of him. He's the show horse of the family. My beautiful boy."

At the moment it was hard to put that together with the guy getting soused at the table even though I knew why he was drinking heavily. Ben's eyes were like blowtorches and it felt like he could see right through me. Over his shoulder, Marvin watched us from the table.

"Welcome to the family," Ben said in a low gravely voice and leaned over and kissed me on the cheek. He was trying to be fatherly and welcoming, but it gave me a chill and reminded me of *The Godfather*, and for a minute I felt like I was being initiated into La Cosa Nostra. He led me over to the refreshment table and cut a piece of cake and poured a glass of wine.

"Here," he said feeding me a bite of cake on a fork. "An old family tradition."

The cake and wine were like ash in my mouth and I could barely swallow. Back at the table Marvin picked up my camera and took a picture of us. I couldn't imagine what I looked like; I must look like hell. K.D. was up dancing with Cal and the band started playing an Italian polka. Ben thanked me for the dance and I walked back to the table. I couldn't believe I was actually going back there but I didn't know what else to do. It wasn't exactly like I had anywhere I could go.

CHAPTER 19

Marvin kept downing Dixie cups of wine and smoking cigarettes with the same goofy smile on his face, and I glared at him because I didn't see what he had to smile about. I didn't see anything funny in the situation, except that if I was as drunk as he was I might, so maybe he had the right idea after all.

The skin was stretched tight across Jason's cheekbones and he looked like a skull grinning back at me across the table, and with a jolt I remembered it was the Day of the Dead. Cal had his pocketknife out and snapped it open and shut like a nervous tic, till Marvin told him it was getting on his nerves. Jason pulled out a deck of cards and I thought, I don't believe this. I'm going to have to sit here and play cards with these guys just like nothing ever happened. But he didn't deal us in after all, so we sat and watched them play Blackjack for loose change. Marvin's judgment was mightily impaired and he was losing big-time till they finally wiped him out completely.

"Did you know her father was an anthropologist?" Jason said to Marvin. "Didn't you say he wrote a book or something?"

I didn't answer, but K.D. nodded her head emphatically and

said, "Yeah, *Indian Tribes of the Miami Confederacy*. Isn't that what it's called? He was supposedly a brilliant man."

It was probably the first time in recorded history I hadn't carried on like a ninny about my father, and K.D. looked like she didn't know what to make of it. By her reaction, I got an idea of what an idiot I'd been and what they'd had to put up with all along.

"Well, I cleared out of your room yesterday," Jason told me. "It's not exactly spotless, but it's better than it was."

"You had to give up your room for me?" I said. "I didn't know that. Thanks. I was wondering which room I would have."

"We thought of putting you down in the coal bin," Cal said. "but decided against it."

Jason smiled.

"It's not that big a deal," he said. "Besides, it'll give me a chance to get to know my big brother better. Right, Cal?"

He elbowed Cal in the ribs and Cal glared at him and said gruffly, "Yeah, right."

"Although you're going to have to find someplace else for your band practice now."

Cal rolled his eyes like it was another in a long series of accommodations.

"What's the band?" K.D. asked.

"Just some friends of mine get together to play rock 'n' roll at parties and dances occasionally. No big deal."

"Do you have a name?"

"The Rainmakers."

"I had a feeling there was more to you guys than crystal meth," K.D. said smiling slyly.

"You'd never know it from watching him, though, would you?" Cal asked, gesturing to Marvin.

The reception was winding down and the guests were beginning to leave. The empty tables were covered with crumpled paper napkins and paper cups. In the corner, a little girl ground lasagna into the floor with the heel of her black Mary Jane.

"Goodbye, Miami, dear," Mrs. Quinn said in a singsong voice when she came over. "I've told your mother, it was a beautiful wedding, one of the nicest I've seen."

Her father patted me on the shoulder and said he was confident he was leaving me in good hands with these fine looking young stepbrothers.

"I'm going to miss you," K.D. said. "Come back and visit soon and I'll come over to see you too. Your brothers are really neat. It's going to be good."

I nodded but I was like a stick; I couldn't say anything. She was cheerful and clueless and made me feel that much more far gone by comparison. She handed me a present but her face crumpled as she caught my expression.

"Keep in touch," Jane said. "Call us."

Then she disappeared down the stairwell after K.D. and her parents.

When it was time to go, Ben and Lilah came over to the table, and she chucked me under the chin, and put her arm around me, and kissed me playfully on the nose. She was clearly in her element. I got in the car with her and Ben, and the boys piled in Marvin's Cadillac and it swerved and backfired out of the lot. He'd had way too much to drink to be driving, but it wasn't my place to say anything. In my present mood, I couldn't have cared less if he smashed the car into a telephone pole. It would have taken some of the pressure off me.

The dogs ran up to us when we got to the house, and I had to push them away to keep them from ruining my dress. Carton boxes and moving crates were stacked everywhere, and our furniture was mixed haphazardly with theirs. Their furniture was a boxy style from the fifties with squared off armrests and end tables, and it would be interesting to see how it blended with my mother's antiques.

I sat down on one of the sofas and looked at the boys' athletic trophies lined up on the mantle.

"Well, it's all over now," Ben said. "And we can just relax and unwind. It was fun, though, wasn't it? Did you have a good time?"

I nodded and tried to smile.

"How about all that food? It was something, wasn't it? They pretty near cleaned us out, although that's what it was there for. Boy oh boy, we'll be paying for that for some time. Oh, well, you only live once. After all, how many times does a person get married in this life?"

"I guess that's one of those things you never know," I said.

"Well, it's the second time for me, but I've no hesitation it'll be the last. I can't decide which of these we'll keep," he said, pointing to the two sofas. "Maybe we'll just keep them both. After all, there's almost twice as many of us now."

"Not really," I said. "There were four of you here—five when your wife was alive—now there's six of us."

"You kids are so smart," Ben said. "I don't know what we'd do without you. Just blunder through, I guess."

Ben tussled with the dogs and they leveled their heads with their paws and growled playfully.

"Good dogs," he said. "Donner, Blitzen. Don't be afraid of them, Miami. They won't hurt you. They're hunting dogs, you know. In Norse mythology, they lead the souls of the departed heroes across the river into Valhalla."

The dogs sat back on their haunches panting. With their

long tongues hanging out of their mouths and their pointed teeth, they looked completely ghoulish and reminded me of Mrs. Gannett's rottweilers.

"Come on," Ben said. "Let me show you up to your room. I spent most of yesterday installing bookshelves for you. I thought you could use them after I saw all those boxes of books."

"You should have seen all the ones I gave away," I said. "We don't have to go up there now, though. I'll find my way up later."

"Suit yourself," Ben said, sitting back down. "So you like to read. What do you read?"

"Just about anything," I said. "Twentieth-century poetry and novels, mostly, and of course mysteries."

"Mysteries, huh? Which ones?"

"Oh, the usual," I said. "Agatha Christie, Ngaio Marsh, Marjorie Allingham, Dick Francis, and Raymond Chandler."

"Not Dashiell Hammett?" he asked.

"I'll read him but he doesn't really do anything for me," I said. "He sounds like he was a wonderful man, though."

"*The Maltese Falcon* was always one of my favorites. Sam Spade and Brigid O'Shaughnessy. I love it when he turns her in at the end and says he'll be there waiting for her when she gets out. Now that's wry humor. It made one hell of a movie, too."

"Ever try Rex Stout?" Ben asked and I shook my head. "I like him sometimes. Nero Wolf is his detective. I'll pass some on to you."

He looked at his watch and then he called upstairs. "Come on, Lilah, aren't you ready yet? I want to get going."

"I'll be down in a minute," she called back.

"Our honeymoon," he said to me and winked.

I half heard it and half didn't. I got up and looked at the

photograph of the Grand Canyon on the calendar. It was the usual staggering vista in vermilion, gray, terracotta, and pink.

"I wonder where those boys are," Ben said. "I guess they just went off somewhere."

I imagined the boys parked out in the woods, their long legs sticking out of the windows of the pink car, popping beer cans while Marvin entertained them with the story of the party at Sylvia Hamlin's, and they all had a good laugh about it.

I heard the click of my mother's high heels in the hall and she came in wearing a tomato red suit and a cream-colored silk blouse I'd never seen before.

"Well," Ben said getting up. "I hate to leave you alone here your first night, but the boys should be back soon. I guess I should have told them to come right home, but it never occurred to me they'd go off somewhere."

"Where are you two going?" I asked.

They stood in the doorway. Ben held her overnight bag and a bottle of champagne.

"On our honeymoon," Ben said. "Like I told you."

"Honeymoon?" I repeated. "Nobody said anything about a honeymoon. What are you talking about?"

They exchanged glances and Ben raised his eyebrows.

"I'm sorry, Honey," Lilah said to me. "Don't you remember I told you yesterday? We're not really going away. It's not like we're going to Hawaii or anything. It's just an overnight to the Holiday Inn in Modesto. We'll be back tomorrow afternoon before dinner."

"It'll be nice," Ben said. "You can have the place to yourself for a while, and then the boys'll be back and you'll have a chance to get to know them better. They'll take you to school in the morning and show you the ropes and the whole works."

I already knew one of my stepbrothers a lot better than they would want me to, only I couldn't tell them that. I didn't think I could physically get the words out of my mouth if I tried.

After they left, I went upstairs to find my room. It was the small one at the end of the hall and my furniture from La Grange had been arranged inside. Ben had assembled four bracketed bookshelves on one wall and my desk fit neatly underneath. Other than that, I thought it was a dismal little room. The walls were painted an institutional green like a mental hospital, and the only window in the room looked out on a utility pole with a "Danger: High Voltage" sign hanging from it.

I sat on the edge of my bed and opened the present K.D. had given me. It was a pen and ink drawing in her signature cubist style of a man grimacing, with one arm bent over his head, bordered by the questions: "Who are we? Where do we come from? Where are we going?" She had set it in a simple black frame. The card said, "Tomorrow is the first day of the rest of your life," under a photo of a beachscape and she'd written, "I hope you'll be happy with your new family" inside.

I looked at the drawing for a while and then pulled out the book containing "Goblin Market" Ms. Richmond had given me, but I didn't have the energy to read, and the book sat on my lap. I closed my eyes and tried going to my power place to change my mental imagery. I don't know that I accomplished anything, because I wasn't able to summon the picture of the hummingbirds that I wanted, but at least I might have kept my mood from deteriorating further. I must have sat like that for a couple of hours. Then I lay down and pulled the blankets over me. I didn't bother putting sheets on the bed. I didn't think I was going to be able to sleep, but I must have dozed off, because the next thing I knew, the front door slammed and the boys were back and I heard them tromping through the kitchen.

They came upstairs and I thought they were going to bed, but I heard them shuffling and muttering outside my door. The doorknob turned and I held my breath and thought, Shit, they're actually trying to break in here! Jason let out a high-pitched giggle like a girl, and then I knew for sure that Marvin had told them, that slime. I was afraid of that when I saw them drive away from the restaurant together, but it was so fucked, it was still hard to believe he'd actually done it. I lay perfectly still and watched the doorknob turn again but the door didn't open. There were more muffled noises in the hall, and then they must have gone off to bed.

Outside a siren blared and my heart pounded so hard my pulse filled the room. I was in shock and didn't understand why this was happening to me. They hadn't gotten in but the fact that they tried was almost as bad. I lay on the bed and felt small and twisted and misshapen, like one of Arbus's freaks and remembered her quote about them having been born with their trauma. It felt like mine had just tried to force its way into the room. Ms. Richmond and her warnings had not been for nothing, it turned out. I must have violated some fundamental principle of the universe and now the sky had come crashing down on me.

I still couldn't figure out what I'd done to deserve this. I remembered my apprehension about the quote on the church, and I wondered if it was some kind of Catholic thing. The siren faded and I looked around the room. My boxes and suitcases stood out in grim relief, and it was hard to imagine how I would ever be able to pick up the pieces from so much rubble and ruin. It was hard to fathom doing anything at all.

It wasn't a Catholic thing, I realized. There was nothing remotely esoteric about it. I had trespassed the most basic, fundamental principles, and violated my own core beliefs. I'd really gone for the jugular in my competition with Glenda over *The Record.* My competitive streak had always been my downfall—my Watergate and my Waterloo. Then I'd gotten foul mouthed and unpleasant about Kevin, thoroughly alienating Glenda so she hadn't even come to the wedding. On the rebound from Kevin, I'd thrown myself into the make-out session at the party, probably also motivated by sexual insecurity after the trip to San Francisco. I jumped the gun with Marvin rather than waiting for a genuine romantic opportunity to present itself, and it had blown up in my face, destroying any chance of an easy relationship with the boys or a comfortable entry into the house. I had good reason to fear the consequences of my actions, and I hadn't exactly been spared anything.

Halloween was the time when the Veil Between the Worlds was thinnest, so the past life stuff out in the cornfield that day must have been true after all. I never heard of witches betraying each other before, it was always other people betraying them. Maybe they did sometimes under duress to avoid getting burned at the stake, but I wasn't being persecuted. It was simple jealousy and fighting over boys and everything they'd been saying about women all along. It was the worst possible stereotype. I was competitive and had a possessive streak a mile wide, and now I had lost my best friend, so what could be left for me other than this hell I'd gotten myself into?

I tried to get a grip on myself in my rivalry with Glenda, but I hadn't been able to. It would probably take some ordeal to reverse it all, and maybe that was the purpose of all this. If it *was* some Catholic thing, at least they believed in Purgatory, I knew that. One of my friends in middle school, Maria Munoz, had told me about it. She was probably worried about my soul even then and rightly so, as it turned out. She said Purgatory was a giant mountain with a tier for each of the seven deadly sins and on each one, penitents performed labors designed to correct their particular vice—the proud walked with downcast eyes, the covetous were prevented from looking at each other, the lazy made to carry heavy burdens and break up stones, etc. At the time, it sounded like a medieval torture chamber, proof of how out of step Catholics were. Jane said mystics view the world itself as Purgatory, and current sufferings as karmic payment for past-life sins. What goes around comes around.

I lay twisted up in the blanket with my head turned to one side and my legs to the other. I thought of the crucifix at the church with Jesus looking like he'd been beaten up and both his legs had been broken. It just seemed like some dead religion to me, but now I was living it myself. I was a living testament to it, so it wasn't dead at all, although it felt like maybe I was.

Light began to trickle through the venetian blinds. I don't know if it was morning already or just the streetlamps, because it was still very faint so it was hard to tell. I looked around the room and it looked like a negative, because everything was inverted and was dark where it should have been light. I had a feeling yesterday morning that someone was going to take a picture of me, and it had finally happened, so I was right about that anyway, and it looked like that was the only thing I was right about.

CHAPTER 20

I thought the boys went to school the next day. I wasn't sure because they didn't come and get me, and I didn't venture downstairs. I stayed in my room with the door locked and didn't leave except to go to the bathroom. When I looked in the mirror, my mascara had been smudged into two black eyes and I looked like I'd been beaten up in a fight. There were a couple of rusty razor blades in the wastebasket and I didn't like the idea of dropping my Kotex in there, so I wrapped it in toilet paper and took it back to my room and stuck it in the back of my closet.

My mother and Ben didn't come home till late afternoon. I must have made Lilah feel properly guilty for leaving me alone, because she came straight to my room to look in on me, but I wouldn't open the door. I told her that I had cramps and was resting. Ben muttered something about that not being a reason he'd ever heard of to stay out of school before, but I told him as a football coach with three sons, it would have been pretty strange if he had.

I spent the day reading "Goblin Market" and *Touched by Fire*, a thriller about an industrial spy, Archie Layton, who had to descend into the contaminated inner chambers of a failed nuclear reactor in order to stop the leakage. Geiger counters were clicking around him as he lowered himself toward the melted core, but he sloughed it off as if it was no more than the humming of insects. The only thing between him and the contamination was a sheet of heavy plastic, and he was just wearing a surgical mask for protection. He managed to keep the radiation from getting into the water table, but for months afterward he couldn't sleep and felt as if he was being stung by a thousand scorpions. Archie went in for tests and checkups, but doctors couldn't help him. He finally found a shaman in a remote village of Siberia who exposed him to fire and ice and put him on a diet of raw fish, seaweed, boiled rice, and herb tea. He gave him amulets to wear—a tiger's tooth, a mammoth-fur pouch, and pendants of carved malachite and lapis. Just as he was finishing the treatment, Archie was apprehended by the KGB who sentenced him to seven years of hard labor at a prison camp, and by the time he finally completed the sentence, he had his health back.

I felt a little better after I finished the paperback. Archie's trials and tribulations mirrored mine and the book actually had a semi-happy ending. It was the middle of the night, and I thought everyone was in bed and it was finally safe to leave my room. I hadn't eaten all day, and I was starving so I tiptoed downstairs. The kitchen countertops were still covered with leftovers from the wedding, and the poached salmon and ham crowded the refrigerator. I ate deviled eggs and garlic bread and drank a glass of milk and went back upstairs.

The next morning my mother made me get up and go to school. I ran into Marvin in the kitchen. We stood staring at each other as though we were caught in a freeze frame, till he broke it and wheeled out of the room. The boys drove to school in Marvin's car. I was going to take the school bus, but before I could leave the house, Ben said he would drive me—he'd already arranged to be late to work. We drove to Mission and he got me registered in the office and introduced me to the principal, Mr. Gerwitz, who promised to look out for me. I signed up for English, Gym, French, World History, Drama, and Community Development. I missed homeroom but managed to make it to class by the beginning of first period.

Mission High was dark and low-ceilinged and smelled like Pine-Sol, and practically all you heard in the halls was Spanish. The soft, fluid tones sounded like secrets I had been shut out of, everything that was most essential, and I regretted studying French, but I was already a senior so it was too late to change now. It wasn't until the end of the day I realized the place was practically 70 percent Chicano. The day went all right; it wasn't as bad as it could have been—at least none of my stepbrothers were in any of my classes.

When I got home, Jason was in the kitchen eating the last of the wedding cake and drinking milk out of the carton. He asked me how my day went and I told him it was OK—I was going to try to get out of Drama so I could work on the school paper. The principal hadn't been able to sign me up for it. He nodded like that was a good idea and then bolted out the door for soccer practice. It was the first time I'd talked to any of them since the reception, and it made me feel a little better. I shook some of the tension out of my shoulders and went upstairs.

A sign on Marvin's door read CAUTION: HAZARDOUS NUCLEAR MATERIAL under three black triangles arranged in a circle against a yellow background. The door was half open and I didn't think he was home yet, so I looked inside. The room was a mess like the other time I'd seen it, and the picture of the beautiful Chicana girl was still hanging over the bed. She had big dark eyes and long black hair falling over one shoulder, and I felt a twinge of jealousy when I looked at it. I couldn't believe I still felt that way after everything that had happened. I must really be sick or something.

I went to my room and changed into jeans and a sweatshirt and got my camera and took off on my bike. It was overcast and looked like rain so I took my poncho but didn't let it keep me in the house. I followed Thorn Hill Road out of town for five miles and turned onto a loose gravel road that led down to the El Valle Tomato Cannery. It was closed for the season and the windows were all boarded up, but I found a loose board and took a couple of shots of the dusty canning equipment and conveyor belts inside. Then I slid down the steep embankment to the river. Newspapers decomposed next to rusty tin cans and unidentifiable, rotting trash, and there was an ugly, yellow foam on the water. I seemed to have an unerring nose for blight. The rain finally started a slow, steady saturation and I pulled up the hood of my poncho. Tears beaded in the corners of my eyes and spilled onto my cheeks as raindrops pelted the plastic hood.

I lived out of boxes and suitcases for the next few days, and it wasn't until the end of the week I finally started unpacking. My room was small and irregular and the furniture took up most of the space. It looked like the wiring for the entire block was attached to a porcelain fixture on the pole outside the window. I'd never seen so many cables, and it was probably dangerous as hell, and I would get cancer from sheer proximity to it, but I moved the bed under the window anyway. It was really the only place for it.

I put K.D.'s picture above the chest of drawers next to the mirror, and Diane Arbus's photograph of the albino sword-swallower on the opposite wall. The folds of her satin blouse glimmered with light, and her outspread arms gave it the composition of a crucifix.

I was in the midst of hanging a gold sari in a canopy above the light bulb when Ben stuck his head in the door and looked around the room.

"Hmmmm," he said. "I like the way you're fixing it up in here. Sort of early coffeehouse chic. How are those bookshelves holding up? If you want any of them raised or lowered, just let me know."

He made a sour face as he sniffed the air and saw the apple cores, banana peels, and cereal bowls stashed around the room.

"I hereby retract my former compliments. Say, what are you operating here, a compost heap?" He picked up a glass and a couple of plates to take downstairs, but he stopped at the door and turned as if he'd just gotten an idea.

"I thought maybe you and I could take in a movie sometime," he said. "So you can keep me up to date on how you're doing at Mission. What do you say? *Serpico* is playing in town, and if that doesn't appeal, we could always drive over to Fresno and see *Godfather II*."

He smiled and I was momentarily taken aback by his friendliness. But I shook my head no.

"OK, Miss Sticks to Herself/Stays in Her Room," he said. "Suit yourself. What are you reading these days, anyhow? *Le Misanthrope*?"

He glared at me and left the room. I felt a twinge of regret at not accepting his invitation, but I was too bogged down with my own problems to try to relate to anyone else. It might have gotten my mind off things, but it seemed like a burden to have to make conversation, and I couldn't risk feeling any worse than I already did.

The winter rains started in earnest and kept up relentlessly for two weeks, battering the roof and pelting the windows. I rode the bus to school in the mornings and home again in the afternoon. It was far too wet to go out on my bike—I just lay on my bed and looked out the window at the "Danger: High Voltage" sign. The weather suited my mood and kept me company.

I felt worse now that I didn't have my room to focus on anymore. At first I stopped eating, and probably lost a couple of pounds, but then I was ravenous all the time, sometimes devouring entire packages of cookies in a sitting. Crackers, cookies, ice cream, chips, sandwiches—even trayf like ham and salami. My mother gave me weird looks when she noticed a week's worth of desserts and snacks disappearing a few days after she had brought them home. I don't know how she knew it was me—boys were the ones that were supposed to have the big appetites, but she had me pegged.

My dreams were feverish and disruptive. In one, Marvin and I were caught in bed together by Lilah and Ben and dragged in shame before Mr. Gerwitz. I woke gasping for air, momentarily relieved it wasn't true, before I sank back into the doldrums. I was hooked by an undertow that took me to depths where I clambered among mollusks, eels, and mute, slimy creatures. I recognized Marvin's tread in the hall and was painfully aware of his comings and goings. I saw him in passing in the living room or the kitchen, but we barely acknowledged each other. I ran into him once in the upstairs hallway in the middle of the night. It had the moonscape look and feel of a dream and when I realized it wasn't, I rushed into the bathroom and slammed the door and when I came out he was gone.

Ben gave me some Rex Stout mysteries like he said he would and *The Maltese Falcon*, all of which I read and returned without comment. I read *King Lear* and *Hamlet* for my English class, both experiences of jaw-dropping intensity that unleashed torrents of tears. I was actually moved to forget my own troubles for a time, either that or go deeper into them. *King Lear* brought Grandma Heaney to mind and the ills that had befallen her after giving her property away, and I wrote an impassioned paper called "More Sinned Against Than Sinning." My teacher Mr. Byrd didn't think too much of it, but writing it was a personal catharsis and probably the best I'd felt since we moved there.

I created an altar to Derek Montague on my chest of drawers, because I had lost him just as surely as if he was my real father. I made a photo collage from a few *National Geographic* pictures of the Adena burial mounds and some caballeros and one I took myself of a little girl in a white dress leading a horse out of a corral. I put out the copy of his book and a jar of fresh marigolds, and at night I burned sage and a yellow candle in front of it and watched the shadows jump around on the walls.

I thought about my real father and again tried to visualize what he might be like. All I saw was a faceless man in a gray flannel suit sitting in a cubicle like a section of an ice cube tray in a big insurance office. I didn't feel like I was channeling any real information and it didn't feel like a psychic reading of any kind.

I went back to El Valle and took more pictures and thought about doing an expose on the place for the local newspaper. I got on the school paper, *The Herald*, but they didn't have their own darkroom, which was a setback. The darkroom at *The Record* had gotten me through my last disaster and I needed it more than ever now.

I didn't know if I would be able to set up a darkroom by myself, but Kevin obviously thought so or he wouldn't have given me the enlarger, so I went down to the basement to look for a site. I hadn't been down there since we moved and I'd forgotten all the junk that was piled everywhere. There was a rusty lawn mower, bunches of carton boxes, and an old jungle gym. It didn't look like they'd cleaned the place in years.

There were several boxes full of dusty liquor bottles—Johnny Walker, Jack Daniels, Jose Cuervo, Jim Beam, Gilbey's, and Canadian Club. I don't know what they kept those around for, and I figured they must have had some wild parties over here. I remembered what Cal and Jason said about their mother's drinking problem so I figured they were hers, and they'd never gotten around to getting rid of them.

I opened one of the boxes and pulled out a flowered cotton housedress and held it up to me. It was only slightly too big, so she and I would have been roughly the same size. No one had ever mentioned her having a job and judging by the clothes, she was probably a housewife.

I looked through a box of old books—there was a Bible, Kahlil Gibran's *The Prophet*, *How to Be Your Own Best Friend*, James Baldwin's *The Fire Next Time*, Karen Horney's *The Neurotic Personality of Our Time*, Doris Lessing's *The Four-Gated City*, Zora Neale Hurston's *Their Eyes Were Watching God*, *Jane Eyre*, *Heart of Darkness*, and *Silas Marner*. There were a couple of Agatha Christie mysteries—*Appointment with Death* and *Murder in Mesopotamia*. The Bible dated all the way back to the 1880s with names handwritten on the brittle yellow flyleaf—Doreen and Eduardo Del Mar. The wedding of Dolores Dempsey and Benjamin Beasley was recorded as July 13, 1955, and Marvin Beasley's baptism on June 15, 1957. Jason Beasley was baptized on March 5, 1960, and that was the last entry in the book. There were some pamphlets in the box—"The Catholic Guide to Marriage," "The Sanctuary of Marriage and Family Blessings,"

"Marriage in Trouble" by Father Eugene Alfonso, and a couple of secular marriage manuals. There was a crucifix in another box, several strands of rosary beads, and some little religious statues—a bronze Buddha and figurines of the Virgin de Guadalupe, St. Peter, and Mary Magdalene—and the Waite Tarot deck.

The books were so eclectic it was hard to get a sense of who she was except that she was a Catholic with a marriage problem, in which case, she was in trouble since they didn't believe in divorce. I picked up a mottled composition notebook filled with spidery, elongated handwriting. It was clearly a journal. I could have deciphered her handwriting easily enough and a part of me was tempted to read it, but I was uncomfortable prying into her secrets and I put the journal back.

Another box was full of dolls—baby dolls with rubber heads and old, antique porcelain-headed dolls with blinking glass eyes and taffeta dresses and starched collars. There was a black doll, an Indian doll, a Chinese doll in a blue coolie outfit, a Raggedy Ann, a Madame Alexander Shirley Temple doll, and a set of nested Russian dolls. I didn't know what she was doing with all of them in a house full of boys. Maybe she had been saving them up for a girl all along.

"Well, here I am," I whispered out loud. "I finally made it."

I saw a quick flash of light overhead, but when I looked again, nothing was there, and I don't know whether I'd seen anything or not.

A corn dolly was wedged deep into the corner of the box, and I picked it up and shook the dust off it. It was handmade and looked like it was almost seventy years old. They'd used a corncob for the base and made the rest out of husks and clothed it in a red calico dress. It reminded me of the one my friends and I buried in the cornfield during the ritual, and my past life recall came back to me. It seemed a miracle she would have something like this, and goose bumps spread up my arms. No wonder that karma had been visited on me my first night in the house with something like this down here.

The doll brought up painful memories but also offered an opportunity to fix them. It seemed like a second chance somehow. After all I wouldn't go down that same road with my friends again, after everything I had been through. The doll was light as a feather but felt like it had heft and substance in my hand. I half expected someone to reach out of the shadows and take it away from me, but all was quiet and still. I stacked the boxes back the way I found them and blew the cobwebs off the doll and took it, along with the two Agatha Christie mysteries, back to my room.

CHAPTER 21

A couple of days later I inspected the basement with an eye to setting up the darkroom. It was dark as pitch without the overhead light on, and there was a double sink in the corner with a clothesline over it, so it was practically custom made. More important was the fact that nobody ever came down there, so I would have the place to myself. I set the processing tank and overflow pipe in the sink, and used a couple of my mother's seed trays for the developer, fixer, and stop bath. I cleaned the place up a bit and when I was through, I thought it looked almost professional.

I developed the series I took of the cannery and runoff. One of the rolls was so streaked and blotchy I had to throw it out. The remaining roll was underexposed so I had to burn them in. It wasn't until Sunday night that I had a set of ten prints in shape to submit to *The Bee*, and I bundled them up and mailed them off the next day.

When I got back from the post office I called Jane. It was the first time I'd talked to her since the wedding. I'd waited until I had something positive to report. But I didn't have to worry about keeping up my end of the conversation. I barely got a word in edgewise because all she wanted to talk about was her college applications. She'd mailed off six the day before—to Stanford, Pomona, and the rest to schools back East. She had another six to get ready, in addition to lengthy financial aid applications.

I'd been so absorbed in angst I'd forgotten all about college, and my mother had dropped the ball as well. Jane said I'd better get on it or I'd wind up going to Modesto J.C., just like they said all along. K.D. had an audition at the Conservatory in a few weeks and Jane was thinking about going back East for interviews.

I was in a different state of mind after I got off the phone. An old part of me roused itself and came back to life. College had always been our salvation and in all the turmoil I'd forgotten all about it, but now it loomed ahead of me like the promise of a way out right when I needed one. I emptied out the contents of my desk looking for my applications. I'd only sent away for two. I wasn't going to saturate the market like Jane. Fortunately, I hadn't missed the deadline on either one. In fact, I was within the cutoff period for spring quarter at Berkeley.

It dawned on me that if my SATs were high enough they might even admit me in the spring before graduation. I would eventually have to make my peace with Marvin, but something told me he would look a lot different to me after a quarter away at college. In fact, he looked different just at the prospect of it.

I spent the rest of the week assembling my applications. The Art Institute required a couple of essays in addition to a portfolio, and I began roughing them out. They were the usual schlock, but I poured my heart and soul into them anyway—my philosophy of life as a quest to capture hidden truths with my camera, help poor people, and improve society. I decided to spare them my Wiccan philosophy if I wanted any chance of getting admitted. I mapped out the rest of my strategy—a letter of recommendation from Ms. Richmond, copies of the photo essay I'd submitted to *The Bee*, and a couple of my CAC prints.

Wednesday after school, I went down to the basement to print out my portfolio. The dogs barked sharply as I started down the steps—I didn't know what had gotten into them. They seemed to be warning me off something, and when I got to where my darkroom had been, the whole darkroom had been dismantled. The clothesline was down, my trays and enlarger were missing, even the sinks had been boarded up. I was staring at the empty counter wondering what could have happened when I heard the front door slam and footsteps in the kitchen and recognized the tread of the heavy construction boots Marvin wore. I thought, *Marvin*. And he must have just come down there and taken everything. He really seemed to have it in for me for some reason. It wasn't my fault that we'd had that stupid tryst; I was just as much a victim of it as he was, if not more so. I couldn't imagine why he was out to get me or what he had done with everything, and I stood there for a full minute before bounding up the stairs, taking them two at a time.

Marvin was making a tuna fish sandwich at the kitchen table and had a jar of mayonnaise in his hand. Lilah was at the stove cooking bacon, and Ben was unloading bags of groceries from the car. He turned to greet me when I came in.

"What's this?" Ben asked. "A visit from long-lost sister Susie? Joining the family at last, are we? Nice to see you again. How've you been?"

"Not too good," I said. "Because my darkroom's been messed with. OK, Marvin. What did you do with everything?"

"Do with what?" Marvin asked turning around. "I don't know what you're talking about."

"Yes, you do," I said. "I want all my stuff back. Everything you took. The trays, the chemicals, my enlarger, all of it."

"I didn't take anything," Marvin muttered. "What would I want with any of your stuff?"

He looked at me blankly, trying to pretend he didn't know what I was talking about, but I didn't back down. Before I knew it, Ben planted himself between us.

"Hold on a minute," Ben said. "If you're talking about that mess down in the basement, Marvin didn't take any of that junk down there. I did. I cleaned it all up."

I stared at him.

"You?" I said. "What would you do that for?"

"I see a bunch of chemicals lying around and to me it's like a pile of oily rags," Ben said. "It's a fire hazard, pure and simple. Maybe I should have realized it was yours and asked you about it first."

"You most definitely should have," I said. "Those chemicals aren't combustible. They're just standard darkroom chemicals. Kodak HC 110 and paper developer. Besides, I always clean everything up whenever I work down there, and I use my own measuring cups not hers, so there's no danger of my contaminating your food if that's what you're worried about. This isn't just some hobby of mine, you know. I need to print out my portfolio for my college applications. I've got deadlines coming up."

I expected him to see reason and offer to give me my things back, but he didn't. He was being strangely obtuse and his usual friendly manner was gone too.

"Next time better check with me before you go setting something like that up in this house," he said. "You don't just go turning the place upside down, doing as you please. Besides, I don't want you prowling around down there, getting into things."

"Why?" I asked, flaring up. "What are you afraid I might find? Some old letters or a journal?"

He pulled back and narrowed his eyes and I thought I'd touched a nerve. Some of the things in the journal probably weren't too flattering to Ben, and I was sure he wouldn't want me reading it. Maybe that's what his whole thing with the darkroom was really all about.

"What are you talking about?" he said. "What have you been getting into? That stuff down there isn't any business of yours."

I fixed him with a silent stare. My mother stood by the stove, her face pale and strained.

"Ben, that's enough," Lilah said nervously. "Miami, you too. Come on. Let's us go upstairs now and get a start on your homework."

Her voice lacked conviction and neither Ben nor I paid any attention to her. We glared at each other, then something in me snapped and before I could stop myself, I hurled myself at him.

"Give me back my enlarger and my trays," I screamed.

I hammered on his chest with my fists till he caught my wrists and pinned them against the refrigerator. He held them there and a hush filled the room that was scarier than if he was yelling in my face. I looked from Ben to Marvin to my mother and they were all frozen in place. Smoke poured from an empty skillet on one of the burners and finally my mother grabbed it off the stove.

"Didn't anybody ever say anything to you about asking nicely?" Ben asked. "You're not going to get anything back carrying on like this. Now I'm glad I got rid of all that stuff downstairs, because I think you're a danger to the rest of us. You could have blown up the house just like I thought."

His face was inches from mine and his blue eyes hissed and the muscles in his neck were taut.

"I'm afraid we're going to have to lay down some ground rules around here," he said. "Or the rest of us will wind up having to take karate classes for self-defense. You're grounded for the next two weeks, do you hear me? And as far as the darkroom goes, that's history."

He threw my wrists down and pushed open the swinging door into the living room. He turned on the TV and the news blared into the room, something about Patty Hearst being sighted somewhere. Normally I would have stopped to listen to the broadcast, but I ran upstairs and threw myself on my bed. I was too upset to even cry. I hugged my knees to my chest and rocked back and forth trying to comfort myself. I knew from the start that moving here was going to be trouble, but it had turned out far worse than I could ever have imagined.

After I calmed down a bit, I didn't know if I was madder at Ben or myself. Ben was the only person who'd been nice to me since we moved here and now I'd alienated him. I looked at the "Danger: High Voltage" sign and figured that was what it must've been warning me about all along. My temper. As usual, I got the message too late to do me any good. The sign was there, big as life, but I went blithely on my way, paying no attention to it.

I was about to go out of the house for a cigarette when there was a knock on the door and my mother came in. She wore a turquoise knit dress with a Guatemalan sash tied around her waist. Her cheeks were flushed and she sat down on the bed next to me.

"How're you feeling?" she asked. She reached over to brush a strand of hair out of my eyes but I pushed her hand away.

"How do you think I feel?" I said.

"You've been so secretive about everything," she said. "I didn't know you had all that set up down there. Why didn't you tell me about it? Or more to the point, why didn't you tell him?"

"I guess you can see why now, can't you?" I said. "He finds out and look what happens."

"He told you he wanted you to check with him first," she said. "You should have asked him, that's all. Why don't you try communicating instead of holing up here by yourself not talking to anyone? Ben tells me he's reached out to you several times and you haven't wanted to have anything to do with him. It might have hurt his feelings. We're all trying to be a family here, you know."

"The same goes for him, doesn't it?" I said. "Why didn't he ask me before he went in and tore the place up?"

"You're right," she said nodding her head slowly. "He should have. He as much as said so himself. You were in a strong position but I'm afraid you relinquished it when you lost your temper. Now you're the one who needs to apologize to him. What does that tell you?"

"It tells me I had a mother who crawled into a bottle at every opportunity while I was growing up, and I was effectively raised by wolves," I said. "So excuse me if my manners aren't up to Emily Post's standards."

There was a brief silence. I jarred something loose with that and she lost her sacrosanct, preachy look and seemed momentarily shaken.

"Is there someone you'd like to talk to?" she asked. "Not me, maybe, but a counselor or therapist of some kind?"

"No," I said acidly. "I don't want to talk to anyone."

I was foisting my problems onto her and now she wanted

to fob me off on a professional. It was a cheap shot and she had sent it right back at me.

"You, the big advocate of higher education," I said. "If it hadn't been for Jane, I might still be in the dark and could have missed the application deadline completely. I *still* might miss them if he has his way."

"I'm sorry," she said. "I've been very remiss."

"I need the darkroom to print my portfolio for my application to art school," I said. "That's why I got so upset. Don't *you* care about that even if he doesn't?"

"I'll talk to him about it," she said. "Of course you need to complete your applications. In the meantime, do you want to go back to Alamo and see if you can use the darkroom there?"

I didn't answer. The situation with Kevin and Glenda was an equal fiasco. I was surrounded by my handiwork and it felt like it was closing in on me.

"How are you getting along with the boys?" she asked and I rolled my eyes. I'd been expecting that question ever since we moved in. I wondered why it had taken her this long to get around to it.

"Is there anything you want to talk to me about?" she asked quietly.

"No," I said. "We don't have that much to do with each other, that's all. We stay out of each other's way. Why? How've you been getting along with them?"

"Fine," she said smiling for the first time. "I think they're adorable and they seem to appreciate me—only Marvin's been holding out. But I expected some of that, and he has a right to his feelings. He may come around eventually if I don't force myself on him."

She frowned at me again.

"I'm serious about this, you know. We could find someone—a therapist or psychologist, some nice professional person who has nothing to do with this place. They might be a real comfort to you now."

I shook my head again.

"It was too much to spring on you all at once," she said sadly. "This move. I see that now. You wanted me to wait that extra year and I should have. It just seemed to make sense with the sale of the house and all. I thought Ben needed me too much, and in all honesty, I felt as if I'd waited my whole life for that wedding, and I couldn't wait any longer. I'm sorry, Honey."

Tears beaded in the corners of my eyes. It was the first time she'd done anything other than blame me for everything, and it was a relief even if I'd had to shame her into it.

"Things will get better for you here eventually," she said. "You'll see. Trust me."

My mother hugged me and left the room.

CHAPTER 22

Wednesday the phone was ringing when I got home from school and I ran to answer it. My mother had put up a lace curtain in the hall window and hung a Chinese scroll, a picture of a roan horse tied to a willow tree, in the phone alcove. The hallway was filled with light, and I held my breath when I recognized Glenda's voice on the phone.

"Glenda," I whispered. "How are you?"

"I'm OK," she said. "But it's not the same around here without you, you know."

"I miss you too, Glenda," I said.

"I'm sorry I didn't make it to your mom's wedding," she said. "I wasn't really that mad at you, I just felt like I had to stop being around you for a while. You got so competitive with me. You didn't want me to join *The Record*—you made it clear you were very possessive and threatened about that. Then when Kevin and I got together, you got even weirder."

"I'm sorry, Glenda," I said. "I was totally out of line. I guess I was just jealous and I tried to make it your fault rather than own up to it. To be honest, I was so drunk I don't remember the whole episode very well. I'm kind of cloudy on exactly what I said."

"Apology accepted," she said.

"I had a crush on Kevin," I admitted.

"That was obvious," she said. "So I also had to be away from you while Kevin and I were getting to know each other, because I knew you couldn't handle it."

"I'm sorry I was jealous, Glenda," I said. "It's one of my worst faults, but I've missed you and really learned to value our friendship. You certainly mean much more to me than Kevin does, so I've learned my lesson and I hope to be a better friend from now on. Maybe I can make it up to you somehow."

"Forget it," she said. "It's over. The other thing was it seemed like the slightest thing I'd say—even a joke—you'd take to heart. You can be so sensitive sometimes."

I didn't know what to say to this, so I didn't answer.

"I try to remember how sensitive you are," she went on. "So I'm sorry, too. I know I can be kind of critical sometimes, and my teasing gets on people's nerves. Linda's always getting on my case about that."

"Yes," I said quietly. "Sometimes it does."

"So how are things over there, anyway?" she asked. "What's it like living in a household full of boys? You must be in seventh heaven."

"It's OK," I said but my voice was constricted and tight.

"Only OK?" Glenda asked. "Why? What's the matter?"

"Nothing," I said. I was glad to be back on good terms with her again, but my days of confiding in her were over. Our break had weaned me of that habit.

"I've been taking a lot of pictures, even more than usual. I'm doing an environmental sequence on a toxic dumpsite that I'm trying to get published in *The Bee.* What have you been up to?"

"Not much," she said. "We all went to Fresno to hear Joan Baez at the amphitheater but it was *sold out*."

There was an insinuation in her voice when she said "sold out" that reminded me of the past life regression and I winced.

"I'm preparing an audition for *West Side Story*," Glenda said. "Are you ever coming back here for a visit?"

"I don't know," I said. "I'd like to."

"Or we could come over there and see you," Glenda said. "*Blow Up* is playing at the Clayborn Theater in Guadalupe Friday night. Want to go? It's supposed to be really good. It's maybe seven or eight years old. Vanessa Redgrave is in it, and it's about a photographer, which is why I thought of it."

"Sure," I said. "Let's go."

I was thrilled to be getting back together with Glenda and my friends, but then I remembered and stopped myself.

"I can't," I said. "I forgot. I'm grounded."

"Grounded?" Glenda laughed. "Oh, oh, sounds like a real groovy stepfather you've got. He's the strict type, huh?"

I stood still in the light from the hall window and thought, No. There was no way I was *not* going to go to that movie. I had to see Glenda, Jane, and K.D. again, because they were the only friends I had and I'd been afraid I'd lost Glenda for good.

"Wait, a minute," I said. "I'm going after all. I've changed my mind."

"That's the spirit," Glenda said. "Resist tyranny till the end!"

"So do you know how to get over here?" I asked.

"Kevin has a car," she said. "He'll know."

It never occurred to me Kevin would come and the scene from the party washed over me, but I could handle it this time and I pretty much *had* to, because Kevin was the least of my problems after what I'd been through. Besides I was so happy about seeing Glenda and K.D. again, I could put up with anything.

"Sure," I said. "That'll be great."

"We'll pick you up in front of Mission after school on Friday," she said.

The rest of the week I was both excited about seeing Glenda and nervous about defying Ben, but I didn't back out. Friday came and I stood in the driveway outside Mission looking for Kevin's car, and when I didn't see it right away, I was afraid they weren't going to show up. Finally I saw Glenda wearing jeans, a denim jacket, dark glasses, and red lipstick getting out of a dusty blue Mustang at the end of the driveway. "Glenda," I called out, and she rushed over and hugged me. Kevin stood next to her smiling at me. He wore a turquoise flannel shirt that brought out the blue in his eyes, and his hair was slicked back as though he'd just gotten out of the shower.

K.D. grinned at me with the sun glinting off her glasses.

"What happened to you?" Glenda asked. "You look like you've been hit by a truck."

"I'm OK," I said, but there were tears in my eyes and my voice cracked.

"Why didn't you call us?" Glenda asked, but I just stared at her because she'd made it pretty obvious she didn't want to have anything to do with me.

"Jane sends her love but she's still tied up with her college essays and couldn't make it," K.D. said with a bemused smile.

"What are your stepbrothers like?" Glenda asked and I shrugged.

"I don't spend that much time with them," I said. "They sort of keep to themselves."

"What do you think of Cal's band?" K.D. asked.

"I haven't heard them yet," I said. "They practice somewhere else and he's practically never at home. There'll be a horn in the street, and he's out of there. The car looks like a black hole in space, with a matte finish. Sometimes he'll be gone for days at a time, and I'll run into him at school, but that's about it."

"Maybe they weren't kidding about the methamphetamine," K.D. said.

"Who knows? Anything's possible," I shrugged. "He's skinny and he has kind of a haunted look. Maybe he just has a girlfriend or he's a sex hound or something."

"How about Marvin?" K.D. asked grinning. "The one who was drinking the whole time at your mom's wedding. Marvelous Marv."

"Marvin turned out to be a jerk," I said. "A real asshole."

"I'm not surprised," K.D. said giggling. "Why? What happened?"

"I want to know what you did to get yourself grounded," Glenda said.

A smile tugged at the corners of my mouth.

"I got in a fight with my stepfather," I said. "I think I might have pushed him or something."

Glenda and K.D. looked at each other and grinned.

"Watch it, Miami," Glenda said. "Temper, temper."

"I know," I said.

"Good going, Miami," K.D. said. "Nice way to get to know the family. What'd he do? Touch your camera or something?"

"He took away my enlarger," I said. "The one Kevin gave me. I was right in the middle of printing my portfolio for my college applications."

"That's completely fucked," Kevin said. "I ought to come over there and deck him myself. You know you can always come back to *The Record* and print them there, if you need to."

"Thanks," I said. "I may take you up on that."

I asked Kevin what had happened with the farm labor bill he was talking about at the party. He said it had failed in the legislature, but the Chavez forces were working on a more moderate version they hoped to get through the assembly next year. He'd begun writing about it regularly in *The Record.*

The movie theater in Guadalupe was high ceilinged and ornate with gold bric-a-brac and art deco trim. A dusty afternoon light filtered into the lobby and the theater was practically empty, but there was a guy playing the Wurlitzer up front anyway. He played "There's No Business Like Show Business" and "The Sound of Music" for us with a flourish and then the movie started.

It was an offbeat mystery story about a fashion photographer. He took pictures of Vanessa Redgrave and her boyfriend having a fight in a park and when he developed them, he noticed a blur off in the corner of one of the prints. He kept blowing it up, and when he went back to investigate, he found a corpse lying on the grass, so he had been photographing a murder the whole time.

His apartment had been trashed and the prints and negatives were missing, and when he went back to the park, now the corpse was gone too. He stood with his camera in the inbetween, half-dark and half-light, as the sun was coming up. Then a mime troupe started playing an imaginary game of tennis without a ball, and now he *really* didn't know what was real and what wasn't anymore, and you didn't either because the whole thing totally messed with your head.

It was twilight when we got out of the theater but the lights on the marquee were already on, and across the street the window of the bridal shop was lit up. Glenda was reading the credits and Kevin lit a cigarette, and K.D. balanced by her heels on the curb watching the cars go by. It looked like they were still under the spell of the movie. Meanwhile, a line formed for the next show and an usher in a maroon cap started letting people in. It felt like the movie wasn't over, and we were still in it, and the projector was running and the credits were rolling.

Glenda said she wanted to get something to eat, so we crossed the street to Mama Pasquale's Seafood Squid Grotto and sat in a booth at the back of the restaurant. There was a fake swordfish and plastic grapes hanging from the latticework on the wall and an electric Olympia sign over the door.

"I think it was a statement about the subjectivity and alienation of the artist," K.D. said. "After all that, he was left totally stranded, and it ends with the image of a mime troop. The best they could do was *pretend* to have a game of tennis. That's the height of consensual reality right there."

"It looked like he was using his camera to hide from the world," Glenda said smiling at me.

"Gee," I said. "I wonder why anyone would want to do that?"

"Vanessa Redgrave was good," Kevin said.

"She was great!" Glenda said. "She hasn't made that many movies since then, though. She's been blacklisted for being pro-Palestinian."

"That's fucked," Kevin said. "Everybody should be able to think whatever they want."

"I read somewhere that Antonioni had to paint the grass in the park to get it that green," Glenda said.

"Like *Alice in Wonderland*," K.D. said. "'Painting the roses red.'"

The waitress finally showed up with our order. She had a dour face and put a plate of pasta primavera in front of me. After she left, Glenda whispered that she'd heard somewhere that the restaurant was controlled by the Mafia.

We finished dinner and the waitress came back with coffee and Kevin started putting quarters in the jukebox. He must have played "I Heard It Through the Grapevine" five times. I don't know what was with him or where he got all that change. K.D. ordered some spumoni and the waitress brought the check, and between the four of us, we barely scraped together the money to get out of there, even shorting her on the tip.

They dropped me off at the curb, and I walked slowly toward the house. The lights were all out except for one in the back, and the house looked dark and somber like Bluebeard's castle. I tiptoed inside and got up to my room without seeing Ben or anyone else, and I thought I might have gotten away with it.

The next morning I languished in bed a long time, bathing in the shafts of light from the window. I still had a larger-than-life feeling of being in a movie, and I savored how good it felt to have patched things up with Glenda.

I didn't go downstairs until noon. I was sitting at the dining room table eating buttered toast and soft-boiled eggs when I noticed Ben in the doorway. His red Forty-niners cap was pulled low over his forehead and he was looking straight at me. I obviously hadn't gotten away with anything, and I bent over my food, avoiding his eyes.

"I thought I made it clear you weren't to leave the house," Ben said folding his arms over his chest and walking toward me. "Where did you go last night?"

"I went to a movie with my friends from La Grange," I said pushing the toast away. "We went to see *Blow Up*."

"*Blow Up*," he said. "How appropriate. What's that about? A girl with a nasty temper?"

"No, it's about a photographer who discovers a corpse with his camera," I said insinuatingly. "In the darkroom, actually. He keeps blowing up the print until he sees it tucked away in the corner."

He looked momentarily uncomfortable. I remembered my own darkroom and all of his wife's stuff and again I wondered if I had gotten close to zeroing in on something myself.

"What did I tell you about leaving the house, young lady?" he said sharply. "When I say grounded, I mean *grounded.*"

I got up and pushed my chair back from the table.

"Get off my back," I said tossing my hair out of my face. "Ever since I came here, all you've done is boss me around, and I've had enough of it. Leave me alone!"

He had a lot of nerve getting on my case when he had quite a temper himself, and I was just expected to bear the brunt of it. I was becoming everybody's convenient little scapegoat.

"Don't tell me what I can and can't do in my own house!" he snapped. "You're not used to having a father or any discipline whatsoever from what I can see, and I'm not going to sit back and let you raise hell around here."

"Well, at least *you're* not my father," I said. "And I can thank heaven for that. Sometimes I think you think you are. I have my own father and he was an anthropology professor, and I'd rather have him even if he is dead."

I don't know what possessed me to bring Derek Montague up. I was on weak ground here and I expected Ben to come back down on me hard, but he didn't say anything at all. He stood there silent with a peculiar expression on his face and turned and left the room. He probably didn't have a clue what I was talking about. I'd never seen Ben at a loss for words before and I felt momentarily light-headed and spacey from getting the upper hand when I hadn't expected to. I sat at the table a little longer and then went upstairs.

Having had a taste of freedom, I wasn't going to stay pent up in my room anymore. Ben had taken away my darkroom equipment and that was punishment enough. It was clear he didn't have my interests at heart, and Lilah was so blissed out, she couldn't be counted on for much either, and I was going to have to take care of myself.

I changed into a pair of pink corduroy jeans and a brown mohair sweater. I hadn't been out with my camera in over a week and a half, and I got on my bike and rode out Route 7. Since I'd already stood up to Ben the night before, I didn't see the point in going along with his restrictions now. It didn't seem like a big act of defiance on my part, and I thought that would pretty much be the end of it.

I rode over to Rio Road and took a couple of rolls of film of the Guadalupe Bridge. I got down in the sand and shot the underbelly up through the girders, and then I stood on the frame and shot the cement pilings in the riverbed down over the railing. The bridge had been built by the WPA during the Depression, and it was a challenge to shoot, because it was a totally utilitarian structure, so it had to be all in the photography to make it come out looking like anything.

It was dark by the time I got home and I didn't even bother to sneak in. I walked through the front door and didn't care who saw me. I was coming out of the bathroom in my flannel nightgown with a towel wrapped around my head around ten o'clock when I overheard my mother and Ben talking downstairs. Their voices were low and I was just about to go back to my room when I heard my name mentioned, so I tiptoed to the balustrade to listen.

"It wasn't all that bad," my mother said. "You're making too much out of this. She's just upset, that's all. She's been lonely and isolated ever since we moved here, and it was too strict to keep her in the house like that. She needed to see her friends. I think it was good for her."

"If it were *only* that, maybe… ," Ben said.

I couldn't see either one of them, but I saw his shadow moving from wall to wall as he paced the room.

"She's either morose and sulking or else totally out of control. You were there the other day when she attacked me. She's holed up in her room since she's been here and it's littered with old paper plates crusted with food—definitely not a healthy atmosphere. She's hunkered down in there and sees everyone else as the enemy. I try to impose a little discipline, and she flouts that, and then she was rude and insolent this morning when I reprimanded her for it. I don't see that we have any choice but to get some professional help. It's not that I want to, Lilah, but I've tried everything else and I'm all out of ideas. Frankly, I don't see any signs that you know what to do either."

I heard the word "professional" and stiffened. My heart started pounding and I sat down on the stairs and the towel unwrapped and fell at my feet.

Marvin's door opened and he came out wearing a white shirt, black leatherjacket, and cowboy boots. He stopped short when he saw me.

"You don't understand how different this is after all those years when it was just the two of us," my mother said. "She's confused. Let me talk to her."

"You already tried that, remember?" Ben said. "You told me she was completely unresponsive when you suggested a counselor."

"What exactly are you suggesting?" my mother asked.

"A psychiatric evaluation," Ben said. "I'm concerned about her. She may even need to go away somewhere for a while, to a clinic or a home for adolescents. Is this the way she usually behaves? You tell me."

Now my mother got up and I could see her shadow on the wall pacing the room opposite Ben's.

"Look here, Ben," she snapped. "Just because of your experiences with Dolores, you have no right to talk about Miami that way. Maybe I was in too big a rush to sell the house before we moved in here. I'm beginning to think it was precipitous, because I don't like the way you're talking right now. But house or no house, I'm warning you, if you make so much as a move to try to institutionalize my daughter, she and I will be out of here before that can happen."

"Relax, Lilah," Ben said. "Nobody's talking about institutionalizing her."

"No? I just heard you say it two minutes ago."

"Well, then I misspoke. I'm sorry. My nerves are on edge too. That's not what I meant at all. Forget I said it."

"What exactly *are* you suggesting then?"

"An evaluation, like I said. That's all. You told me you were worried sick about her yourself. That's what this is all about—helping your daughter. She could use some help. I think we both agree on that."

There was a moment of silence, and I held my breath. I sensed that they had reached a place of agreement where they could hash out and hatch my fate. Ben had backed down some but I didn't feel reassured. I felt like a sacrificial lamb that was being trussed up and prepared for someplace like the Harris Ranch. I guess I'd always had a sixth sense about the place.

"She's in the middle of sending applications to art school, and she was printing her portfolio. That's why she was upset. She needs the darkroom. It's important to her future, it wasn't just a fit of pique."

"Maybe she is under strain," Ben said. "I try to appreciate that, but so am I. And I can't have her talking to me like she did today. I have my limits too, you know."

Marvin was standing right next to me so I knew he could hear them just as well as I could. I don't know why he had to be around every time something terrible happened. What was he, my nemesis? But there was a minute when it looked like sympathy on his face.

"What's the matter, Lilah?" Ben asked. "You act like you're still wavering."

"Where exactly do you want to take her?" my mother asked.

"Over to Valley Central in Fresno for an evaluation for starters, and we'll see what they recommend. I would think it would just be standard, classical psychotherapy. What's so scary about that? Only she won't be able to weasel out of it this time. It won't be optional."

"I don't know, Ben," Lilah said. "Let me think about it for a while. I already asked her about it, and she said no. I'd like her to get some counseling but I don't want to force it on her. I'm not sure how productive it would be entered into in that spirit."

"OK," Ben growled. "But you know what I think."

Suddenly Marvin was clattering down the stairs. He made so much noise, they couldn't help but hear him and stopped their talk. The front door slammed and I heard his car start up, and it spat and backfired as he backed out of the driveway.

I went back to my room and sat on my bed. It was cold in the room and my hair was wet, and I was shivering and started biting my fingernails. I was more scared than I was the first night in the house with the boys. It occurred to me that Ben was right, and I *was* crazy because everything was beginning to unravel and my vision was blurring. I was depressed and nervous and had headaches, so I fit the profile. Maybe that had been my problem all along and I just never realized it before. My bedroom reminded me of a mental hospital the first night I was there and now it seemed like it was panning out for real. I always knew there was something deep and twisted and crazy inside me, and it was just a matter of time before it came out.

I thought about how Diane Arbus and Sylvia Plath and Virginia Woolf had all gone crazy and killed themselves. I figured I was going to wind up that way one way or the other, because if even people who were talented and I admired were like that, what hope could there possibly be for me?

CHAPTER 23

The other thing that kept going through my mind was that I had gotten too close to something down in the basement, and Ben was trying to ship me off to Napa to shut me up about it. It may have been a paranoid thought, but it was the closest thing to sanity I could muster at the moment and I clung to it tenaciously. Phyllis Chesler considered the psychiatric profession little more than an institutionalized "gaslighting" of women just like the movie and I had no interest in being subjected to it. Ben had been OK at first but turned out to be a control freak and a heavy-handed power tripper. I was glad Lilah had stood up for me, but who knows how long she'd be able to hold out or what she would eventually decide on her own? My only hope was getting admitted to spring quarter at Berkeley, but the deadline was approaching and I hadn't even completed my application.

When I got out of school, Marvin's old Cadillac was pulled into the Mission driveway and he leaned out the window and beckoned me over.

"Come on," he said. "I'll give you a ride home. I need to talk to you about something."

"What do you want to talk about?" I asked. I stood at the

curb shivering in my green cotton dress and corduroy jacket. It was the first time he'd said a word to me in the month that I'd been in the house, and there was still an uncomfortable charge between us.

"Just get in," he said. "It'll take too long to explain it."

The inside of Marvin's car was a wreck—the lining from the ceiling was hanging down in strips and a spring was coming through the upholstery on the back seat. He wasn't taking the same route the bus took, and he drove fast and the car swerved on the curves. The engine sounded like it was missing on one of the cylinders.

A pack of Camels slid back and forth on the gritty dashboard and Marvin pulled one out and lit it. I tore off a hangnail and bit the jagged fingernail down to the quick.

"Where are we going?" I asked. "I don't feel like going on any joyride."

"We're not going on a joyride," he said. "I need to talk to you about something. I heard what he said last night, you know."

"Yeah," I said. "I figured you did. Look, if you're worried about me or something, forget it. I don't know how to say this exactly, but if you're feeling bad because of what happened between us, don't. It's not your fault or your problem."

Marvin's eyes were bloodshot and he looked like he had barely slept. I was taken aback by this show of concern on my behalf and hardly knew what to make of it.

"I never thought it was anybody's fault—mine or yours. I just thought you got a raw deal moving in here the way you did. And of course I'm the only one who knows anything about that, and I felt too uncomfortable to say anything until now, but after last night, I knew I had to. I thought it might help to talk since things have been so… uh,… awkward between us."

"Oh, they've been awkward, all right," I said. "Thanks. It does mean a lot to me, actually. I'm sorry if I was resistant to it at first. I'm kind of paranoid these days."

"It's not paranoia when they really are out to get you," Marvin said with a laugh. "I was there, remember."

It was an old joke but it established something like rapport between us for the first time and I smiled.

"I'm sorry about attacking you over the darkroom that day. I guess I just lost it with you and Ben. I really do have a temper, as it turns out. It's funny; it's something I'm only beginning to realize about myself. I always thought I was the wimp of the universe, and I had to protect myself with a tough act so I wouldn't get completely trampled underfoot. I was just trying to defend myself and now it turns out everyone sees me as the perpetrator. "

"Maybe you've been overdoing it a little," Marvin said. "Is that what's called being passive-aggressive? The whole thing was really fucked up. Like I said, I think you were just on edge because of what happened with us. If I'd spoken up sooner it might have taken some of the pressure off so you wouldn't have flared up at Dad like that. As far as I'm concerned, the whole thing was perfectly understandable. But like I said, it was easier to ignore you, even though I knew you weren't going anywhere. Of course, Dad doesn't know anything about it, so he wasn't going to cut you any slack on account of it."

"Praise God for that, anyway," I said. "Then he'd have me committed and throw away the key."

"He kind of overreacted to the whole thing," Marvin said. "Probably because of everything he went through with my mother. My advice is to lay low and stay out of Dad's way for a while and maybe he'll get over it. That's the way he is—sometimes, anyway. He's quick to flare up, sort of like you are, but then he gets over things too."

"I heard them talking about your mother last night," I said. "Dolores? Was that her name? Was she supposed to be sort of crazy too?"

"She was kind of fucked up," Marvin said. "I don't know that I'd call her crazy, but she had a drinking problem and they didn't have a good marriage. You can call anyone crazy if you have no compassion for them and just write them off. I think she may have been going to a psychiatrist, I don't know. She was just a housewife and she didn't have any real hobbies to speak of, so she just bottled everything up. She didn't have any outlets—I always thought that was her main problem. All she had was us and we could never give her back anything close to what she needed. I guess she felt pretty unappreciated. I can't really say as I blame her."

I thought of all the bottles I'd seen down in the basement and guessed she had a lot to bottle up.

"Lilah used to be a big alcoholic too," I said. "But she gave it up a long time ago."

"Fucked up, huh?" he said, giving me a sideways glance. "It didn't hurt me none, though, did it? I ain't no damaged goods. Not like you."

Marvin gave me a little smirk.

"I found out at an early age that no one was going to take care of me, and I was going to have to do it myself," Marvin said. "You learn to rely on yourself more, I guess. Become more independent."

"That's good, isn't it?" I asked. "It builds character."

"I don't know how good it really is," Marvin said. "You learn not to rely on people or let them get too close. In the end, you can't get along with anyone."

It felt like Marvin might as well have been talking about me. We were even more alike than I'd ever thought.

Marvin almost missed his turn and veered onto a dirt road, and the tires churned up mud and gravel. The grass was so green, it looked like the park in *Blow Up*, and there was a lake at the end of the road bordered by a row of yellow aspen. We got out of the car and walked along a narrow strip of beach by the water. We were the only ones there. The clouds had dissipated and the sun was already low in the sky, and the light picked up the gold flecks in Marvin's eyes and the highlights in his hair.

"Where are we?" I asked. "It feels like we're a million miles away from everything."

"That's the general idea," Marvin said. "I drive over here when I need to get away. It's called Russet Lake. I come here to fish or bring my camera. You're not the only one who likes to take pictures, you know."

"I know," I said. "I saw your picture of the church at the County Fair last summer before I met you. It was great. I was incredibly envious because it won the blue ribbon, and none of my prints got anywhere. "

"Maybe they weren't any good," Marvin said. "Just kidding, of course. I'd like to see some sometime. So, you're the competitive type, huh? Maybe that's something you can talk to the psychiatrist about."

Marvin smiled at me mischievously.

"We used to go swimming here in the summer when we were kids, with a picnic and beach balls and shit. Most of my childhood I was convinced we were the typical, all-American family. We went skiing at Mammoth in the winter, and camping in Yosemite in the summer. Dad would take Jason and Cal and me up to the John Muir Trail and we'd climb Mt. Darwin or the

Hermit while Mom kept the base camp below. Then we'd return after three days with a string of rainbow trout and she'd cook up a big fish fry and hash browns on the Coleman stove."

"I'm glad to hear there were some good times," I said.

"Oh, yeah," he said. "Plenty of them."

He kicked a rock zigzag along the sand and the sun sank lower, and artificial lights from the houses on the other side of the lake began to flicker through the trees.

"Dad wasn't as nice to Mom as he is to your mother. They had some problems they never worked out. Maybe he never really loved her. They should have gone to a marriage counselor or something. They'd have these big fights, screaming and yelling and throwing things around. I used to wonder why they didn't just call it quits and get a divorce. That way, she might have had a chance instead of…"

His voice trailed off.

"Instead of what?" I asked. "What happened to her, anyway?"

"She killed herself," Marvin said quietly. "She hung herself down in the basement."

"When did she do that?" I asked.

My voice was hushed and the wind let up, like the wind and me both were holding our breath.

"At the beginning of this year," he said. "In January, I came home and the house was empty, and I kept calling 'Ma,' but she didn't answer. I thought she'd been drinking and was passed out somewhere and I was going to have to call Detox again. I went through the whole house looking for her, and finally found her down in the basement.

"She was hanging by a rope she'd tied to one of the rafters, in the back corner by the sink, swaying slightly back and forth. I called Dad and I got her down and couldn't let her go. I sat there rocking her in my arms until Dad came home. He tried to do CPR, but it was much too late for CPR. She was cold even when I got there."

"How awful," I said. "I'm so sorry. I had no idea or I never would have brought it up."

Marvin stared across the lake.

"It's better to talk about it than to keep it a big secret and live side by side with her ghost and act like nothing happened," he said. "It was awful, though. Mainly you wonder if there was anything you could have done that would have prevented it, which I guess I'll never know."

"I'm sure you did everything you could," I said. "Some things are just beyond our control."

We sat on a damp log and the cold went straight through me. I didn't know what to say in the face of a tragedy like that, so I didn't say anything, and we sat in silence for a long time. The sky darkened and a big crescent moon rose over the other side of the lake, as though nature was paying homage to his mother, and the beauty and stillness were a more majestic tribute than anything I could have hoped to say. There was a splash of silver and a fish leaped into the air, and I stood up to look and Marvin got up too.

Then he suggested we head back.

"Your mother's probably got dinner ready," Marvin said. "Are you going to start eating with us now or keep taking your meals up to your room? 'She's a vegetarian'— That's what your mother always says when Dad complains about it. But we all know you're really wishing you were back in your old house. I think that's what frustrates Dad more than anything. After all, he's the coach, and if you're separating off and not part of the team, he takes it as an affront."

"I'll probably keep eating in my room for the time being,"

I said. "But yeah, we'd better head back. After all, I'm still on restriction, technically. But it's been great to talk. Thank you for bringing me out here."

The trees arched over the headlights as we drove back down the dirt road to the highway. I treasured the time I'd spent with Marvin and dreaded returning to my isolation in the house but was too shy to say so.

As it turned out I didn't have to, because the next day he was sitting in the car waiting for me after school again.

"Where to this time?" I asked but he said it was a surprise and refused to tell me.

We drove out past the strip malls on Highway 9 and on to Modesto, and he pulled into a parking lot at the junior college.

"What are we doing here?" I asked. "This place used to be a standing joke with me and my friends in La Grange. It was our worst-case scenario that we'd wind up going to college here."

"Oh yeah?" he said. "I guess your future just caught up with you."

He opened a door in the art building and we walked into the biggest darkroom I had ever seen. There were twelve enlargers and stainless steel sinks and there must have been at least fifty trays; there was even a drum dryer and a Beseler enlarger.

"Wow," I said. "This is where you get to develop your prints? No wonder they're so good."

Marvin nodded.

"I'm taking a Fundamentals class so I get to use the darkroom. I thought you could develop your portfolio here."

"That'd be great," I said.

"See?" he said. "Isn't this a lot better than that setup you had down in the basement? Everything happens for a reason, they say. Funny how things work out sometimes, isn't it?"

"I guess so," I said. "I'm so used to things not working out that I'm pretty much flummoxed when they do."

I printed copies of my portfolio and got the applications in by the deadline, which took some of the pressure off me. After that, Marvin and I just had fun together, something I hadn't experienced in so long it felt like we were inventing it. We worked in the darkroom, went to the movies and the A & W root beer stand, and hiked up El Viejito, with its staggering vistas along the arduous switchbacks, and climbed the slippery rocks next to Tolusa Falls. In the house, we watched dumb TV shows together.

My restriction was over and Ben and my mother seemed pleased to see me spending time with Marvin. I felt more understanding and forgiving of Ben now that I knew about Dolores. I'd set up the darkroom in the precise location where she'd killed herself, so his reaction made more sense. I located a corpse with my darkroom like in *Blow Up* after all.

Marvin's favorite photographer was Walker Evans, who had pretty much defined the medium back in the early days with Steichen and Stieglitz, as well as being a big influence on Diane Arbus. He loaned me his copies of *Let Us Now Praise Famous Men* and *Many Are Called*, both out of print. Marvin's composition was always good, with some new angle and the image close to the edge, and I learned a lot from him about that and selective focusing, framing, and seeing stuff that wasn't there. The invisible picture, he called it.

Marvin said he got into photography because it took him out of the house and away from the bickering between his parents. A guidance counselor had suggested it. He liked having something to focus on (literally) while he was out on his hikes instead of just wandering around. He thought of it as a positive addiction and a better way of dealing with problems than his mother had found. It sounded like Lilah and her gardening. I told him I had stumbled onto my camera on the rebound from some guy. He suggested it was a consolation prize, but I shrugged and said he was the one with all the prizes.

Marvin took it upon himself to teach me how to drive. He thought it was hopelessly geeky not to at my age, and it was something concrete he could do to improve my situation. At the end of the first lesson, he said, "There, that wasn't so bad was it?" Considering I had nearly ripped out the gearshift, I thought he was pretty magnanimous. I started getting behind the wheel occasionally in the parking lot at the junior college at night, and out at the lake, and even on the highway a few times. After a while, I got better control of the steering, although I still had trouble with the contact point on the clutch, and he said I had a tendency to ride the brake.

I was touched and incredulous that Marvin was going to all this trouble on my behalf. He was really trying to help me and it wasn't just talk. I wanted to do something for him too and after a little thought, I knew what it would be. I gave him some frankincense and myrrh, a clay incense burner, and a statue of the Virgin de Guadalupe from the box in the basement, so he could make an altar for his mother. I thought it would help him to honor her, and incense resins were traditional for banishing ghosts. I briefly considered showing him the journal down in the basement but decided it might freak him out too much. After all, who knows what was in it?

I didn't know whether he would follow through or not, but the following week I smelled the frankincense in the hall and peeked inside his room. He'd covered an orange crate with a piece of yellow taffeta and put a jar of Peruvian lilies and an old black-and-white snapshot of his mother in front of it, along with the ritual objects I'd given him. The altar bore the touch of a natural warlock. The yellow taffeta established a baseline of sunshine and happiness his mother hadn't found in this life, and in all likelihood she was in a better place now. His intention helped to make it so, which was what altars were all about. They were essentially affirmations.

It was the first picture I'd ever seen of his mother. It had been taken when she was young, perhaps on one of their picnics at Russet Lake, and she was wearing Bermudas and squinting into the sun. She looked happy enough then. She had short, curly brown hair and a strong, determined face with a slightly protruding jaw. I thought she looked a little like me.

The following week I got a letter from the California Arts Council in Sacramento saying one of my photos won Honorable Mention in the Young Photographers Photo Journal Contest. The one they chose was a hand of solitaire over a fuchsia bush. They called it the "best treatment and most original use of a double exposure." I don't think it was necessarily a separate category. They were going to have an exhibit in January and a luncheon for the prizewinners beforehand.

That same week *The Bee* printed my photo essay about the El Valle dumpsite under the title "Gutsy Teen Blows Whistle on Cannery." It all seemed serendipitously associated with patching things up with Marvin, but the accomplishments themselves were my own. Ben was so proud of me, he showed the paper to the neighbors and took us all out for a tamale dinner. He returned my enlarger and said he had underestimated my seriousness or that I knew what the hell I was doing, but he could see that I had a head on my shoulders.

The whole incident told me a lot about him too and how important symbols of success were to him. It seemed a shallow way to judge someone. Nonetheless, I would take it. It was better than having him on the warpath.

I thought it might turn everything with Ben around for good, but just when I thought it was all behind me, my mother told me she had set me up with an appointment with a psychiatrist. Two weeks from Friday was the soonest they were able to fit me in, which should give me time to get used to the idea. She'd decided to go through with it after all. I guess she was only waiting for Ben to back off so she could make the decision on her own.

CHAPTER 24

Saturday night, Marvin and I went to Alamo to see Glenda in *West Side Story* and at the last minute, Cal and Jason decided to join us. Even Cal was genial and friendly these days; genial for him anyway. We met up with Jane in the lobby. K.D. was inside warming up with the orchestra. I wore a burgundy velvet dress with an empire waist and Jane told me how much better I looked than when she saw me at the wedding. I said "Thanks," and told her I'd had a breakthrough with my stepbrothers and we'd finally started hanging out together.

"So I see," Jane said. "Good."

I caught sight of Brian Quinn at the other end of the lobby and figured he'd come to hear K.D. play. It seemed like he was spending more time down here now. It was the second time I'd seen him in a little more than a month.

It was a great production and I had fun picking out the cast members and seeing my old classmates again. I almost didn't recognize Glenda as Maria with her hair dyed black. Jose Delgado was Tony and they sang "Tonight" together in two spotlights, and they were so good it gave me goose bumps to listen to them. I must have heard Glenda sing a million times, but I'd never heard her sound like that before. I'd always suspected she was a real talent.

The play ended with her down on her knees crying over Tony's corpse with a mantilla over her shoulders. She went into a speech against violence, and in the end that was what the play was about more than anything. It wasn't trite or clichéd, because that's what happened sometimes. Things escalated and before you knew it, there was Maria with Tony on her lap like the Pieta. I was crying and when I looked down at my hands, my palms were bleeding. I was so tense I must have been gouging myself with my nails the whole time.

It took me by surprise that I reacted so strongly, but the play hit close to home about the importance of not fighting and being scrappy and going around raising hell. It was only the second time I'd seen my friends in over a month, and I had narrowly avoided being institutionalized because of my fight with Ben. I suppose it was still actually a possibility.

The cast party was at Eddie Vasquez's house. Marvin, Jason, and Cal didn't know anyone, so they played DJ while Jane and K.D. and I congratulated Glenda. She was still in costume talking to Jose and Cecilia, and grinned when we came up. It was like being friends with a celebrity.

"You were great, Glenda," K.D. said. "You were better than Natalie Wood even."

"Really, Glenda," I said nodding. "You should go to Hollywood, because you're good enough to make it. I can see it."

She beamed and lapped it up and then went off to dance with Kevin.

"It's funny the way they mixed everything up," K.D. said. "Because here's Glenda this Scandinavian blond supposed to be a Puerto Rican girl and Jose Delgado is a super La Raza activist and he plays the sidekick of a WASP gang leader."

"Maybe they did it on purpose," I said. "To make a statement."

"I don't think so," K.D. said. "Glenda said whoever was best got the part and Mr. Mendez didn't care who was an Anglo and who was Chicano, even though that's what the play was all about."

"If you didn't know you might not even notice," Jane said. "With the hair dye and all."

"The orchestra was really good too, K.D.," I said. She was wearing a black dress with an orchid corsage on her shoulder and made an exaggerated, theatrical bow.

"Did you know they changed the lyrics on 'I Feel Pretty'?" K.D. asked. "The way Bernstein wrote it was 'I feel pretty and witty and white,' and they changed it to 'I feel pretty and witty and bright.' I guess they thought it was too controversial."

"How about 'I feel pretty and witty and gay'?" Jane asked.

"Out of the frying pan into the fire," I said. "He ought to know, anyway."

"I heard about a production of *Romeo and Juliet* once where Romeo was played by a woman," K.D. said. "It was an opera by Bellini. He wrote both parts for soprano voices. Romeo killed himself because Juliet wouldn't elope with him out of family loyalty."

"That's a new twist on the Elizabethan thing where men played both roles," I said.

"I thought Sarah Talbot was good," Jane said. "What was her character's name again?"

"Anybody," K.D. said.

"Anybody," I repeated. "What's that supposed to be, the working-class Everyman?"

"Everywoman, please," Jane said. "The protean feminist hero."

"Are you kidding?" K.D. said. "I thought she was a classic victim."

The lights were dim and I was searching the other side of the room to see how my brothers were faring when Brian Quinn stepped in front of me. Brian had a tall, lanky build and was wearing a light green T-shirt under a brown corduroy shirt. His hair had grown out since the last time I saw him and he had shaved his beard, and he looked more like the Brian of old with his otherworldly eyes, although his hair wasn't down to his shoulders anymore.

"Hi, Brian," I said. "I thought I saw you at the play earlier."

"I was staring at you from across the room and it took me about five minutes to realize who you were," he said.

All that grief that I went through a few years ago, and it seemed like I had barely registered. It was almost comical now.

"I came over to see how family life was agreeing with you. I hear you're not the only one anymore."

"No, indeed," I said. "There they all are. My stepbrothers."

I gestured to them gathered around the turntable.

"They look like fine, strapping lads," Brian said.

"Yeah, they're pretty nice," I said.

"My sister always thought it might be a bit on the lonely side with just you and your mom."

"It's hard to believe it's only been a few months," I said. "It seems a lot longer."

I looked around for his girlfriend Susan or some recent incarnation but didn't notice anyone.

"You're still up at Chico State, right?"

He nodded. "For now, anyhow."

"Are you still in that religious community?" I asked.

Brian nodded.

"How's that working out?"

"Great," he said.

His eyes radiated warmth that bespoke happiness and commitment.

"We're all living together in shared housing, the Agape House. We pool our funds and use consensus in conflict resolution—we're trying to put into practice the teachings of the gospels. We offer services on campus and in the poorer parts of town with free after-school care and tutoring, a food bank, and a clothes closet.

"School is less of a success story," Brian said. "The church takes up a lot of my time so my grades are pretty average. The mater and pater are not particularly pleased. They don't think they're getting their money's worth. At least that's how I think they're feeling. It might really be more honest to just drop out at some point and follow my heart."

"I'm sure they're happy to pay for school, Brian," I said. "It's not that much money and they just want you to be happy. I doubt they're expecting anything else from you."

"You're certainly a supportive soul," Brian said. "I'd forgotten that about you."

I'd always seen myself as nurturing and supportive, but with the hell I'd been through lately it was possible I had become more empathic.

"Are you still going out with that girl Susan?" I asked on an impulse, and he shook his head.

"No," he said wistfully. "We broke up over the summer. I guess she just wasn't into sticking it out—either with me or the church. She said she wanted to see the rest of the country and transferred to the University of Maryland."

It was unlike me to be so forward. My question seemed to end the discussion and prompt him to ask me to dance. His arm circled my waist, and it was probably the closest I'd ever been to him physically.

When the song ended, I wasn't sure what to do with myself. I stood there quietly for a few minutes, until another song started and Brian pulled me back toward him. Marvin and Jason were still picking the records, and they were hitting a lot of my favorites—"Higher and Higher," "Your Precious Love," "Unforgettable," "Rock the Boat," "I Just Want to Testify" by the Parliaments, and "This Old Heart of Mine."

The news about him and Susan was good. It was exciting but at the same time potentially hazardous. We had started out alone on the dance floor but stayed for song after song, and now it was crowded with couples. I caught Marvin's eye watching us closely.

"What are you studying?" I asked.

"Just general education requirements," he said. "I haven't declared a major yet. I was thinking about Economics at first but I wasn't that taken with it."

"How about religious education?"

"I have taken a couple of those courses," Brian said. "It was really interesting to learn about the early history of the church, the Council of Nicaea, etcetera. All those crazy disputes about doctrine and how many angels are dancing on the head of a pin. It makes you wonder how they could have gotten so side-tracked from the essential teachings. They don't have a major in it, though. Can't say as I'm particularly disappointed."

Now Marvin was at my shoulder telling me they were ready to leave. I couldn't believe the party was over, but Glenda, Kevin, Jane, and most of the cast had already gone home. Only my step-brothers and K.D. were still hanging around the turntable, and they were probably ready to leave an hour ago. Eddie Vasquez's parents were back and everyone looked bleary-eyed. Brian kissed me on the cheek and told me how great it was to connect with me again. He said he'd call me that week and try to come down the following weekend, and see if we could get together. He sounded genuinely enthusiastic.

"You two seemed pretty chummy," Marvin said on the way home.

"That's the guy responsible for my getting into photography," I said.

"He's a master photographer?"

"No, I mean on the rebound."

"Uh, oh," Marvin said. "Well, it looks like you can put the camera away now."

"You think?" I said.

"I do," he said. "You might as well chuck it completely. On the other hand, you could have the best of both worlds. What's the matter with that?"

"Nothing," I said. Except that Marvin clearly didn't know me very well if he thought of that as even a remote possibility. I just didn't have that kind of luck.

CHAPTER 25

I felt a rare excitement whistling through me that week as I waited for Brian to call, quite certain that he would. I wasn't the same girl that had been so crazy in love with Brian Quinn, yet I couldn't deny that the exhilaration I felt was essentially the same. Strangely, I wasn't so enamored of my past heartbreak and disappointment but felt a curious sure-footedness this time around. I couldn't go back to what had been, which both was and was not, like the magical beast in the Book of Revelation, because it hadn't been at all. It was only a secret, one-sided crush in my own mind. There was a Goldilocks element to the whole thing now, where it wasn't too good to be true and he wasn't too good for me, pinch myself this can't be happening. It felt like the timing was finally just right.

Brian called midweek, on Wednesday night. He asked me what I'd been doing other than getting to know my stepbrothers and adjusting to a new high school. I told him I'd been applying to colleges, Berkeley and the San Francisco Art Institute, and I'd developed an interest in photography and went out on photo shoots whenever I could.

"Are you into nature photography at all?" Brian asked.

"No," I said. "I've never really pursued it."

"I only ask because the countryside up here is as beautiful as anything you're ever going to see—full of Douglas fir, laurel, apple orchards, and live oak. That's why they called it Paradise. Perhaps you'd like to come up for a visit somctime? I could show you some gorgeous places."

I told him I'd like that. I'd never developed my nature photography sufficiently. It was a whole world waiting to be tapped.

"I could also document some of your church programs, if you liked. I could do a spread on it for your local paper and give you some publicity."

"I don't suppose Chico State is on your list of the colleges you're applying to?"

"No," I said.

Brian said he was coming down that weekend and we decided to get together on Saturday night. I still hadn't heard Cal's band, The Rainmakers, and as luck would have it, they were going to be playing at a party that night, and Brian and I decided to go.

Brian showed up wearing a bright blue shirt. I didn't know how he would get along with my stepbrothers but I needn't have worried. They fell into an easy camaraderie and I had to run to catch up. They sat around the living room exchanging sports stats and music trivia. Then Brian asked to see some of my photos and Marvin showed him a few of his as well.

When Brian realized the party wasn't till later in the evening, he suggested we all go bowling beforehand. I sat on the front seat next to Brian on the way to Merced. The sunset was prolonged and beautiful, drenching the road in pumpkin-colored light. We were the only car on the road and it was rattling like crazy. Brian's car was in better shape than Marvin's but sounded like it needed shocks or something pretty bad. The radio was playing

Ravi Shankar, counterpoint to the clatter, and Jason drummed his fingers against the back of my headrest.

The anticipation I'd been feeling all week came to a head, and it felt like we were hurtling down the road toward some final showdown, and it was the end of the world. I'd had some heavy karma with all four of them, which I'd managed to reverse and the moment felt spectacular.

The sunset was so picturesque it didn't look real. It looked like a canvas and you could almost see the brush strokes. The fields on both sides of the highway were empty and spotted with rocks, but it turned out they were crows, and when we drove by they rose up and flew off all at once. We drove through the center of town past the hardware store, the post office, the Merced County Fire Department, and Brian turned into the parking lot for the Rip Van Winkle Twenty-Nine Pins bowling alley. "Ripped Van Winkle," Jason said, laughing. As we got out of the car, I heard change jingling in Marvin's pocket.

It was a big bowling alley with over forty lanes open, and there was a crash of pins getting knocked over that sounded like continuous thunder. The kelly green carpet was as bright as a pool table and the fluorescent lights as vibrant as day. They decided we were going to bowl with duckpins. I didn't care if it was duckpins or any other kind of pins. I'd been bowling maybe twice before in my whole life. At first the ball went in the gutter every time, but after a while I got so I could clip a few off the ends.

The guys were really good, though. They slid down the lane and stopped on the white line with one foot poised in the air like ballet dancers. Brian was having an especially good night. I looked over Jason's shoulder at the score pad and he had a perfect score—he'd been bowling strikes and spares all evening. I didn't know Brian was some kind of crack bowler like that, but then there was a lot about him I didn't know. Brian said he was usually pretty good but it was an exceptional night even for him.

I stopped after a while and then Jason and Marvin dropped out too, and we all sat there watching Brian bowl. Pretty soon people came over from the other lanes to watch him. Brian had a flush of victory on his cheeks, and I thought he's going to mess up. This winning streak couldn't last forever, but Brian wasn't like me and the attention seemed to sharpen his focus and gave him an edge.

Finally he stopped and slipped into the seat next to me. The show was over and people cheered and gradually drifted back to their lanes. Jason bought us each a Coke and sat down next to Marvin and we toasted Brian with our drinks. Some of the lanes were going dark and we finally got up to go.

The party was being held at a Chevron station for the novelty of it. A stage had been set up in the corner of the lot, and Cal and the other band members were tuning their instruments and warming up on stage. There must have been at least forty people milling around the lot smoking cigarettes and talking, waiting for the music to start. Meanwhile cars were still pulling into the station and attendants pumped their gas, and a couple of people used the self-service pumps, just like business as usual. When we got out of the car, one of the attendants waved at Marvin like they were old pals. I recognized a couple of people from Mission who said hi to Marvin, and we stood around drinking beer and talking. He introduced me to Lupe Ramirez who I recognized as the girl in the photo over his bed. She looked like a vision in her white coat and dress, and they linked arms and smiled sweetly and I wondered why he'd never said anything about her. He was such a sensitive guy; it was like he'd waited till I was with someone myself to let me know he had a girlfriend.

Lupe clucked her tongue at me, and I figured she was teasing me about the beer. She wasn't drinking herself and either it came across as unladylike or else she was just joking.

There was a red Chevy van and a vintage Fairlane at the service pump, and the blue and orange lights from the Chevron sign reflected off the oil slicks and bled into the night. There was almost a halo around people's faces from the lights, and it looked like a stage set or an Edward Hopper painting. It was so timeless that we could have been anywhere.

Cal was the lead singer of his band and he was like a different person on stage. The sullen, hangdog look was gone and he seemed totally in his element—he had amazing stage presence, star quality even. They played a couple of classics—"Louie Louie" and "Gloria"—and an instrumental version of "Proud Mary," and some songs I didn't recognize that I figured might be original compositions. They had a bluesy sound I liked, but the instrumentation was so dense I couldn't catch any of the lyrics.

"Not bad, huh?" Marvin said to Brian. "My kid brother. I think he's got big ambitions."

"No," Brian said. "Not bad at all. He's pretty fantastic, actually. He might even make it."

I loved the music and the buzz from the beer didn't hurt either. I compared the pleasant, relaxed way I felt to the night after *West Side Story* when I was practically getting the stigmata. All the old hurts and conflicts I had worried about had curled up and slunk away. It felt good to be part of a family instead of being on the outs with people all the time, and being with Brian was best of all. I looked around at the glowing auras of the others and thought briefly of the religious community Brian and his friends had in Paradise.

Brian was drinking a 7-Up and I put my beer down because I

thought maybe Lupe Ramirez had the right idea, and I needed to sober up. I didn't want to be tripping on the music in a drunken revel and sleeping through a revolution like Rip Van Winkle, somehow getting it wrong. All these insights and ideas were floating around, and if I had a clear head I might be able to grasp them. I needed to let my best Virgo characteristics come to the fore and break through, so I wouldn't repeat my mistakes. Besides, I was probably as high as I was going to get from the music and being with Brian, and the beer was just muddying the waters.

Brian squeezed my hand and in the artificial light his face looked broad and expansive as the moon. It seemed like a miracle that I was getting a second chance with him, and I planned on making the most of it. The last set ended and he beamed down at me.

"It was great, wasn't it?" he asked enthusiastically and I nodded.

Brian put his arm around me and we watched while the band members packed up their instruments and amplifiers. They were taking down the lights and dismantling the stage when we left. Jason, Marvin, and Lupe were getting a ride home with Cal, and a girl with short blond hair I had seen him with earlier in the evening.

Brian took the long way to Coombs, meandering down a series of backcountry roads, stopping at every gate. He said there was someplace he wanted to show me. He finally pulled into the Waycliffe YMCA Summer Camp. It was closed for the season and the gate was padlocked, but he found a key under a pile of rocks and we drove down the dirt road through dense underbrush into the deserted camp.

Brian had worked at the camp several summers, leading the

singing after dinner and as a counselor for the older boys. He played Woody Guthrie songs, traditional American folk ballads, and spirituals, and had fond memories of the place.

"I can see why you like it so much," I said.

He knew his way around at night from all the summers of prowling around after the kids were asleep. We crossed a wide open meadow and headed back into a semicircle of trees, past the boarded-up cabins and the main lodge. He pulled me toward him against the shaggy trunk of a eucalyptus tree.

The moonlight reflected off his face and his eyes were soft and his breath was warm. His face brushed mine and I had to stand on tiptoe to reach him. His lips were warm and wet and when we stopped kissing, I looked up and a deer stood in the meadow, maybe ten yards away from us. It was perfectly still and the moonlight shone off its coat and velvet antlers. It looked at us unfazed before ambling away.

There was real chemistry between Brian and me, as I'd always suspected, and we gradually made our way down to the ground. There were a couple of occasions to put the brakes on, and even more reasons to use them, but I let them pass me by one by one. At the back of my mind, I was thinking, don't people ever learn anything? But then again, maybe some mistakes you've got to make twice, and some things you never do learn. Then when it really was too late, I followed Brian back to the car and he nudged me into the back seat. He climbed on top of me and started unbuttoning my blouse. It felt like my whole body was coming to life now, as if it had just been numb or sleeping until then. It was the beginning of December, but we weren't cold even with our clothes off. He ran his hands over my face, my nose, my mouth, my cheeks like he was reading Braille.

The urgency took over everything now, even the pain,

because it was my first time, but the pleasure was still stronger. Our breath was coming hard and fast, and when it happened and something tore through me and the sky opened up, it was like rain, only it wasn't raining, because Brian was; Brian was the rain. We lay tangled up in each other's arms and I felt his skin next to mine and the rhythm of our breath was so close, you couldn't tell whose was whose or which was which. My knee was bent double and he lay on the inside of my thigh and pulled an old army blanket over us.

My face was wet with tears.

"You're crying," Brian said. "Why are you crying?"

"Because I'm so happy," I said.

The euphoria of the moment gave me the courage to tell Brian I'd been in love with him years ago, and this was an old dream of mine.

"Yeah, I could have gone for you too if I hadn't been involved with somebody else," Brian said. "Susan wasn't exactly a flash in the pan, but you seem like you could be the real thing."

It was just what I wanted to hear and I allowed myself to take it in.

We lay on the backseat listening to the radio and finally roused ourselves and put our clothes on.

"Steal Away" was playing on the radio. The gravel on the dirt road crunched under the tires, and I sat as close to Brian as I could without actually climbing into his lap. We bounced along in his old Chrysler with the worn-out suspension system, and it felt like the car was cradling us in a mystery that was older than the hills and came straight from the center of the Earth.

CHAPTER 26

The memory of Brian's touch left me in a gravity-defying field and I mentally marked off the days till he'd be back for vacation. The juice was turned on and my spirits were on high beam, and before I might as well have been looking out at life from a dark cave. It was like the arrival in the Emerald City in *The Wizard of Oz*, when it shifts from black and white to color. I was glad I had waited to fall in love before I had sex, because with Brian it was a spiritual thing. He was my soul mate, and it was like the philosopher said about the yolk and white of the same egg. For the first time I felt whole, so I understood why I always felt so fractured before.

Friday was my appointment with the psychiatrist, and Lilah took the day off work and drove me to Fresno. It was like her to wait until I was at the top of my game to send me to a shrink. She always did have a strange sense of timing. Jane said I was a Contrary, but if so it was no secret where that came from. Although perhaps she knew what she was doing after all, because it may have been my only chance at a clean bill of health. I was morose enough that my moods could have been mistaken for a serious disturbance and for all I knew I actually had one.

The clinic was in a temporary building that looked like it had been an army barracks at one time. The psychologist, Dr. Janice Gainor, had heavy legs and wore sensible shoes. A Huichol yarn drawing of a deer hung on the wall behind her and a squat, terracotta figurine stood on her desk, arms akimbo. Her dishwater blond hair was cut in a Dutch bob and she looked stable to the point of stolidity. I didn't think she was much of an advertisement for the wonders of mental health. Looking at her, I was almost relieved to have something aberrant and pathological to distinguish myself.

She didn't exactly warm up to me either. She asked a lot of questions about my feelings about my mother's marriage and having siblings for the first time at age seventeen. I told her that after some initial resistance and difficulties I was happy about the move. I had been suffocating and was half-smothered to death in our little bungalow back in La Grange. I found it a lonely and gloomy place. My mother thought I was jealous of the attention she paid the boys, but actually the reverse was true, because it was a relief to have less responsibility for her for a change. It had been a tremendous burden being an only child. I hadn't even known I felt that way until I heard myself say it. I thought I was just making it up to have something to talk about, but I knew it was authentic.

After that, I tried to act noncommittal and guarded without coming off as defensive. First I told her about the photography prize, and learning how to drive so I'd be able to go back and see my friends. I told her I hadn't made any friends at school yet, but I was working on the paper and spent a lot of time with one of my stepbrothers. I decided not to tell her about Brian. It was new and vulnerable and iffy enough as it was, and I didn't want to jinx it.

Dr. Gainor's hands were folded in her lap, and she nodded

her head from time to time. I figured I'd made a good enough impression, until she punctured my illusion.

"Your mother tells me you've had several angry outbursts since the move," she said. "And otherwise have been very anti-social, although that's improved recently. What do you attribute these outbursts to?"

"Frustration," I said. "Frustrations build up and compound themselves. Of course no one helps you or anything. They just increase their expectations, and then come down on you hard when you finally explode. What do they expect of a person, anyway?"

"What kind of frustrations are we talking about here?" she asked.

I didn't know how to answer. I couldn't tell her about getting together with Marvin at the party or my first night in the house, and I didn't want to talk about Brian. There were a lot of things I couldn't talk about, which was how I'd wound up in this predicament to begin with.

"Hard, impossible things are being demanded of you," I said. "Things you can't possibly do, and you're all alone and there's no one around to help. So you're isolated, lonely, and terribly burdened. And there is absolutely no one to talk to about it."

She looked at me steadily.

"Your mother told me a little about your childhood—she's concerned that it had some long-term effects on you. I see a lonely little girl in a hotel room, whose mother is on a prolonged bender and doesn't come back for days at a stretch.

"What happened to that little girl, do you suppose? Is she all grown up or still somewhere inside you?"

It smacked of being a rhetorical question, so I didn't answer.

"You must have a terrible fear of being overlooked as a result of those experiences," she said.

Fear of being overlooked had driven my resistance to Glenda's joining *The Record.* Of course she had been the one to get together with Kevin, but the fear and rivalry themselves had turned out to be the worse problem, costing me my friendship with Glenda for a time. I didn't know if it qualified as an "aha" moment, but it explained a lot.

"Your mother is concerned that you may have the beginnings of an eating disorder," she said. "It's called bulimia in the clinical world."

"I don't think it's really that much of a problem," I said. "After all, I don't go on these binges that often."

She let me know that she thought it would be a good idea if I came to see her for a while. Then she took me into another room and gave me a No. 2 pencil, a test book, and an answer sheet. There were ninety-nine statements on the test and they asked you to rate them from "always" to "frequently" to "occasionally" to "never" true. The questions pretty much ran the gamut: "I feel nervous or anxious," "I have trouble sleeping," "I feel I have been chosen by God to help carry out His special plan for the world," "I enjoy parties and other social gatherings," "Sometimes I think it would be best if I just ended it all." That kind of thing. It struck me that you had to be careful how you answered some of them or they could land you in the loony bin.

Dr. Gainor scheduled my next appointment with my mother. My mother and I stopped for lunch at an old-fashioned luncheonette on the way home. She asked how the meeting had gone and I told her I had dismissed Dr. Gainor early in the session but wound up liking her. I was just as glad to be seeing her again, although I resented Lilah's talking to her behind my back. At the very least, she could have told me about it, which would have spared me going into my well-adjusted spiel at the beginning of the session.

I felt drained and exhausted when we got home and went to my room and took a nap.

I woke up feeling groggy and disoriented and the room was stifling. It was an unusually warm day for early December but the heat had been left on, and it felt like the walls were closing in on me. I opened the window and looked at the power lines outside. On an impulse, I headed down to the basement and looked around for Ben's tool kit. He kept his tools in an old fishing tackle box, and I pulled out a Phillips screwdriver and took it back to my room.

I got up on the windowsill and leaned out as far as I could, supporting myself against the utility pole with my free hand, and started unscrewing the "Danger: High Voltage" sign with Ben's screwdriver. I half expected to get an electric shock in the process, because I took the sign at its word. I lost the screws in the process but managed to wrest the sign free. I sat still for a minute looking at it on my lap.

Out the window I saw my mother digging up her winter beds at the back of the yard. She had changed into cutoffs and a purple T-shirt and was turning the sod with a shovel and working the fertilizer into the soil. The bag of fertilizer, a trowel, claw, and possibly a hundred bulbs were scattered on the lawn behind her. She worked hard but even at that distance I could see she was in her element. She'd planned the bed since before we moved in. I remembered her talking about it in the car the first time we came over.

Dr. Gainor was more astute than I'd given her credit for, and I'd even had a minor epiphany in her office. Her approach had been fundamentally about my overcoming my isolation and learning to express myself. It seemed kind of pathetic that my mother had told her things she was unable to tell me, and then

I went in and did the same. It was as if we were using her as a go-between and were unable to have a serious discussion on our own. Dr. Gainor implied that I needed to reach out to people and that my mother was no longer the incompetent drunk of my youth, but that on an unconscious level I still saw her that way.

I watched her out the window for a while and thought about the fact that Lilah had told me Marvin's mother had died of cancer of the pancreas, when it turned out she had committed suicide. There were all these secrets and lies floating around, and I wondered what else she might be hiding. I never believed the story about Lilah and Ben meeting at the school auction in the first place, and now I'd found out his first wife had killed herself right around the time they first got together, so their relationship seemed the likely explanation for her suicide.

I waited a few minutes and went downstairs. I felt like I was putting the session with Dr. Gainor to use already. My mother was so wrapped up in her gardening I must have stood behind her a full minute before she sensed I was there. Then she saw my shadow and turned abruptly.

"Oh, it's you," she said, relieved. "I'm putting in an English border garden against the back fence. I won't get much done today, I'm afraid. I'm going to let it take shape gradually. It's a little late for the bulbs, but I'm going ahead with them anyway—ranunculi, freesia, tulips, daffodils, hyacinths, and narcissus. In the spring, I'll plant the blue bells, yellow yarrow, goldenrod, phlox, and Solomon's seal."

She nattered on, gesturing toward the bulbs, but her face clouded over when she saw I wasn't smiling or interested.

"I know about Ben's first wife," I said. "She didn't die of pancreatic cancer like you told me, so you lied about that. She killed herself. Did she know about you and Ben, is that it? When did you two meet, anyway? You never did tell me when this school auction was. Didn't the two things happen at the same time? Why else would she have killed herself?"

She gathered herself up off the ground and stood a few feet away from me. The sun beat down on us unobstructed and we were both sweating. The darkness of the freshly dug up earth loomed behind her and the air was musky and fertile.

"Is that what the boys told you?" she asked.

I nodded my head.

"They told me she killed herself, but they didn't say why."

She didn't look guilty or defensive like I had expected. Her eyes were soft, as if she was almost relieved to have been found out.

"It wasn't because of us," she said. "We got together after her death, like I told you."

"Except it wasn't how you told me, was it?" I said.

"No," she acknowledged, dropping her eyes. "It wasn't."

"So how about telling me how it really was this time. I never really believed that hokey story about the auction, you know."

She took a deep breath like she was girding herself for something.

"I first met Ben back in college. I worked as a bartender at Oberon's at night while I went to school. It was a local watering hole in Turlock where the Cal State crowd used to hang out."

Her eyes were big and luminous, and I stared back at her hard.

"One night in the midst of all the "Rah, rah," college crowd—that's the way college kids were in those days—I noticed a man in a shabby brown jacket sitting at the end of the bar. He looked very dignified sitting by himself in a pool of light, oblivious to everything going on around him. He was a bit older than the rest of us, and definitely not one of the regulars. There was something intelligent and thoughtful in his manner, and he had a wise expression on his face, so that you wanted to be let in on his thoughts. I assumed he was one of the professors."

"Sort of like Derek Montague?" I asked.

"The same," my mother said. "Just what we wanted Derek Montague to be like. I thought he was a professor who was outlining the following day's lecture in his head. He wasn't writing anything down.

"He didn't nurse his brandy as much as he seemed to be studying it, and when I came back an hour later he still hadn't touched it. Usually they just threw them back when they were having troubles. He was lost in thought and seemed to have the cares of the world on his shoulders."

"He showed no signs of going anywhere, and I didn't have the heart to turn him out when I closed the place up, so I let him stay while I swept up and washed glasses. When he finally opened up and started talking, it was quite different from what I'd been expecting. It wasn't a problem he was solving, or philosophical issue, and he wasn't composing a lecture or a speech. Instead, it was a sad story of domestic violence and emotional unrest and a rift between him and his wife. He told me about a violent confrontation earlier in the evening. He was in a state of despair about his marriage. Things had been rocky for some time but now they'd come to a head.

"It was an ugly story, but I was impressed by his humanity, his compassion for his wife in spite of his anger, and he was pummeled by regret for his role in the incident. He was upset enough that he had hit her."

"The sun was coming up and I had scrubbed everything so hard the place was practically threadbare. I dried all the glasses, which I usually didn't bother to do, and he still showed no signs of leaving. He clearly didn't want to go home, and he had nowhere else to go, so I invited him home with me.

"He slept on the couch. I provided a sanctuary, nothing more. Our relationship was something that developed quite naturally over time out of the sympathetic affection we felt for each other."

"So it's him, isn't it?" I said quietly. "Ben. He's my father, isn't he?"

I don't know at what point in her story I knew for sure. There was no sense of being thumped on the chest by illumination, no clap of thunder. It dawned on me gradually while she spoke. There was simply no one else it could be.

She nodded and her eyes got big and liquid like seawater. She sank back down on her knees and I sank down on the grass with her.

"Yes, dear," she said. "He's the one. He's your father."

Again, she seemed relieved to hear me say it. I don't know if she ever would have gotten around to it on her own.

"He was a cut above the Cal State students I was going out with. In spite of everything he had been through that night, he actually fed the cat and watered the plants. I guess he felt at home. I wasn't used to such thoughtfulness, I can assure you. Those sorts of things make someone welcome in your home, and incline you to give them a key and tell them they can use the place, whether you're there or not. And when he did come over, he always managed to give something back. Either there was a roast and potatoes in the oven when I came home, or he was fixing the latch on the screen door that hadn't worked since the day I moved in, or building a flower box outside the kitchen window. That's the kind of person he was. Is. A giver.

"I remember the day everything changed between us. There

had been a heat wave and I was wearing one of those off-the-shoulder sundresses and he showed up unexpectedly with a liter of cold beer and a bouquet of dahlias. While I was arranging them in a vase, on an impulse I broke one off and stuck it in my hair. After dinner we danced in our bare feet to the radio in the living room till one a.m. That was our first night as lovers and the beginning of our eight-month affair. He was going to leave her. We were already making plans for a life together.

"I was totally shocked and unprepared for what happened next," she said. "He showed up one night at Oberon's, distraught and beside himself. Things with Dolores had taken an unpredictable turn. She was worse off than he realized. She was completely delusional. At the moment, she was on the psych ward practically imagining herself the Virgin Mary or the Bride of Christ. In reality, she was pregnant with Marvin and it seemed to have tipped her over the edge.

"He wasn't able to leave her in her present condition. It would be unconscionable under the circumstances, so he was leaving me instead. He hoped I would understand; it certainly wasn't what he had intended. Of course I understood, but I was still devastated. He was totally beside himself, poor man. He was upset enough as it was, so I spared him my own melodrama. Maybe he planned it that way, telling me at work, in order to avoid a scene, in which case it was a smart move. He'd been up for days. He'd already thought it through and he didn't want me to try to talk him out of it.

"I was in mourning for well over a month. And it wasn't until three weeks after that that I felt the quiet knitting in my belly, a sort of quickening, and I was puzzled as hell for a while. I tried not to think too much about it, because I had enough on my mind. It wasn't till later I realized it had been six weeks and my period still hadn't come. Then the morning sickness started, so by the time I went in for the test, I already knew."

The tears streamed down my face in a solid sheet. They wouldn't stop and my nose was running too.

Lilah gave me a quick look.

"Oh, my God," she said. "Look at you. I shouldn't be telling you this. What would that shrink today have to say if she heard me? I'd be declared an unfit mother and you'd be taken away from me, that's what."

"Why didn't you just tell me all this when I asked that night in the car?"

"I almost did tell you, in fact," she said. "Ben thought the boys were upset enough by Dolores' suicide. Cal and especially Marvin were severely traumatized, and he didn't think they could handle any more surprises, so we decided against it. Jason seems to be one of those kids who come through things unscathed no matter what happens, but the other two were having a hard time, each in their own way. You sprang it on me in the car the night of the wedding rehearsal, and I didn't want to tell you without consulting Ben."

"Telling me isn't the same thing as telling the boys, you know," I said. "I wouldn't have said anything."

"Yes, I can see that now," she said. "I suppose I should have thought of that. Anyway, eventually, over time, the disappointment and loneliness I felt after he left vanished, because you came along and made it all up to me. I was in disastrous shape for a long time. I was a terrible mother. It took me a while to get over it, and I'm afraid you bore the brunt of it. You remember a lot of that, I'm sure. I know it must have been hard on you. That's why I thought it would be a good idea if you saw someone for a while. I thought it would help you deal with the adjustment to the new house. You seemed to be struggling so."

She looked at me steadily, and I gradually stopped crying and nodded.

"Did you bring me over here one time?" I asked looking around. "Once in the very early morning, back a long time ago, before we got a car. Did we ever come over here on the bus and look at the house from the street? We didn't even go inside."

My mother frowned and shook her head.

"No," she said. "I'd never seen the place myself until this year. He kept those two sides of his life completely separate.

"If I'd told myself I'd have forgiven him just like that, I never would have believed it," she said. "I swore myself off him a long time ago, and then I took him back instantly. I looked up one day and there he was standing in front of my counter at Yarborough's with those eyes of his that look like something that came down out of the sky. I looked up from my counter at Yarborough's, and there he was. After all that time, seventeen years it must have been, and my heart sped up and skipped faster in that same old crazy way just like being a girl again. And there was a little breeze as if I was in the presence of a god or something awesome and strange.

"He told me that Dolores had killed herself a few months back and he'd come looking for me. It didn't take him long. He approached me at work again—I suppose he wanted to find out if I was free before he went about causing complications for me. I never thought I'd see him again, that was for sure, after seventeen years. And there it was happening all over again, just like the first time I met him.

"He came back into my life and the whole thing came rolling back over me full force. All the first throes of happiness and passion, and the difference he made—how he touched my life and changed everything for the better. It was like a miracle all over again."

"But he left you," I said.

"Yes," she said. "He left me. And I was hurt and even hated him for a while, but I always knew why he left. He wasn't rejecting me. He left me because he had a wife who wouldn't be able to bring up a child on her own. So he was sacrificing his own happiness and yours and mine in the process, although he didn't know about you then, for the good of Dolores and Marvin. After I became a parent, it made a lot more sense to me, because I could have used some help myself, and I wasn't nearly as crazy as she was. I couldn't believe it when he told me they went on to have two more kids.

"I hashed it and rehashed it all more times than I care to go into, believe me. I went over it with a fine-toothed comb with a bottle of Seagram's 7 next to me."

"Funny," I said. "He seems to have that effect on people. His first wife had a drinking problem too."

It was weird hearing what a good father Ben was when I had always felt so bereft. Of course, he was off being a father to someone else, so it required a leap of faith to see it.

Get over yourself, I thought. That was what it was all about, and it was the archetypal leap we all had to make at one time or another. Or else time and time again, because it wasn't all about me. How many times did I have to remind myself of that? Maybe that was just the great philosophical issue of our time and every time. End of story.

"But then the hands of the clock turn," my mother went on. "And it got to be my turn to have this wonderful husband who's such a good family man, which was all I ever wanted to begin with."

She turned to me suddenly.

"Do you think in my wildest dreams I ever imagined I would

wind up with someone of his caliber? I was a bit in awe of the man, yet his manner inspired utter confidence."

I wondered why she should feel in awe of Ben. He was a nice guy and all but I didn't think he rated that. It was no secret where my inferiority complex had come from all these years. I hoped other women weren't as insecure as my mother and me, as quick to put themselves down.

I heard a commotion behind us and it sounded like Ben or the boys were home. The backdoor slammed and the dogs scrambled down the back steps. I didn't look up right away. When I turned, Ben stood on the backstairs, arms akimbo, looking out over the backyard like he was surveying his estate. The steps were rickety and practically falling off the house. Ben was thin and wiry and looked as rickety as the steps as he stood there smiling at us. My mother stood behind me, barefoot among the bulbs on the lawn.

"Hi," he said, looking down at us. "What's up?"

The sun had begun to set behind the house and I had to squint to look at him.

"Hi," he said again. "How are my two best girls today?"

He looked back and forth between my mother and me. He looked a little confused at first, but she must have signaled something to him, because I could tell he was clueing in. He pushed his hat back on his head and his eyes widened and he slowly climbed down the steps and gave me a strong, soulful hug. Ben wasn't tall like Marvin, he was about my height and smelled slightly of mothballs, as if his jacket had just been taken out of storage.

"So you two had a big heart-to-heart today, is that the idea?" Ben asked gently, patting my back because I was sobbing again.

"Here, let me get a good look at you," he said holding me a

little away from him. "That's my girl. That's my good girl. Well, we've had a time of it, you and I, haven't we?"

He had tears in his eyes too.

"I'm sorry, Ben," I said. "I'm sorry I was so awful. I wish I'd been a better daughter to you."

He didn't say anything about wishing he had been a better father. My taking it all on myself seemed to be what he expected, and he took it at face value.

"That's all right, Hefalump," he said quietly. "We've got all the time in the world."

There was a reverberation on the stairs and I looked up and Jason and Cal stood at the top of the steps. They didn't say anything. They just looked down at us puzzled like they didn't know what to make of the whole thing.

CHAPTER 27

It wasn't until Marvin got home and some of the emotion wore off that I got the full impact of the situation. We were sitting around the living room, except for Lilah who was in the kitchen making dinner. Cal slouched in an overstuffed chair, and Marvin perched on the back of it and Jason stood by the fireplace. I was sitting next to Ben on the couch when he took it upon himself to make a general announcement. I knew it would have to come out eventually, but I don't know why he had to rush into it now. After all, they'd waited this long. Maybe Ben was afraid I would say something to the boys, and he wanted to make sure they heard it from him first.

He started off slow, stumbling, and inarticulate.

"I've got something important to tell you kids," he said. "That is that Miami's not your stepsister after all. She's your actual sister. Actually, she's your half-sister."

There wasn't an audible gasp like I expected but silence instead, and everyone froze in place like a tableau, one of those Christmas pageants or nativities we used to have back in elementary school where the main object was not to move.

"It turns out Lilah and me—well, Lilah and me go back a

long way. We knew each other before you kids were born. Your mother and I were having some problems in those days and separated briefly, which is when Lilah and I got to know each other. Now, Marvin, hold on. I know what you're thinking but it wasn't like that. It was only for a short time, but it was long enough…

Ben stopped for a gulp of air and continued. "To conceive a child. Even though I didn't know of this child's existence until we got back together again after your mother died."

Marvin stood across the room glaring at Ben and I caught his eye for a minute. The next thing I knew he turned and stormed out of the house, and Lilah came in from the kitchen holding a dishtowel to see what was going on.

"I'm sorry, kids," Ben stammered. "I know it must be a shock to absorb this all at once. But after your mother died, I looked Lilah up again and we decided to get married. We hadn't seen each other in all that time, seventeen years it was, but we still felt the same. Time hadn't changed that. That's our history in a nutshell."

He and Lilah exchanged a sympathetic look and he raised his eyebrows and sighed.

I couldn't get used to the idea of Ben as my father. I'd been imagining this pathetic guy, and it turned out he was neither a cipher nor as grandiose as Derek Montague, but somewhere in between. If Ben was my father, it somehow made me just like anybody else, neither as brilliant as I'd hoped nor as much of a nebbish as I feared. I might actually be normal, whatever that meant. Maybe not so hypersensitive, because that's what everyone always hinted, and that's what Glenda was getting at on the phone that day. I could even see a bit of a physical resemblance to him around the mouth and the bridge of the nose. I may be fragile in some ways but I could be pretty stern myself, flinty almost, perhaps too much so.

I felt more defined, right where I was supposed to be. My whole life I'd felt so marginal, like I was barely hanging in there, so this was a novel concept for me. Still, it would be nice to have Dr. Gainor to talk to while I was getting used to the whole thing.

"Half-brother, half-sister, like a hermaphrodite," Cal whispered to me out of nowhere. The smile on his face reminded me of the barker at the county fair and gave me a rush of déjà vu. I don't know why he would say something like that—he was so off the wall. Maybe he was psychic himself.

Cal went off with some of his friends, so it was just Jason, Ben, Lilah, and me for the family dinner. Lilah went all out, though, and we had a late meal. I even had some pot roast for the first time in two years. I guess I was open to anything. It tasted delicious although I didn't plan on making a habit of it.

There was dark natural woodwork in the dining room and Lilah had put up burgundy drapes and there was a floral stained-glass panel in one window. It was the first time I'd sat down to a meal with them since we'd been there, and with the candles lit, it felt like one of my rituals with my friends. Jason and I drank wine too and there was a warm, rosy glow to everything. If this was what it meant to have a family, it was good and I liked it. Lilah beamed at me as she passed the pot roast. She was clearly in her element.

I didn't see Marvin for a few days, but I finally ran into him in the living room after school on Monday. The blinds were down and he was reading a magazine in the dark and had his feet up on the coffee table. He looked up when he saw me and then went back to thumbing through *Psychology Today*. Up close, Marvin looked tired and distraught. His eyes were bloodshot and his expression made me melt inside. I knew the news had triggered his issues about his mother's death and confirmed his suspicions that Lilah and Ben were responsible for it. After all, I'd thought the same myself.

"Hi, Sis," he said giving me a half-hearted smile.

"Little did we know, huh?"

"Yeah," he said. "How are we supposed to know? They don't tell anybody anything and keep all these secrets."

"I guess that's why you aren't supposed to bend the rules to begin with," I said. "You never know what's lurking in the shadows, and you could stumble onto a mined playing field."

It was dark in the room but I combed Marvin's face for resemblances, following the curve of his jaw and the line of his nose. I always saw myself in Marvin anyway but it never occurred to me it was because we were actual flesh and blood.

"I know what you're thinking," I said. "About Lilah, Ben, and your mother. But I don't think it happened that way."

"How would you know?" Marvin asked. "Just because they say so? Do you really believe them, after all this? Why start telling the truth now? What's their incentive? Whereas the other explains her suicide completely."

"Believe me," I said. "I thought the same thing myself, and I confronted Lilah about it the other day. That's how all this came out. She finally told me the whole story."

I leaned over and gave Marvin a hug.

"I'm glad," I said. "Not just because of Ben, but because it explains the connection between us, and it makes me feel even closer to you. I'm sitting here looking at you thinking, This is my brother, and it sends goose bumps down my spine. We really are a family. And Lilah is a mensch. She's not the wicked stepmother you're thinking."

"Maybe," he said. But he hugged me back and I actually got a smile out of him for the first time.

Brian called that night to inform me that he would be home that weekend and invited me to a Christmas/Solstice party his family was giving. I was relieved to have a chance to talk to someone outside the house and tell him what was going on.

"I've had an intense week in the family drama department," I said. "My mother has me seeing a shrink now."

"I've always wondered what that would be like," Brian said. "It seems kind of weird to go in and pour your heart out to a complete stranger, especially one wearing a button-down collar and polyester suit. Let alone paying them. I don't know if I could do that."

"It was a little strange," I said. "But it turned out better than I thought. It inadvertently wound up leading to some big family revelations. It turns out my stepfather is actually my real father."

"Wow," Brian said. "And you didn't know?"

"No," I said.

"That's heavy. In a good way, I hope. Do you like him?"

"I do," I said. "We had a period of conflict, but I think that was largely because I hurt his feelings and he thought I was rejecting him. When I was a little girl, I was *convinced* that my father would come back someday, even though my mother had told me he was dead. It's like I instinctively knew the truth."

"Out of the mouths of babes and idiots," Brian said. "That must be a lot to take in all at once."

"When are finals?" I asked.

"Not till the end of the week," Brian said. "I'll show up for them for sure but I can't say I'm exactly studying. There's been some big doin's up here, and we've been in nonstop meetings all week."

"What's going on, Brian?" I asked.

"I'll tell you about it at the party," Brian said. "I don't want to overload you on top of all your family stuff. I'm hoping it may eventually involve you as well."

I didn't see what about Brian's religious community would involve me, and I thought it was some scheme to get me up to Chico State.

Friday school was out for Christmas vacation, and I coaxed Marvin into going to the Quinns' for their party, which featured quintets by Mauricio Vasquez, Ginny Lopez, Candy Salzman, Mark Gundersall, and K.D. Brian was home and greeted us at the door. He didn't look like he'd shaved in a couple of days and looked rugged and handsome. He said he'd rolled in around one and they'd immediately enlisted his help putting up the tree and decorating the place.

The living room was festooned with evergreens and lit with so many candles it looked like a church. We drank eggnog from cut-glass punch cups and decorated a Scotch pine with strands of popcorn and cranberries and glazed cookies in the shape of hearts and stars. It had a nice old-fashioned look. The quintet played Handel, Bach, and Mozart in front of the fireplace and accompanied us on Christmas carols. Glenda sang solos of "Ave Maria," "The Holly and the Ivy," and "O Holy Night." She wore a dark-blue velour pants suit, and her hair had been plaited like a medieval maiden's. K.D. sang "The Little Drummer Boy" and "Dominique" with Brian accompanying her on the guitar.

When the chamber music started again, Brian and I filled a plate with cookies, fruitcake, and salted nuts, and sat by the fire.

Brian's eyes glowed as he began unspooling his news.

A friend in the community had offered their fellowship the gift, or more precisely the long-term loan, of 15,000 acres, most of it virgin forest. The catch was that the land was in northern Minnesota. Some of it was fertile farmland, already cleared, and it was just a matter of time before it could become a self-supporting farm. There was a barn and enough pastureland for a sizeable herd of dairy cows. There were a few farmhouses and other buildings on the property but they were all in a state of disrepair and would require a lot of work before anyone could live in them. The roofs all leaked and barn swallows roosted in the rafters.

The community was in meetings for a week trying to decide whether to accept it or not, because it would require an enormous commitment that would change their lives completely. They would all have to drop out of school and move out of state for starters. On the other hand, not taking it would mean the loss of an incredible opportunity to do some good for a lot of people. How often did something like that come along? Never. They were incredibly lucky to have it. They were up in all-night sessions discussing it and praying for guidance. They asked themselves what Jesus would want them to do, and the answer came through loud and clear that this was a chance to establish a little bit of His kingdom on earth, which they couldn't in all conscience pass up.

When the place was ready, they intended to open it up as a religious community and sanctuary to all kinds of people who'd never had a chance in this world—street people, foster kids, high school dropouts, welfare mothers, immigrants, even old folks — anyone who had a hankering to live communally out in nature.

"It would basically be free food and shelter with the expectation that people would want to lend a hand or give back in the form of work," Brian said. "We're going to be looking for people, so you can start putting the word out to everyone you know. How does that sound to you?"

"It sounds fantastic," I said.

In the background, K.D.'s quintet played "What Child Is This?"

"You'll have to come visit," he said, "and see the place for yourself. Who knows? You may end up wanting to move in. That's what I'm secretly hoping. Of course the main draw is all the good we'll be doing with the place. Does it sound like something you might want to get involved with?"

"I don't know, Brian." I said. "Maybe."

Brian was momentarily silent, as though anyone hard-hearted enough to resist this opportunity was beyond his imagination.

"You brainiac girls all have your hearts set on going to Vassar, I guess," he said.

"That's part of it," I said.

"You're all into witchcraft now."

"That too," I said. "But the main thing is what happened to my grandmother. She started a religious community once and it proved to be the ruination of her. She lost every cent she had and then got conscripted into working for the community in indentured servitude for years. She was impoverished till her dying day."

"What's the matter with that?" Brian said. "I would think she would have embraced it. Volunteering and community service are the basis of most religious communities. They're certainly going to be the cornerstone of ours. Vows of poverty are also pretty standard for religious communities. Look at the Catholics."

"I don't think she would have minded if the others had pitched in, but she was the only one, and she was exploited and taken advantage of. She gave much more than she planned on to the community and she wasn't treated very well in return. Those who didn't outright exploit her completely abandoned her."

"So you're leery of the whole thing because of that?"

"It would be foolish not to be, don't you think?" I said. "After all, once burned, twice shy."

"Maybe, but I'd hate to see you turn this down because of what happened to your grandmother twenty-five years ago," Brian said.

"Of course I still have to go out there and see the place myself," he went on. "A couple of us are planning on going back early after Christmas. I was hoping that you'd come with us."

"Maybe you could initiate us into some Wiccan rituals on the land," he added. "Not on this visit, but eventually. In time."

"Yeah," I said. "If you think people would be open to that kind of thing."

"We're open to all of it," Brian said. "Buddhists, lamas, Sufis, Moslems, Mennonites, Quakers, fakirs, yogis, witches, witch doctors, shamans, tribal elders, pipe carriers, Hasids, Ashkenazi, Hindus, Sikhs, Jains. Have I left anyone out? Probably. I guess we draw the line at out and out worshippers of Satan.

"I hope seeing a therapist won't hold things up," Brian said. "From what I understand, that can go on for years."

"I don't think the shrink is a big problem, but I am applying for early admission to Berkeley."

Brian stared at me like I was losing my marbles.

"Maybe there's a community college you could go to out in the wilds of Minnesota."

I wondered if I was ready to give up my plans for college for a back-to-the-land hippie commune. College had always been my version of the Promised Land. Of course my mother would have a cow—one because of the Jesus freaks and another on account of not going to college, but it was really my decision. Joining a Jesus commune was such a reversal of my usual modus operandi, it made Modesto J.C. look like the big time.

We left the cleanup to his parents and K.D. and drove to Coombs via the YMCA camp again. We broke into one of the cabins this time and made love on the dusty mattress ticking of a lower bunk bed. Afterward he fell asleep in my arms, and I studied his silhouette with its rugged jaw and pronounced cheekbones. I couldn't believe my bad luck. No sooner do I finally get a boyfriend than it turns out he's leaving the state.

I decided to join Brian in visiting the place sometime in the next couple of weeks. Other than that there was no hurry to decide. After all, they hadn't entirely committed themselves to it yet. I let Brian sleep for an hour before waking him. I told him I'd love to go out to Minnesota for a visit with him.

The sun was practically coming up when he dropped me off at home, but I still wasn't tired. My head was buzzing with ideas, and I was happy to be the only one up and have the place to myself, so I could sort them out.

I sat on the sofa and looked around the living room. There was a sheen to the upholstery that picked up the blue in the area rug and the floors had all been polished. My mother was working her way through the house room by room, as she had with our place so long ago. With the dark wood coffee table and natural woodwork, it had become an almost beautiful room. She had put up a print of one of Dante Gabriel Rosetti's portraits in the corner of the living room and I thought it looked a little like Jane with her petulant lower lip and deep-set, farseeing eyes. The dogs were doing a skittish dance trying to get my attention, and I scratched them behind the ears and let them lick my hand. It was the first time they'd asked for any affection from me since we'd moved there. Perhaps they were picking up on my mood and were sensitive creatures after all.

I noticed Marvin's car keys on the coffee table and on an impulse I decided to go out for a drive. I would be breaking the law without a licensed driver in the car and I'd never even bothered to get a learner's permit, but I was feeling more daring than usual. There shouldn't be a lot of cops out this early, and as long as I avoided a full-scale collision, I'd probably be all right.

The roads were deserted except for a couple of trucks full of early morning agricultural workers. It was actually easier to drive without Marvin in the car telling me what to do and I felt more self-confident than usual. It had rained for the better part of a month and the bean fields were saturated and the air had a fresh, clean smell.

I took Rio Road out to the Guadalupe Bridge and parked on the shoulder. The sky was mauve and yellow and I walked out to the middle of the bridge and leaned against the railing and looked out at the horizon. I didn't think I'd ever been out there without my camera before. Maybe Marvin was right about my hanging the camera up when I got back with Brian. I always thought it made me see more, but there were things you missed too, looking through lenses, adjusting the meter, and focusing all the time. It fragmented everything, because you were so busy trying to pass the image on to somebody else, that you never really got to enjoy it yourself.

It was dizzying looking into the inky abyss of the river below. A wind whipped up from nowhere, blowing me into the guard-rail. It seemed there was no end to my being buffeted about, but at the moment it felt somehow invigorating.

I wondered if I'd get the spirit again and throw over my Wiccan ideas and return to my Pentecostal roots. Actually none of it seemed that important anymore and I was against any kind of sectarianism. There was something to be said for loyalty to one's traditions, but other than that, adhering to them blindly just seemed like an excuse to create divisions between people.

It made more sense to inspire people with an alternative reality rather than badgering them about sexism or inequality.

If everyone was as open minded as Brian about the Goddess, paganism, and nature worship, I shouldn't have a problem at the commune. I'd always believed all religions were one—that they were talking about the same thing and only quibbling over terms. It wouldn't surprise me if their ideas dovetailed somehow with our feminist views.

The two faces of God, the masculine and the feminine, united in sacred marriage. The hermaphrodite. After all, He had created them in his own image, which was male and female, even Genesis said that, and the Buddhist thangkas were hip to it too, although in both of them women occupied a subservient role. That was where they got it wrong.

Perhaps my grandmother hadn't been so off base in her prophecies. It gave me a rush of satisfaction to think of my grandmother vindicated after all she had been through. I'd always felt like she was trying to pass her messianic legacy on to me and maybe she knew what she was doing after all. I was only a kid in those days, but I had come of age.

What could be more exciting than putting our ideals into action and trying to establish utopia? It didn't get any better than that, and it was no wonder Brian was so jazzed. Even if my grandmother had come a cropper in the effort years ago, the worst we could do would be to fail again.

I looked down into the darkness of the riverbed again. It was the solstice, I realized. I had survived the longest night and from now on the days would be getting longer, and in four days it would be Christmas. There was an old tradition of keeping a vigil on the solstice and drumming up the dawn. I'd forgotten it until now but serendipitously wound up keeping it anyway.

I turned and walked back to the car. The sky was rosy now and alive with chattering birds. I still wasn't the least bit tired. I definitely wanted to go out to Minnesota to visit Brian and meet his friends and check out the community. Marvin might want to go too. He hadn't applied to college and may get interested in the place himself, and K.D. would probably want to at least see it.

I wanted to get my license right away too. That would be my next order of business. Maybe I'd even get a job, perhaps at *The Bee*, so I could buy some kind of broken-down old clunker like Brian's to get me out to Minnesota. Actually, I would need a pretty decent car if it was going to get me all the way out to the Midwest.

bothered to get a learner's permit, but I was feeling more daring than usual. There shouldn't be a lot of cops out this early, and as long as I avoided a full-scale collision, I'd probably be all right.

The roads were deserted except for a couple of trucks full of early morning agricultural workers. It was actually easier to drive without Marvin in the car telling me what to do and I felt more self-confident than usual. It had rained for the better part of a month and the bean fields were saturated and the air had a fresh, clean smell.

I took Rio Road out to the Guadalupe Bridge and parked on the shoulder. The sky was mauve and yellow and I walked out to the middle of the bridge and leaned against the railing and looked out at the horizon. I didn't think I'd ever been out there without my camera before. Maybe Marvin was right about my hanging the camera up when I got back with Brian. I always thought it made me see more, but there were things you missed too, looking through lenses, adjusting the meter, and focusing all the time. It fragmented everything, because you were so busy trying to pass the image on to somebody else, that you never really got to enjoy it yourself.

It was dizzying looking into the inky abyss of the river below. A wind whipped up from nowhere, blowing me into the guard-rail. It seemed there was no end to my being buffeted about, but at the moment it felt somehow invigorating.

I wondered if I'd get the spirit again and throw over my Wiccan ideas and return to my Pentecostal roots. Actually none of it seemed that important anymore and I was against any kind of sectarianism. There was something to be said for loyalty to one's traditions, but other than that, adhering to them blindly just seemed like an excuse to create divisions between people.

It made more sense to inspire people with an alternative reality rather than badgering them about sexism or inequality.

If everyone was as open minded as Brian about the Goddess, paganism, and nature worship, I shouldn't have a problem at the commune. I'd always believed all religions were one—that they were talking about the same thing and only quibbling over terms. It wouldn't surprise me if their ideas dovetailed somehow with our feminist views.

The two faces of God, the masculine and the feminine, united in sacred marriage. The hermaphrodite. After all, He had created them in his own image, which was male and female, even Genesis said that, and the Buddhist thangkas were hip to it too, although in both of them women occupied a subservient role. That was where they got it wrong.

Perhaps my grandmother hadn't been so off base in her prophecies. It gave me a rush of satisfaction to think of my grandmother vindicated after all she had been through. I'd always felt like she was trying to pass her messianic legacy on to me and maybe she knew what she was doing after all. I was only a kid in those days, but I had come of age.

What could be more exciting than putting our ideals into action and trying to establish utopia? It didn't get any better than that, and it was no wonder Brian was so jazzed. Even if my grandmother had come a cropper in the effort years ago, the worst we could do would be to fail again.

I looked down into the darkness of the riverbed again. It was the solstice, I realized. I had survived the longest night and from now on the days would be getting longer, and in four days it would be Christmas. There was an old tradition of keeping a vigil on the solstice and drumming up the dawn. I'd forgotten it until now but serendipitously wound up keeping it anyway.

Acknowledgements

This book bears the union label. Special thanks to Dev Green, whose wisdom has informed so much of this book and who was so helpful in bringing it to publication.

With many thanks to my writers' group for their critique and input: Naomi Cooper, David Belden, Melinda Dart, Henry Hitz, Mark Lapin, Jo-Anne Rosen, and Ruhama Veltfort. My previous writers' group also provided valuable assistance: Christine del Sol, Judy Koretsky, Elaine Starkeman, and Harriet Ziskin.

I'd like to thank members of my family—Christine Luisi, Cappy Coates, and Veronica Selver—for their support, as well as that of friends Beverly Connor, Erica Elliott, and Harriet Matter-Jones.

Thanks to the good people at the Squaw Valley Community of Writers for financial assistance and literary guidance, and to numerous others for inspiration and moral support.

Printed in Great Britain
by Amazon

80125423R00174